Success Is Not An Option

Warren Alexander

Copyright © 2024 by Warren Alexander

Layout design and Copyright © 2024 by Next Chapter

Published 2024 by Next Chapter

Edited by Tyler Colins

Cover art by Lordan June Pinote

This book is a work of fiction. Names, characters, places, and incidents are the product of the author's imagination or are used fictitiously. Any resemblance to actual events, locales, or persons, living or dead, is purely coincidental.

All rights reserved. No part of this book may be reproduced or transmitted in any form or by any means, electronic or mechanical, including photocopying, recording, or by any information storage and retrieval system, without the author's permission.

To Andrea

Acknowledgments

I wish to thank Cliff Conner for volunteering to proofread this thing. Cliff made some excellent editorial suggestions. I want to thank my long-suffering friend Teresa Chan, with whom I worked for many years, who endured my myopia when it comes to corporate America.

I would also like to thank George Fisher, Susan Biderman Montez, Alan Drucker, Gail Alexander Beilin, and Imelda Fagin for listening to me yabber on about this book for years and years.

And without Howard Birnbaum, Lloyd Birnbaum, and Jeff Birnbaum, and their mother and father Florrie and Jerry, we would not have a Seder chapter.

Chapter 1

Sweetened Paper

THE BOARD OF DIRECTORS shuffled out of the elevator, hesitant that they had reached the correct floor. Rarely did we get a single unannounced visitor, let alone a herd that glistened with importance. Each held my photo in their hand. They headed in various directions. Their eyes darted back and forth between my picture and anyone they encountered. One finally held my likeness next to my head and said, "It's him. It's definitely him."

Without a second opinion, the others ambled over and shook my hand. They congratulated me but with a greater enthusiasm, they congratulated themselves. I was their first new idea in years.

When A. J. Spaulding, CEO and Chairman of Remora Property & Casualty died, the Board wanted to bury his stranglehold on the company alongside him. With their newfound freedom, they now favored a leader who was neither an MBA nor a seasoned insurance professional, not even a conservative. They wanted a creative liberal type who could think outside the box. Why the hell were so many people afraid of this imaginary box? A box with dented cardboard sides and filled with little else other than self-imposed restraints. But let us praise their fear, for it gave me this undeserved opportunity.

They found me on the twenty-third floor, where I have sat for the past twenty-seven years, working as the company's principal graphic artist. Ironically, just the week before, I helped compose Spaulding's obituary. I had to choose the best photo of him from various eras, events, and sentiments. He looked ghastly in the latest ones and disinterested in others. I selected an older shot—a practiced pose with his eyes to the side, chin up, and sporting thick black glasses usually worn by middle school principals and pedophiles. I repositioned his head a few times for the official release until he looked dignified. The entire creation was, at once, both a lie and a revelation.

In order to justify my promotion to CEO, the Board had to interview me. I reminded them, with an odd mixture of firmness, humility, honesty, and incredulity, of my obvious lack of skills and inexperience to head up a formidable company. But that only encouraged them. I told them that there should be term limits for CEOs to preclude an 11th decade of rule. They agreed and seemed oddly amused. I half expected one of them to take a fish from his pocket and throw it toward my mouth. They emphasized that they wanted someone who both sounded and thought differently but who could still represent the insurance company proudly. Not only was I to be the new CEO, but a potential alternative to the talking mascots and the Presbyterians of Comedy employed by the other insurance companies for their ads.

Of course, I was leery of their intentions and motives and realized this new position could be a stunt, a progressive as gimmick. They knew there were many difficult, if not unsolvable problems, that I could not change. This way they could say they tried something different, but it failed. On the other hand, I was sure they wanted to avoid public humiliation, depressed staff, and an even more depressed stock price. After an all-night conversation with my wife, Cassia, we decided it was a reasonable risk. It reminded us of us when we were younger and would do things not only because they seemed stupid but the opportunity might never arise again. This was the adult edition. The Board never suspected the main reasons for my daring. We lived in a rent-stabilized apartment in a well-maintained building in the middle of Manhattan. Cassia had an excellent health care plan, and since we did not have children, there were no additional unreasonable expenses for things like food and clothing. No matter what might happen, we had a quiet place to sleep, could summon a plumber at midnight, and stumble to our local ER.

Spaulding's office was a shrine to mid-to-late 20th century masculinity. Buttoned leather chairs and sofas, a liquor cart cluttered with thick-cut glass bottles adorned with dangling silver necklaces, and an inlaid cigar box littered his suite. A first edition of Moby Dick illustrated by Rockwell Kent sat atop a lectern, opened to the sketch where Ahab is tethered to the great whale by his own harpoon. I did not touch or move a thing; it was still his office. Books bound with Moroccan leather stood shoulder to shoulder on the shelves. As only a few had a cracked spine, I wondered if the books had words at all. I still had not opened any drawer for fear I might find the trophies of a serial killer. Among the most loyal employees I inherited from Spaulding was Gladys Pierson, his 86-year-old Admin. She watched me gawking at the trappings of his success.

"A.J. was particularly fond of the *Dalbergia latifolia* paneling. And the rug was handmade at the Royal Tapestry Factory in Madrid where Goya once worked."

I had no clue what *Dalbergia latifolia* paneling might be but edged away from the rug. I did not want my worn heels to touch anything that Goya blessed.

My personal docent continued, "As for that Moby Dick thing, he wouldn't admit it, but some days, A.J. thought he was the whale, and other days he was the guy with the peg leg." As Gladys represented the old guard, I did not mention that Rockwell Kent was a raging socialist.

I lifted the lid to an ice pitcher behind the desk only to find it freshly filled. I tilted it toward Gladys. "Flown in this morning by puffins?"

"Just another Spaulding touch," she said.

"Do you know the word in Yiddish, *ungapatchka*?" I asked. When she did not respond, I did not explain that it meant a blinding garishness of which you should be ashamed.

"You need to meet somebody," said Gladys. With that, a man with raptor eyes materialized from nowhere.

"This is Sladka. Sladka, this is Rob Stone."

"Hello, Sladka."

Sladka said nothing in return, just nodded.

"Sladka was A.J.'s bodyguard for years. He almost quit after A.J. died but thought he'd better stay, at least until you're comfortable. You being an artist and all, you probably don't know how to defend yourself."

"Against what?"

Sladka and Gladys exchanged that he-has-a-lot-to-learn look.

"A.J. was a beloved figure, but even beloved figures have enemies," said Gladys. "And I'm not including all the people who wanted your job but didn't get it."

"I'm sure. But for that I need a bodyguard?"

"Spaulding used to get death threats from time to time," said Gladys.

"Death threats? What kind of death threats?"

"Mostly from people who were denied claims," said Gladys, as if that was reassuring.

"Maybe we should change our claims procedures?" I asked.

"Not necessary. Sladka will protect you," said Gladys.

Until this dramatic introduction, I did not know Sladka even had a name. He was as familiar as the Remora logo, prowling the halls with his menacing wiry mien, stiff back, shaved head, and icepick smile, when he smiled. No matter the weather or temperature, he wore a windbreaker zippered to the neck, which concealed his latest assignment. He also toted a bulging blue duffel bag. Everyone in the company speculated what lurked inside, dying to escape. Guns and knives went unquestioned, explosives and nunchakus were real possibilities, while devotees of esoteric weapons, such as falchions, throwing stars, broadswords, and poisons, hoped they filled his rucksack. One underwriter, who thought Sladka carried a small nuclear device, said, "It's my job to think of the worst-case scenario."

"Don't make a big deal about Sladka. We just don't want the stakeholders to get nervous about these threats. And remember," said Gladys, as if she was wagging her finger, "Sladka has no tongue. It was cut off when he was a boy in Bulgaria."

"Cut off?"

"Relax. You just have first-day jitters," said Gladys.

Sladka sent me a text. "I will take care of you."

How did Sladka know how to text me? Who would want to harm me? And why weren't these two worried about death threats? Missing tongues? What sort of job is this?

"What kind of name is Sladka?" I asked.

"My mother call me Sladka, which mean sweet in Bulgarian. I do not want to change my mother's name." He wrote with an accent. Sladka wriggled his eyebrows and added, "I know things."

"Don't be concerned. Sladka will protect you," said Gladys.

Sladka shook his head once up and down in firm agreement. When the phone rang, I naturally picked it up.

"I'm supposed to answer your phone," said Gladys.

I handed it to her.

"Mr. Stone's office. OK. One minute."

Gladys handed the phone back to me. "It's for you."

"No, I'm no longer doing photos and lay-outs. ...No, I got a promotion. ...Speak to Lindsay Ackerman. She's very smart. ...OK, thanks. Bye. Can I hang up the phone myself?"

Meanwhile, Sladka had vanished as quickly as a magician's scantily clad assistant. In his stead appeared Sir Reginald Pigot-Smythe, the head of HR.

"Welcome, Guv. Would you like a salt beef sandwich?" Which he produced from his suit pocket.

Everyone in the company was aware that Sir Reginald Pigot-Smythe was not his real name. Although born somewhere in the United States, few knew his real name, a secret he kept closely guarded. After he had been posted to London and converted to Anglophilia, he thought he needed a title and name to complete his rebirth.

"What's salt beef?" I asked.

"Salt beef is the Brit version of corned beef. *Pickel fleish* in Paris."

As Sir Reginald was well-versed in the various laws that governed equal opportunity and discrimination, *pickel fleish* surely seemed like code for Jewish.

"Thank you. It's only 9:45. I never have mustard before noon."

"Why don't you just taste it and see if it's to your liking?"

"I'm sure it's fine."

"You're an artist, right?"

"A graphic artist."

"What do you think of the art hanging around the company?"

"Innocuous. But that's the intention."

Sir Reginald pulled out some forms from his portfolio with gold embossed initials and mentioned the store where it was purchased as he tried to impress me.

"Posh is lost on me, but if you knew which urologist held the King in esteem, I'd be impressed," I said.

"Because of your change of position, could you please fill in these forms and sign them?" requested Sir Reginald.

"Name: Robert Stone. That's G-R-E-G-O-R-space-S-A-M-S-A."

"Maybe we can finish these later," said Sir Reginald. "What do you think about the inspirational business posters around the company? They were my idea."

"And what inspired you to do that, Reg?"

He insisted that everyone call him by his full name, Sir Reginald, and did not respond to my question.

"Holy shit," I said. "I think that's a genuine Léger over your shoulder. Gladys, is that a genuine Léger over there?"

"Well, it ain't a copy."

"Sorry, Reggie. I was distracted."

"That's hunky-dory. But, if you'll excuse me, Guv, you should only curse in front of the prole. Should we change the art?"

"No. That would be expensive and I'm not sure how many people would appreciate it."

"Brilliant. I never thought of that. We currently have 40,129 employees in 87 jurisdictions."

"87 jurisdictions? I thought we were in 30-something countries."

"We're in 35 countries."

"So, how do you get 87 jurisdictions?"

"50 states plus DC and Puerto Rico."

"Does the 87 also include the ceremonial counties of England and the old gulags of the Soviet Union?"

"Very good, Guv. The ceremonial counties of England. But no, just the states, DC, and Puerto Rico."

"How is morale?"

"Down. After all, we just lost our leader of many decades."

"But how do you know it's down?"

"Because it should be."

"What should we do to improve it?"

"I think an inspirational message from you would help. I would be chuffed if you let me help you write it."

"Let me think about that."

I then added, "But I think we should make a number of changes to become part of the 21st century. Our building and company should be more eco-friendly. We should have real diversity, not BS lip-service diversity. Maybe we should put in a daycare center on the premises. Pay for classes that have nothing to do with business or insurance. Paternity leave. I'll speak to the underwriters about putting incentives in polices for insuring green companies. Do you have any thoughts on these ideas, Sir Reginald?"

"Let me sort them and reckon which are brill and which are

dodgy, if any. And even though this is our first chat, I love our bants. I know Guv, you'll be a ledge."

All sorts of visitors streamed into my office. They represented kings and fools on camels and donkeys, bearing frankincense, myrrh, and trepidation. Conspirators from the Roman Senate, and stutterers with sincere congratulations gathered. Sprinkled among the common gossipmongers and avengers seeking retribution for real or perceived past transgressions, were the merchants of deceit. I began to welcome the mundane discussions of sales, expenses, and the vagaries of projects small and large. All grasping for an advantage, petty or major, and they measured me with their own narrow criteria.

I greeted each with a practiced smile and a firm dry handshake. I toyed with the idea of telling each person I had a different nickname so I could trace any rumor. But no matter how enjoyable that might be, I could never remember what I said to whom.

Then there were those who thought they and they alone held the power and the secrets of the universe, and that if I curried favor with them, my success would be assured, and my demise deferred for at least a week. Such was the case with Mike Tompkins, the head of the International Division, who ended my day.

"I understand you're an artist," said Mike Tompkins.

"I can be."

"We have art in our home."

"Oh yes? What type?"

"The type with wire on the back and those little round metal holes."

"I'm sure they're lovely."

"I dunno know. My cleaning lady dusts them. You have the job that is rightfully mine. But you won't be here long. You don't know sales. Coverages. Claims. Underwriting. Regulation. Legal. Investments. Risk Management. All you know are those newsletters no one reads."

"Here, eat this."

"You want me to eat a piece of paper?"

"Yes," I said.

"Why should I eat it?"

"In some old schools in Eastern Europe, eating sweetened paper represented the joy of ingesting knowledge." I ate one as a tacit challenge but did not tell Tompkins that it was a forgotten Jewish tradition where rabbis would give young boys paper with honey on it to chew when they first started *cheder*, Hebrew school.

Tompkins stared at the paper. As President of the International Division, he felt the need to protect his foreign mercenaries. Being posted abroad was like herpes; once you got it, you got it over and over again.

"What the hell?" said Tompkins and ate the paper. "Grape?"

"No, cherry."

"It tastes like grape."

"Cherry. Do you feel smarter?"

"Not yet."

"It's early."

"What changes are you going to make?" asked Tompkins.

"I'm not sure yet."

"May I make a suggestion?"

"I wouldn't expect anything less," I said.

"Don't change anything."

"Nothing? Are you a supplicant of the status quo?"

"Change nothing. You might upset the stability that exists. Spaulding valued what he called equilibrium. People are afraid of change. Especially from someone like yourself, someone who knows nothing."

"That's exactly why I was chosen. I'm not part of some secret fraternity like some people I know, who think they run things."

"How did you know about that?" asked Tompkins.

"You're not supposed to brag about a secret society," I said.

"I'm just talking about equilibrium."

"Spaulding and his equilibrium are dead."

"I could always use more money for raises and bonuses and to hire more people," said Tompkins.

In business, people were currency and Tompkins wanted to be the richest.

"Maybe we can open an office in Mumbai. India's now the world's largest country," continued Tompkins.

"I thought we had an office in Mumbai," I said.

"Just wanted to see what you knew."

"How is your division faring?" I asked.

"Good. Better than good. We made our quota last quarter, and we look good to this quarter," said Tompkins.

"Great. What about the fraud case in London?"

"Nothing we can't handle."

"Civil and Criminal?"

"Yes, both."

"Have you read the UK Fraud Act of 2006, which discusses the borderline between criminal and civil liability?" I asked.

I did not tell Tompkins that I knew nothing about it either until that morning when I spoke with our General Counsel Mimi Lee.

"You know the company motto: 'We seek an unfair advantage.' Don't worry, Stone. I know what I'm doing in the UK, and this is just the price of doing business."

"Well, read up on it anyway," I continued. "It could save your division real money. We'll meet monthly, but if there are any emergencies, you know where to find me. On the way out, tell Gladys what dates are good for you."

"By the way, there are two ways to assess an insurance risk: frequency and severity. The worst is when both are high. Which are you?"

"You know the names of the two lions outside the 42nd Street Library? Patience and Fortitude. They sit out there in the heat, hurricanes, and snowstorms. Which are you?"

"Do you want to ask me anything else?"

"Like what?"

"Like where the bodies are buried. I know where all the bodies are buried," said Tompkins.

"Well, if they're dead, what harm can they do?" I asked.

"I know your type. You're untrustworthy because you're honest. You see yourself as some caped crusader. Well, at least for now. I could be very useful to you."

"That's probably so. Speak to Gladys on the way out and I'll see you next quarter."

"I thought we would meet monthly."

"We just did."

"Just remember: around here sales matter, not brains. Sales are king and you're a pauper."

"He's in big trouble Gladys," said Tompkins as he made his appointment. "Big trouble. Tell him that. You know he has the job that is rightfully mine."

"You're very agitated, Mike; do you want to sit a minute?"

"I'm not agitated, I'm involved."

Gladys told Tompkins to return in three months, like a dental check-up. She had been Spaulding's secretary longer than the dust on the top shelf. Long before Spaulding made his friends call him Mr. President in public settings.

When I heard Tompkins leave, I walked out to Gladys's desk, "I think that's it for the day."

"You know," said Gladys, "I've slept with just about everyone in the company. Some of the women too. Although no one recently. Getting on in years."

I tried not to give her the satisfaction of acting shocked but did not doubt her. "Everyone? You must have missed someone."

"No, no one important. I didn't screw the lame ones who are happy to be middle managers all their lives. Limp dick in life, limp dick in bed."

"Words to live by," I said.

"Some people are not cut out for the pressures of upper management. They just want to put in a day, pay the mortgage, and spend some time with their family. Watch some football. Do PTA stuff," said Gladys.

"Why are you telling me this?"

"Because you think I'm nothing more than an old biddy who just screens your calls, files papers, and remembers this and that."

"I never even hinted at that."

"Consider this a pre-emptive strike."

"Why are you really telling me this?"

"Why not? We're working together now, aren't we?"

"That we are."

"Well, you're probably the only person in the company who doesn't know about me. You want to know why I had sex with all those people?"

I did want to know but did not answer.

"I did it to protect my financial interest in Remora."

"Why? You don't trust the State Insurance Bankruptcy Fund?"

"I did it because I wanted to know how they think. Who they are. Who they knew. You learn a lot about someone when they're naked. Especially the flabby ones."

"What do you learn about people when they have clothes on?"

"Not as much. Clothes can be like armor."

"What did they learn about you?"

"Not to screw with me."

"Are you recommending this to me as an interview technique?"

"It's better than that stupid piece of paper you had Tompkins eat."

"Long after I started working at Remora, I realized that you should start acting crazy the first day of work. If you do that, then the others will not be surprised or worried when you do start acting like yourself at a later time," I said.

"Is that the reason you give them that stupid little piece of paper?"

"I give them the paper because they don't expect it. That way I can see how they react to unexpected situations and me. It's harder these days to know if someone is nuts with all the legal restrictions on what questions you can ask and what you cannot say. But you still have to figure out if they're nuts."

"That's one reason why I screwed them. But I'm too old to help you with that."

"That's OK. HR frowns on that behavior now."

Gladys unlocked her filing cabinet, removed her pocketbook from the bottom drawer, then locked it again as if the pocketbook was still in there. She applied a new layer of lipstick, looked into her compact for any new flaws, slipped on her mink, and sidled through the doors of the suite.

"Good night," said Gladys. "See you tomorrow."

"That coat is not very PC," I said.

"Let someone try and rip it from my shoulders."

"Good night, Gladys."

"Will you need my services this evening?"

"No, I'm good."

"And try to wear a better suit tomorrow. You are the CEO now."

"I only have two and one is my funeral suit. I took this one home from my old office the other night."

"At least iron the thing. And shake the dandruff from the shoulders."

"I thought the company was business casual."

"A.J. hated that and he only did it so people would think he was modern. But you can't."

"Shouldn't I set an example and dress business casual?"

"Summer Fridays. And the rest of the time, make sure that you wear nice shoes; people forget about shoes. And a nice belt. People forget about belts too."

"It will take time to buy all that and then have them tailored."

"A.J. left a few suits at the office. I think you're his size."

"I'm not wearing a dead man's suit."

"Well, he isn't wearing them, is he? Try one on tomorrow."

Chapter 2

To Air Is Human

BEFORE I COULD FINISH my breakfast of an egg sandwich on a Styrofoam roll, the three consultants, anointed by the Board as my handlers, seated themselves uninvited on the other side of my desk. They reminded me of the First Roman Triumvirate, although I could not determine who was Pompey and who was Crassus. They actually hailed from the prestigious firm of MaKissMe, their slogan, "Judgmental as your Mother. But more effective."

Bill Fine was Caeser, enrobed in a cologne from an era long past. The initials on his hand-stitched cuffs read WTF—William Thomas Fine. I guessed three marriages in and not enough accumulated wealth, meant Bill still needed to work in the field on a daily basis.

I can only describe the outer shells of the other two. To state otherwise would be rude speculation. Not that I was above that. They did, however, remind me of newly-minted physicians, unduly solemn to mask their inexperience in the hope of creating an aura of gravitas.

Fiona McAdam, properly stiff in a skirt, blouse, and reflective-stop-sign-red lipstick, seemingly had her clothes ironed in the lobby of the building. Quinn Buckley must have had a strong blink response, otherwise he would have been able to wear contacts and not have needed glasses. He combed his hair in the opposite direction of his attention.

"Good morning," they said, not quite in unison. "First of all, congratulations on your promotion."

"Thank you. I'm sure you had a hand in it."

"How have you been doing?"

"Not bad." Although this was the first time we had met, I thought they were still at Remora due to an unfinished long-term project.

"Are you adjusting?"

"Well, people seem to treat me like a zoo animal. Some want to pet me. Some think I'm dangerous. Others demand I do tricks on command."

"Is there anything you want to ask us?"

"What are the characteristics of Australopithecus?"

After a brief silence, I continued, "Give up? Small brain and walked erect."

"I believe the specialists at our company would know that. Quinn, make a note to ask them," said Bill. "We're pleased to inform you, we've arranged for you to be interviewed on the *Estrogen and Tonic* TV show tomorrow. The Board wants the world to learn about Remora's new direction."

"Tomorrow? I'm not ready to be interviewed."

"Not to worry. One of the hosts, Blenheim Peabody, is an old friend." That was supposed to assuage my fears? They thought if Bill knew him, this fraternity would naturally extend to me.

"*Estrogen and Tonic* is a new concept in television that combines business and a talk show. They can wind up discussing anything."

"I'm not much of a public person."

"You are now. And that's why we're here. To prepare you for your appearance."

"I can't learn this stuff overnight."

I guessed the consultants thought I would know how to behave on television because, like everyone else, I had watched television all my life. This was like a little kid watching his favorite baseball player and trying to emulate his batting stance, so he too could be a big leaguer.

"They'll ask some basic questions. Like what is the organic growth? What is the R-O-I?"

"What's the R-O-I?"

"It's 8%. Pretty good for an insurance company."

"No, I mean what is R-O-I?"

My ignorance filled the three with worry. "R-O-I is a very basic term. It means return on investment, R-O-I."

"*Vive Le* R-O-I!"

"That's funny. Very funny. You are flippant. But you're going to have to curtail your flippancy."

"The last flippancy ended with Pope Pius XII in 1939."

"What might be funny at a bar or with your friends is not necessarily funny in the business world. The business world will be waiting on your every word."

"Never tell a joke publicly, on-line, or on camera that could offend any human, living or dead. Thus, no mention of the Pope, unless you've had a private audience with him. Accordingly, no Pope jokes. You never know who could be a potential investor."

"Then no Third Reich jokes either?"

"If you say something funny, it could be misinterpreted. Lower the stock price. Arouse the scorn or suspicion of the media, market analysts, the SEC, or stakeholders," said Bill.

This was the business version of what will the neighbors think; no one ever thought the neighbors might like it.

"And never imply something is worse than it appears, even if it is. That seems like you're trying to cover up something," said Fiona.

"Don't get us wrong. We want you to be yourself. We want

you to be clever. You can be clever, but not too clever. Funny, but not too funny. Funny, but in an adult business way funny," said Fiona. "That's why The Board chose you."

My mind wandered and I started counting boards—cutting boards, plasterboard, floorboards, carving boards, Co-op Boards, board games, on board, college boards, draft boards, the Federal Reserve Board, boogie boards, cheeseboards, and many more. Almost all seemed to apply to my situation in one way or another.

"Think of it as hedge fun. Get it? *Hedge fun*?" said Quinn.

"Good one," said Bill. "That's the type of humor we need."

"Have you ever heard of *The Art of a Spontaneous Wit* by Harold 'Pancakes' Chamberlain?"

"We hired Pancakes as our humor consultant. He's the founder and President of Ice Breakers and Nut Crackers."

"He's a highly respected business humor consultant and a world-renowned expert on icebreakers."

"Here's his book. Read it," said Bill, gently sliding an extremely thin pamphlet across the desk. The three stared at me with great expectations that I would read a word or two and have a comedy orgasm and scream, "I'll be here all week. Try the veal."

"Does he really call himself 'Pancakes'? You know, that's a direct violation of the Nickname Rule? You're not allowed to give yourself a nickname. It has to come from someone who loves or hates you."

"People always ask him why he calls himself 'Pancakes.' Most people think it's because he likes pancakes. No, because it's an icebreaker. Isn't that clever?" asked Quinn.

"The only people who need icebreakers and conversation pieces are the people who have nothing to say in the first place."

"Rob, you have to start thinking of yourself in different terms now. Think of yourself as the *pater familias* with a splash of hard-nosed economics and only a dash of humor."

"Acceptable humor," said Fiona.

"You can't be flippant. When thinking of flippancy," said Bill, "picture the dog who runs through an electronic fence but then can't figure out how to get back in."

I was getting advice from people who needed to carry chairs around with a hole in the seat, so the stick had someplace to go.

"You must be prepared for this interview. We'll help you. Here. This is filled with facts and FAQs we've prepared for you."

They handed me loose-leaf binders with colorful coded tabs. Quinn pointed out certain highlights. "These pages explain the forecast for 3Q and 4Q."

"4Q, Quinn," I said.

"This section explains a few of the headwinds we foresee."

"This lays out some of the innovations and initiatives in progress at Remora."

"And when we say Remora, we mean you."

"And while speaking about you, here's a section on you," said Bill.

"On me?"

"When you were at Cooper Union, you took a course called, 'Art and Business.' If you can slip that in, people might conclude that you're not such a novice."

"That course taught us how to break into a gallery and hang our work when no one was looking. You think one course at an art school makes me a CEO?"

"And if you can slip in a reference to the famous Lincoln anti-slavery speech at Cooper Union in 1860, it could be construed as being an inspiration to who you are today."

"Being against slavery is really going out on a limb, don't you think? And a tad gratuitous? Anyway, can't do it. I graduated the year before the anti-slavery speech."

"And how'd you get my transcript? You know being funny can be a powerful weapon."

"You're going to have to put that weapon back in its sheath."

"And wear a better suit. We should have told you earlier, but we wanted to see how you would do on your own."

"Gladys already admonished me for that."

"Good woman."

"You guys haven't even given me a chance to fuck up."

"We're trying to prevent just that."

"We'll even pay for the first round of bespoke suits, shirts, and shoes."

"Will you pay for the belts too? People usually forget the belts," I said.

"Yes, and the belts too."

"And don't forget to read your 'Pancakes.'"

The three left without a goodbye, a peck on the cheek, or an empty, 'I'll call you tomorrow."

The following morning, Gladys told me that a car was waiting to take me to the studio for *Estrogen and Tonic*.

"My sister tapes it for me every morning. What a crazy show. Don't worry, you'll be fine," said Gladys.

I became just another overstuffed cushion in the back of a limo, a car bigger than any of my embarrassments. If I wanted a second breakfast, they installed into the door a lacquered wood bar thick with liquor. The driver belonged to an exclusive fraternity, The Society of Ex-Hitmen. His black suit barely contained his bulging body. His sunglasses bolted to his bald head. His fingers resembled peeled potatoes. The same union which provided him, also supplied hearse drivers born with an uncanny instinct to know the best route to the cemetery. They reminded me of the pool players from decades past who were forced to wear tuxedos to give the game a patina of class.

"Thanks for picking me up."

"No problem, Chief. It's what I do."

"Yeah, this is what I do now too. What's your name?"

"Little Joey. That's the name the boss gave me, because he don't like my real nickname."

"You have a nickname and nickname for your nickname?"

"Yeah. You really wanna know the real one?"

"Sure."

"Garbage Cans."

No story ends well where the main character is named Garbage Cans. I thumbed through the binders the consultants assembled crammed with theorems, astrological predictions, and children's birthdays. We all knew that no amount of tutoring or torture would enable me to understand such alchemy as business equations, let alone apply them properly. I lived in my own reality, not in the middle of someone else's contrived numbers that others placed bets on.

Bill, Quinn, and Fiona met me just inside the stage door of *Estrogen and Tonic*. I flashed the binders at them as if I had read them. They directed me backstage where I was washed and folded into an appropriate guest. I wore makeup for the first time since I played a destitute peddler in a summer camp production of *Fiddler on the Roof*. The consultants peppered me with questions and offered their versions of a proper answer.

"Maybe this wasn't a good idea," said Bill. "Sometimes Peabody drinks too much."

"Now you think of that?"

"Two minutes," someone from the production crew yelled.

I could read a disclaimer on the monitor that neither host owned Remora stock. This statement, while reassuring that no conflict of interest existed, also demonstrated a keen lack of confidence in the company.

"Remember the consequences of being flippant. No flippancy."

The show intentionally featured a misshapen pair, Katje Russell, a young Black Progressive woman, who had worked for a number of NGOs and activists, and Blenheim Peabody, a white conservative who went directly from the womb to Yale. Their contractual obligation was to fight about everything, especially when not necessary. Peabody wore his hoary verisimilitude as armor. He pronounced his name "PIBB-it-ee."

"Don't be nervous. Just pretend we're having a conversation over drinks," Peabody told me. His red nose leached through the make-up.

"Today, we have an exclusive. The first national TV appearance of Rob Stone, the new CEO of Remora Property & Casualty, a large insurance company with offices worldwide. He took over for the legendary A. J. Spaulding," said Peabody.

"Mr. Stone has an unusual background for a CEO. He is a graphic and fine artist who has exhibited his art in the United States and Europe. He is a graduate of Cooper Union, the prestigious art and architecture college here in New York. Let's welcome him this morning," said Russell.

I got the distinct feeling everyone did welcome me, except Peabody.

"Thanks for coming this morning, Rob. Can I call you 'Rob'?"

Peabody did not give me time to respond.

"I must ask the obvious question first. How does your background as a graphic artist prepare you to be a CEO of any company, let alone a staid institution like Remora?"

"I don't think the Board of Remora wants to remain a staid institution. That's one reason they chose me. I think running an insurance company is a lot like running a large art studio. The most skilled people are assigned to the most important projects. Able people need little or no guidance. Those with less experience or initiative need more guidance. You have to be wise enough to know who's who. Rembrandt and Michelangelo had students who worked as assistants. And today Jeff Koons and Chihuly have small armies of able craftspeople."

"That's modern and proven at the same time," said Russell.

"We are trying to create a different type of profitable company."

"Like a Frankenstein," said Peabody.

"Frankenstein is an easy comparison. Is that why the hump on your back keeps moving from shoulder to shoulder?"

Peabody did not flinch while Russell laughed with her eyes. I looked to see if the townspeople, including the consultants, were racing up the hill with pitchforks and torches.

Russell asked me, "How is it to take over for a legend like A.J. Spaulding? He turned a small company into a large one."

I was anxious and fell back on what I knew: art references.

"In art, there is a term, *pentimento*. That's when an artist paints over what has dried but traces of the old painting can still be seen. Sometimes, an x-ray machine is needed to see what is underneath, but sometimes it peeks through on its own. I haven't been accepted as yet. The ghost of Spaulding still roams the halls."

"Very poetic," said Russell.

Peabody jumped in. "But this is a business show, not some airy-fairy art show. We need business answers. What is Wall Street supposed to do with that stuff?"

"I'm just saying that some of things Mr. Spaulding did were evident while others were not. Some are buried in corporate history or by his iron-fisted rule. Thus, the value of pentimento."

"Not so fast. Are you saying Spaulding was a dictator?" asked Peabody.

"Except for a co-op or a kibbutz, every business is some sort of a dictatorship."

"How will you govern?"

"I don't know exactly, but I appreciate unique viewpoints, such as negative space." I knew I sounded like a pompous ass but could not contain myself.

"Oh dear, not more poetic nonsense. The business community has no clue what you are talking about; we know about profits and losses. P&L."

"Well, I want to hear more about negative space," said Russell. "It sounds like it might have interesting applications."

"Yes, what exactly is negative space anyway and what does that have to with the price of tomatoes?" asked Peabody.

"Negative space is the area within, between, and around objects and can be adapted for painting, drawing, and photography. It can help focus the eye. It can evoke its own image or illusion. Different people may see different things."

"Hear that?" asked Peabody. "That's the sound of Remora stock plummeting."

"Oh, don't be yourself for ten minutes, Blenheim, and listen to new ideas. This is original and exciting."

"Businesses thrive on conformity, as I think Mr. Peabody would have it. New ideas don't have to be accepted, but should be seen and considered," I said.

"All this mumbo jumbo sounds to me like the famous painting *The Scream*," said Peabody. Some of the crew laughed. "There are all sorts of global and domestic economic conditions that should be considered before creativity and conformity."

"But isn't this refreshing and possibly a new way to lead?" said Russell.

"Sob-sister BS. You're the reason a major corporation has never been headed by a writer or artist. How about a dancer? They can pirouette and leap all around the office. We need hardened businesspeople."

"Today's MBAs are taught to have a defendable position in case something fails in the future. They are more prepared for failure than success. Intuition and creativity are frightening to businesspeople," I said.

Then Peabody asked a specific question that needed a real response in return. "Remora stock is at 22 times earnings. The industry average is 13. Is that attributable to the leadership of Spaulding? What is your target P/E?"

I had to pull something out of my ass. I had to remember something from the binders besides a Pancakes' joke. Anything that resembled a number.

"There is more than one directional filter that can measure a company. Our 50-day moving average has been a steady up," I said with a great deal of false authority. I also hoped my grammatical inaccuracy would lend to some authenticity. Did that make any sense? Did they buy that? I wished I knew what this shit meant. Please ask me anything but questions that need a number in response.

"You are just filled with hooey. If I were a shareholder of Remora, I would sell my shares, move to Idaho, and become a survivalist," said Peabody.

"Let's open this up to questions," said Russell. "Just speak clearly into the microphone."

I did not realize that talk show meant audience participation. No one warned me about this. The first few questioners wavered from complimentary to accusations that I was creating a new form of business obfuscation. But then a woman about my age accepted the microphone and said, "Good Morning. My name is Joyce Schapiro. But you might remember me as Tandalayo Blossom when I lost my virginity to you."

"Me?" said Russell.

"Me?" said Peabody.

"No, Bobby Stone."

My face reddened from Tandalayo's statement and the heat from the overhead lights. My feet were cold from the studio air conditioner. Due to the temperature differences, I turned into one of Aunt Georgia's culinary impossibilities—a brisket that was burnt on the top and frozen on the bottom. We always tried to pick some meat from the middle with the hope we could chew it. If she had a dog, it either would have been well fed or dead. I did not know what to say. A joke would have been insensitive, and an apology seemed gratuitous or long overdue. I hoped for a nuclear conflagration. A nationwide blackout. Cassia knew I had a life before her. Everyone has a previous life, but this was not the time or place to divulge something like this. Did I walk into an intentional ambush?

"We were young and innocent kids," said Tandalayo.

I had not thought about her in decades but now I thought more about litigation than lust. I had to give her a cordial neutral response, not too personal. But it couldn't be cold either. It did happen over 35 years ago.

"Hello, can I call you Joyce?"

"Sure, I haven't used Tandalayo in years."

"How are you? I hope you've had a wonderful life."

"You were sweet about it then and seem the same now."

She did not mention child support and seemed more wistful than angry. "Thank you," I said. "Would you and your significant other like to have dinner with my wife and myself?"

"I have two significant others. I live with a man and a woman."

"Bring them both. We can order a bunch of things. It seems like you're used to sharing." Nobody laughed and Joyce said nothing. Fortunately, that was the end of my segment, whether planned or of panic.

"We want to thank Rob Stone, the newly appointed CEO of Remora P & C for his most informative and unusual answers. If anyone understands them, send us a text or email at what's-the-world-coming-to.com?" said Peabody.

As I walked off the set, I heard Peabody tell Bill, "That was the most bizarre interview I have ever been part of. Does he really know what the 50-day average means?"

Russell said, "That was kickass. Those Harvard MBAs must be shitting case studies now."

I tried to avoid a postmortem with the consultants by racing directly to the limo. I ran through an adjoining studio adorned with a wall ablaze with green and red squares, indicating a specific stock's value at that particular moment. Christmas lights of both profit and despair.

"Remora up two and half points," someone shouted.

Fiona and Quinn thwarted my plans by jumping into the car with me. The last time I was in the backseat of a car with a Republican girl was in high school.

"You were fantastic. We're getting all sorts of messages about how different and engaging you were. Boy, that virginity thing worked out well. People thought you were a gentleman and she was a bit of a kook."

I had not heard the word kook in decades. I was quite

Success Is Not An Option

surprised that people liked what I said, especially the consultants, who get paid to correct things.

"Now, we want you to conduct podcasts and webinars."

"Webinars sound like an Elmer Fudd production, you cwazy webinar."

"And the producers want you to return next week and talk about virginity."

"Oh, no. Mi virginity no es tu virginity. That was a one-time shot. Besides, that schmuck Peabody hates me."

"It's just an act. It probably goosed his ratings. And Bill said that he will milk your appearance for weeks."

"Hey Garbage Cans, you hungry?"

"I'm always hungry."

"Do you like pancakes?"

"Nah, I can take 'em or leave 'em."

"You don't like pancakes? Some people live by them."

"Nah, they used to serve them every Thursday morning when I was inside."

I turned to Fiona and Quinn, "See, he doesn't like pancakes either."

"Hey Garbage Cans, do you like franks?"

"Do ducks have lips?"

"These are my cousins from out-of-town who've never been to Brooklyn but named their daughter Brooklyn."

"That just ain't right. Who'd name their daughter Brooklyn? That's like naming your kid Gowanus Canal before it was cleaned up," said Garbage Cans.

"What kind of name is Garbage Cans anyway?" whispered Quinn. Both consultants looked confused.

"Do you have time to stop at Papaya Papa?" I asked.

"Your dime, Chief. Ya' mean, the place with the fruit drinks that never met a fruit?"

"Yeah, like someone blessed it by passing an orange and papaya over some cold water. Like some weird church rite."

"Hey, you just reminded me. I got a better idea," said Garbage

Cans. "I know this guy from the can who makes the best dirt water dogs."

"Perfect. Everyone can have a few dogs on me. Should we get rid of the guy in the trunk first?" I asked.

Garbage Cans caught on immediately that I was putting on the other passengers. "Whatta' you, a wise guy? You know we got rid of him already."

I asked Quinn and Fiona, "You guys want to try a dirt water dog?"

They looked at each other with uncertainty but answered, "Sure, we'll try one."

They did not ask what it was and I was not going to tell them.

"You'll love them, don't worry. Hey Garbage Cans, we're not going to the guy who was
cited because he didn't know what was in the dogs?"

"Nah. My guy knows what's in 'em."

The Dirt Water Dog Guy hugged Garbage Cans and they reminisced for a few minutes about guys they once knew but had disappeared. Then the Dirt Water Dog Guy began the metallic and melodic ritual of building a frank. First, he twirled his two-tined serving fork in the air. Then, he stabbed a bun from the display case, slamming the sliding door shut. With the prongs, he next flipped open a piano-hinged lid, speared a dog from a lukewarm pond, and let the cover bang closed. Without the slightest bit of grace, he plopped the dog onto the bun, after which he slapped on the mustard from the end of long dipstick, added relish and tangy red onions, then awarded it to you. And whatever soda you wanted, he fished out of the bottom of the ice chamber. Every vendor, good citizen or ex-con, wrapped the dripping can in a thin napkin which immediately became soaked.

"You don't got no beers, do you?" asked Garbage Cans.

"No, these frankfurter licenses are hard to get, so I don't fool around," said the Dirty Water Dog Guy.

The 300-pound frankfurter cart was a New York institution.

It might exist elsewhere but no New Yorker cared. The dogs themselves were more satisfying than good.

Garbage Cans immediately ordered several rounds of dogs and shared some of them. He sipped his orange drink through a straw like a delicate schoolgirl, slyly emulating Fiona. Quinn took small bites as if that might prevent his poisoning. I lived in the world the consultants created for me and, just for a few minutes, I wanted them to know mine.

"Don't worry. Everybody wonders where they go to bathroom," I said.

Chapter 3

Bread and Circuses

ARGUMENTS AND COMPLAINTS were the price of admission to a corporate cafeteria. The air was filled, not with the smells of the daily specials, but with moans and indignation. No co-worker or boss had ever done anything right since the inception of work. If everyone returned to the wrong office or company after lunch, even those involved in insider trading, money laundering, or office affairs, would not notice the difference.

Younger workers groused in a nasal upspeak. The future of American commerce will pass through the sinuses of our youth. Older workers spoke the language of practiced weariness. At the core of this dissatisfaction was the knowledge, whether this was their first job out of college or retirement in a week, that they all would have to work, for at least another twenty-five years.

As soon as Lindsay Ackerman, my oldest friend at the company, saw me, she secured a seat for me by draping a napkin on the back of an empty chair. White, of course, was the traditional color of surrender and, in some Asian cultures, the color of death.

Gary Gilbert and Karl Hoving, our colleagues who always joined us for lunch, fidgeted. Their eyes darted around The Caf, seeming to ask, "Why the hell is he joining us? What will people think of us?"

"I got your obit. Very subtle," I said to Lindsay.

That morning when I arrived at the office, an envelope from Lindsay sat on my desk. I slit it open and found her more honest, never to be published, obituary of A.J. Spaulding. Scribbled at the top, she wrote, "I wonder if Spaulding started as a nice guy too."

Remora Property & Casualty is sad to announce the passing of their Chairman of the Board and CEO, A.J. Spaulding, Jr. The egomaniacal, tit-grabbing asshole died last Tuesday, succumbing to a horrible disease to the glee of all who knew him. Born in Buttfuck, Kentucky, where cesspools were used for swimming holes, Spaulding began to resent his early hardscrabble life and tiny cock. He thought this gave him carte blanche to claw, lie, and scheme his way to the top, while treating everyone like shit. He dropped out of a college that no one had ever heard of and joined the Army. He would often snigger, "I was too young for the First World War and too old for the Second." He quickly rose to the rank of private.

After his military service, Spaulding became the protégé of Robert Hoover, the benevolent founder of Remora Property & Casualty. Spaulding's management style of inquisition and stomping on live bodies allowed him to reshape the firm from a mid-sized organization into the company it is today. As soon as he could, Spaulding fucked Hoover over by labeling him a Commie homosexual poet. Spaulding, well-known for installing underage girls under his desk and squandering company funds on penis enlargers, also kept at least four sets of books. Married countless times, he is survived by a collection of mutants and reprobates, some of whom still slither across the floors of Remora Property & Casualty.

Donations can be made to the "I Could Really Give a Shit Foundation."

He will be sorely missed.

"You're another one who has no confidence in me," I said to Lindsay.

"It's not that I lack confidence in you. It's just you've never done anything like this before and you don't know what the hell you're doing. It's gentle encouragement," said Lindsay.

I raised my right hand and pledged to Lindsay, "I solemnly swear to be a *mensch*, especially when the schmucks are thick. So help me, cultural Jews."

"Be sure to keep that promise *Übermensch,*" said Lindsay.

"I'm sorry I didn't come here sooner to tell you what happened," I said.

"Missed your old troop of baboons, Rob?" asked Karl.

"I'm glad you're here now, Rob. Maybe you can settle this argument," said Gary. Gary was Lindsay's loyal assistant, a proud Nazi grammarian, and on a first name basis with many dead writers. Gary always feuded with Karl.

Karl had once been my assistant, but went back to school for something or other, then moved to another area, and possibly to another company. He refused to acknowledge for whom or where he worked. Nevertheless, he returned every day to our table, even when he was on vacation. "The prices and fights are better here."

"How many times have we sat here and planned the demise, exile, or hanging of Spaulding and some of the others? Well, now I'm one of those others," I said.

"That TV appearance didn't help," said Gary.

"It was the consultants' idea. Not mine."

"Nuts. That was nuts," said Karl. "Why would you appear on some finance/porn show? What were you thinking?"

"It wasn't porn. A woman asked a very personal and unexpected question. You watched it?"

"Of course, I watched it. How many times does someone I know appear on television? Like never. Especially someone you know, who always gets mayonnaise on his fly at lunch," said Gary.

"Not every lunch," I said.

"Why did you talk about art stuff?"

"I panicked a little and started talking about things I knew. Did it sound pretentious or evasive?"

"Actually, I think it helped. That old fart had no idea what you were talking about and it threw him off his game. He was ready to argue business and you talked art. You were an accidental genius. But don't try it again. They'll be ready next time," said Lindsay.

"Can we get back to what is important? The argument between Karl and me. Don't you think it's wrong to use an ice cream scooper to make tuna balls?"

"What are you talking about, Gary?" I asked.

"The Caf uses ice cream scoopers to make tuna balls for tuna ball salad. And then the scoopers stink."

"You're the only one who calls it tuna ball salad. Most humans call it tuna salad and don't give a shit how the balls got there," said Karl.

"The point is that the tuna smell sticks to the scooper like a skunk."

"Who walks around smelling tuna balls? Besides, don't they wash the scoops every night?"

"Maybe."

"Have you ever heard a parent yell, 'Hey kids, do you wanna go for tuna? YAY. I hope they have albacore. It's my favorite.' No, they scream for ice cream. Ice Cream."

"Tuna and ice cream: it's not a binary choice."

"It is if you get two different scoops."

"You know, you could have told us about your promotion. People expect us to know things," said Karl.

"I barely knew about it myself. Things happened quickly."

"That didn't help us. You made us look bad."

"Excuse me, Lindsay and gentlemen. But I'm going to get something to eat," I said. As I sidled through the tables to the food line, I gathered a few quizzical looks as to why I was here and could I be that guy.

The colors of the walls and furniture of The Caf must have

been clinically tested to brighten the spirits of employees to make them happy, happy, although it never worked. The pea soup and string beans matched the greens of the walls and carpeting, while the hamburger buns and oranges matched the tables and chairs.

I chose my lunch and got on the line to pay. Without lifting her head or the cover of the Styrofoam clamshell, Wanda the Cafeteria Lady said, "Burger and fries. No cheese, right?"

"Yes. How did you know that?"

"And the lime Jell-O. Your ID?"

"Sorry, I don't have my new ID yet and I didn't bring my old one."

"You need your ID if you want to buy anything. Jell-O or turd soup. You need your ID."

"Wanda, you know me."

"I knew you last week. I don't know you this week. NEXT!" said Wanda, without looking up.

Someone at the back of the line yelled, "C'mon, he's the new boss for chrissakes."

"I don't care if he's the old dead boss. No ID. No lunch. NEXT!"

Lindsay saw the skirmish and walked over and offered to pay for my lunch.

"Why are you paying for this man? A man who now makes a lot more money than you," Wanda asked Lindsay.

"See, you know me," I said to Wanda and then to Lindsay, "Thanks, here's the money,"

"My treat. You can buy me some real food one of these days," said Lindsay.

As I squeezed in next to Karl, he said, "You know the vegan and gluten-free stuff they sell now, right? Well, it's a little-known fact that The Glutens and The Vegans signed a secret non-aggression pact during World War II. But it didn't last long because the two sides could not decide who was more self-righteous."

"That's not true," said Gary.

"I'll bet some of their grandchildren are sitting among us now," I said. "So, what else is going on?"

"Nothing," said Gary, like a child when asked what happened that day at school. "What should we call you now?"

"Rob. I'm still Rob."

"How about Big Kahuna? Big Wig? Top Banana? Head Honcho."

Chief Rabbi would be nice, I thought. Unlike most countries with Jewish communities, there are no Chief Rabbis in America. The non-Jews in the company thought that's what I was anyway, so it would be an appropriate form of sacrilege.

"What's the weirdest thing that has happened since you became the boss?"

"I have a bodyguard. You know, the guy who walks around the halls with the blue satchel. He's like my personal hitman. So, treat me right."

"The one who carries a nuclear device, right?"

"Yep, the same."

"You're shitting me?"

"Nope. He worked for Spaulding and they thought I might need him too. His name's Sladka. He's Bulgarian and he had his tongue cut off by pirates."

"Pirates in Bulgaria?"

"They must have gotten lost. OK, but he did have his tongue cut out."

"Aren't you afraid of him?"

"Not yet. He says he's on my side."

"Do you want to split a brownie?" Gary asked Karl.

"No, you never cut them even. And you always get the bigger half."

"Isn't the bigger half an oxymoron?"

"If two people wanted to share something, my great-grandfather would have one person cut something in two, and the other person would choose which piece to eat."

"That's smart. Since you're the new Solomon, why don't you cut the brownie for us?"

"I think you're both capable of a bisection selection."

Karl went to get a brownie and a plastic serrated knife. "They have sporks; why don't they have knorks?"

"What's a knork?"

"A combo knife and fork."

"That's not how you pronounce knork."

"Of course, it is. I invented it."

"Here, Rob. You cut it."

I turned it on its side and cut it through the center, splitting the bottom from the top.

"But I don't like just the bottom."

"Next time, be more specific."

"We've got to get back to work. It was good to see you, Rob. I mean, Mr. Stone, Sir."

When the others left, Lindsay asked, "Why do you think they picked you, Rob? Why not some MBA type? Or at least someone with business experience? And why did you accept? Aren't you leery of them?"

"They thought they would try a liberal, keep a close eye on me, give me doggie treats, and see what happens. I think The Board and the MaKissMe consultants have some sort of deal. If I work out, they can sell the 'Liberal CEO' model to others and makes millions."

"But a graphic artist of all things?"

"I figured, what have I got to lose? I ain't a kid anymore. And in a Pollyanna sort of way, maybe I can do something useful. They underestimate people like you and me and they feel superior because we're not hard-ass business types. But we know stuff that they don't know. They don't know things like crappy artists and crappy writers copy and that great artists and great writers steal."

"What does Cassia think?"

"She's both worried and excited. It's almost as stupid as the things we did when we were kids. And they pay me a shit-load of cash. In a weird way, it's almost liberating. But what I haven't told Cassia yet is that we'll probably have to attend fancy-ass functions ..."

"You'd better. She'll have to buy clothes, dresses and shoes and stuff."

"I'm sure she has something."

"You ignorant male."

"Good to see you in here, Mr. Stone," said a passerby. "I like what you said about negative space on that TV show. There is a lot of negative space going on around here. Maybe you can do something about it?"

"I'll see what I can do."

"Do you know him?"

"Not a clue. Maybe I should have corrected him."

"No, he thinks you're on his side."

Everyone self-segregates at The Caf. The reason could be anything—caste, ethnicity, color, education, position, or even the non-existent descendants of the Vegan/Gluten feud. Ten thousand Remora employees in New York alone and each one sits with the same four every day to avoid sitting with a new or odious substitute. The exception is the Christmas roast beef lunch when employees fly in from Hong Kong and Buenos Aires at their own expense, only to wait on line for 35 minutes for a free meal. Otherwise, The Caf is only used a few hours a day. Maybe the company could fill the unused times with other activities? New ways for the troops of baboons to be with their own kind.

As soon as I returned to my desk, I asked Gladys to summon Barry Belette, while I typed out my new ideas as fast as I could. Belette was another I inherited from Spaulding. A sycophant who gave sycophants a bad name but could act as an effective nettle. If Spaulding needed something done that did not require thinking or large sums of money, he would ask Belette to pester whoever needed pestering until they succumbed or left the company. Belette lived in dread that he might not be able to say "yes sir" to whoever gave him an order. It had to be hard living your life in fear every day.

Fifteen minutes later, Belette appeared as commanded but with his own Sladka: Sir Reginald.

"Good afternoon, Guv. You were brill on the telly. But you did look a bit knackered," said Sir Reginald.

"What's knackered mean?" asked Belette.

"I'm fine, thank you."

"I was having lunch with some old friends in the cafeteria, and I have some ideas that might improve morale and make the company some money." I handed each a copy of my notes.

"I have some ideas I want to run past you."

Gladys came into the office, "Wait a minute. You're not changing anything around here without me knowing about it." She tried to rip Belette's notes from his hands, but he was too quick and held them against his chest. When Gladys glared at him, he turned the pages over to her and read over Sir Reginald's shoulder.

"What's your first idea, Guv?"

"OK, let's establish an 'Asshole of the Month Award.' They deserve formal recognition too and it may modify behavior. We'll have a company-wide vote."

"I see liability issues there," said Sir Reginald.

"Maybe we should hold off on that one," said Belette.

"What are you afraid of? That you'll win every month?" said Gladys.

"Let's try it and see where it goes," I said.

"Another stupid idea. Don't make me give you the ultatomato," said Gladys.

"What's the ultatomato?" asked Sir Reg.

"That's when Gladys threatens me that it's either her or ... I am not sure what," I replied.

"How about if someone stabs a co-worker in the back, steals their work, or spreads gossip, they should have an 'R' for rat embroidered on their clothes for easy identification. Like Hester Prynne's 'A' in the *Scarlet Letter*," I said.

"Who pissed in your cereal? That is really, really, really, stupid," said Gladys.

"You'll need a lot of Rs."

"OK, OK. Too extreme. Forget that one. How about in its place, a Kangaroo Court to settle minor grievances?"

"We'll have a pool of employees who'll act as judges."

"We have to make sure the judges don't know the people involved in the argument."

"What will the punishment be?"

"To talk to you guys," said Gladys.

"That might work."

"Wow. This is really turning into a brainstorming session," said Belette.

"More like a *braingusting* session than brainstorming with this crew," said Gladys.

"OK, how about this one?" I asked. "We should establish a true meritocracy at Remora. We should develop a system where people can advance, not based on who they know or who they went to school with or who they slept with, but on their feats and gests."

"Another brill idea, although a tad idealistic," said Sir Reginald.

"Are you going to have a senior prom, too?" asked Gladys.

"Maybe we can do it like the Police Department and include years of service," said Sir Reginald. "We can weigh annual reviews and peer reviews. Give points for accomplishments. We can give a standardized test."

"Standardized tests yield standard people," I said.

"And besides everybody hates annual reviews," said Gladys.

"I think it's a good idea. I'll work on the specifics" said Belette.

"We need metrics for all your new innovations. Everything is metriced these days." said Sir Reginald.

"Is metriced a word?"

"Abso-bloody-lutely. I'm sure it is, Guv." Reggie knew Americans never took offense at the use of the word "bloody" and it sounded at once both vulgar and sophisticated.

"We don't need metrics. I'm sure everything will work as planned," said Belette. "I'll make it work."

"Barry can't be a secondment. We don't need a Gordon Bennett."

Nobody knew who or what Gordon Bennett meant, but no one bothered to ask either.

"We'll see. I don't want to pay for metrics. I don't want to hire new people, yet. I want people to act like people and use their intuition, not their fear."

"Who are you, Winston Churchill?"

"Let's vote," said Belette.

There were three ayes and a dirty look from Gladys. She might have liked the idea but did not want to be seen agreeing with Sir Reginald or worse Belette.

"This is the last one, I promise. The Caf is only used from approximately 8 AM to 2 PM during the week. Maybe we can find other activities to fill the other hours. How about a poker tournament?"

"What are you, crazy? Poker? Gambling on the premises?" said Gladys.

"Barry, write Mimi Lee and ask her what the restrictions are on gambling on the premises. Maybe we'll have to harden or soften some of the ideas."

"Dance lessons might work," said Sir Reginald.

"They're all stupid," said Gladys.

"The poker would be for charity."

"That's better," said Gladys.

"How about if we have weddings and bar mitzvahs at night and weekends?" asked Belette.

"That sounds a little ambitious."

"At last, this one makes some sense," said Gladys.

"Barry, I want you to head the Cafeteria Committee. See how difficult or easy it is to stage such events."

"Sounds good. Do I have a budget or a deadline?"

"Send any bills to me but create your own deadline."

"No one's ever let me create my own deadlines. Not even in elementary school. And certainly not Mr. Spaulding."

"Well, here's your opportunity."

I knew allowing Belette to set was his own deadlines was a bit cruel. Afterall, any deadline he chose would be self-imposed and more severe than anything I might inflict on him. Yet, this was the perfect assignment for him.

"Thank you," I said to all.

When Belette and Reginald left Gladys remained. She became hesitant, something she usually considered a character flaw in others.

"I know everybody hates Belette because he's a *tuchas* licker. And I'm probably the meanest to him. But people like him make the company go."

"He's smaller than life. How did he wind up working for Spaulding?"

"I really don't know. One day he's in Workers' Comp and the next he's kneecapping people for Spaulding. I don't even think he knows how he got here. Can I show you something?" asked Gladys.

"Of course." I did not know what to expect.

Gladys went to her desk and returned with a book. "Here. You're the first person I've shown this to because you're an artist and I know you'll understand. But be kind."

"What is this?"

"It's a book about Barry Belette. It's called *Barry the Beneficial Nematode.*"

Gladys gave me a handmade manuscript replete with illustrations.

"You're going to hate it."

"No, let me see it."

"I was inspired to do this because I'm a weekend gardener." It was almost shocking for Gladys to display a vulnerable side.

"A splendid title, indeed," I said. "Who did the illustrations?"

"My sister Mary. She could have been a very good artist but was too shy to exhibit."

Gladys started reciting *Barry the Beneficial Nematode* in the sincere, but obligatory, sing-song voice of a child's book reader as she gently turned the pages.

To the Barry I know, I write this ode,
He's a not toad, but a nematode.

Her rhyme was under a drawing of a nematode wagging his head at a frog.

It's a worm, a worm? Is what I found,
Not hook or flat, but one that's round.
It's microscopic, you cannot see,
Like a Remora retiree.

Gladys interrupted herself. "I wanted to make it a relevant poem too, so I added the retiree part."

"Very sensitive."

"And look at the dot. Mary painted even the smallest dot for the microscopic nematode." She continued reading aloud.

Some nematodes are evil but Barry is good,
He kills the bad ones whenever he could.
Like a nematode, he enters their anus for their swift
*   execution,*
And excretes a bacteria called the final solution.

"What do you think? I have been working on it for some time, for years in fact. We can change anything, including Mary's illustrations, if it's inappropriate for children."

42

I looked at the deep wrinkles in her face and could only imagine when she started it. Confronted with the ancient conundrum of critiquing other people's writing, music, or art, honestly or whether to tell them kind lies, I chose kind lies.

"It is quite sentimental and moving."

"And if you tell anyone about this, I will tell everyone you jerk off in your office with the door open."

"I don't do that."

"I know. But I don't care. And you can't tell my sister that I shared it with you. You know we live together and she would be mortified. I don't tell her about my private life, but I think she suspects. But showing you her art and my poetry without telling her, would be unforgiveable."

"I promise I won't say a word. What do you tell Mary when you don't come home?"

"I tell her I'm doing volunteer work at the church."

"An all-night church?"

"What church do you belong to?"

"I don't go to church."

Chapter 4

The Thermometer

The following morning, as I entered the Remora Building, someone grabbed my sleeve from behind one of the marble ornamental columns. The type of brown and white marble that looked like shiny head cheese.

"Sorry Rob. I didn't mean to startle you," said Gladys.

She pulled me through the gaudy lobby with its jumble of mosaics, gilded wood, and mismatched sculptures that was built in the shape of a cross to intimidate or confuse the most hardened of money lenders. She found what she thought was a quiet corner. A corner in the same lobby I had passed through thousands of times before without being accosted.

"We can talk here," she said. "It's private."

"Gladys, people can see us. Especially those two *yentas* over there who run the candy stand. And that gargoyle is taking notes. What's going on? Is there a mob upstairs that wants to kill me after that TV show debacle?"

"Worse than even that. Candy, the head of marketing, had a terrible accident. She's in the hospital and might be paralyzed."

"What happened?"

"Not sure."

"When did it happen?"

"A few days ago."

"A few days ago. Why didn't someone tell me?"

"I'll try to find that out but, meanwhile, you should head over to see her."

"Do you know which hospital?"

I raced uptown to the hospital, although the speed seemed gratuitous and an action of guilt since the incident occurred days before. There were numerous rumors and whispers about Candace's network of spies and snitches. As the story went, she routinely rifled through personnel files targeting middle-aged employees with unrealistic expectations of advancement, especially those with younger children, a mortgage, or low credit scores. She extorted the financially vulnerable and delusional for her network and personal gain. Nirvana to her was finding someone with a past addiction. Part of the legend suggested she actually read the performance reviews. And if all that failed, she would then hang some bogus allegation on her target with the promise of parole if they spied for her. The only people who could be trusted were those who left the company. Even the higher up executives were not immune from her noose. A rumor abounded that she created an off-site weekend meeting, had them pay for it out of their own pocket, and then she brought in hookers, male dancers, and a photographer.

My urgency appeared even more unwarranted as an older woman sat calmly by Candace's bedside. I introduced myself and added, "I came as soon as I heard," as if I had entered stage left in a bad play.

"She knows who you are. I'm Candy's mother, Alice. Thank you for coming. Even if you are late."

"How is she?"

"They tell me that she's paralyzed from the waist up."

"I'm not a doctor but I never heard of that."

"Well, they're saying it's the first case they ever heard of, too. She's medical history."

"What are they going to do?"

"They're not sure."

Because of her condition, she could barely move. Her white woman's brown Afro provided a second pillow. She could have been the sister of the artist on TV who whispered art lessons into his brushes as he painted the same tree over and over again.

When Candace roamed the corridors of Remora, she reminded some of a forklift with her feet pointed straight ahead, a beeping sound if she backed up. Every day at work, she wore something resembling a paramilitary outfit, sans medals or a general's stars, but the effect was the same. Now, she appeared vulnerable and immodest in her hospital gown.

"How are you, Candace?" I said to her. "I brought you some flowers."

"You better give them to her feet. Her hands don't work anymore."

"Her feet?"

"Just give them to her toes."

"Which toes?"

"The big one and the one next to it."

I placed the flowers as best I could between her toes. Candace grabbed them with the force of a crab's pincers.

"Everyone is pulling for you," I said.

"She can't answer."

"OK. I'll speak to her later."

"It won't make a difference."

"Do you know how this happened?"

"Don't you know?"

"I would like to hear it from you."

"Why?"

"If it's too painful, you don't have to tell me."

"Somebody hit her in the back of her head with a bagel during a marketing seminar. They waited until her back was turned."

"A bagel did that?"

"Yes, someone threw a bagel at her. An everything, lightly toasted, I believe. The doctors ruled out a muffin because she had cream cheese in her hair. It hit the back of her head, and now she's paralyzed."

"What's the prognosis?"

"They don't know. They gave her a CAT scan, an MRI, an electro something, and the NCV test."

"I'm not familiar with an NCV. What is it?"

"I don't know either, but they said it was bad. And they gave her the Bubinski."

"What's a Bubinski?"

"I don't know that either, but they said that one was good."

"Candace is appreciated at work, and I know how important Remora is to her."

I did not know or could not recollect Candace's real last name. Around the company, everyone secretly called her Quisling.

"Excuse me. I'll be back in a few minutes."

I stepped into the stairwell and called Gladys.

"How's Miss Angry Tits doing?"

"You have to stop talking like that."

"No, I don't. I'm 88-years-old."

"You told me 86 a few days ago."

"Spaulding will protect me."

"Spaulding's dead."

I explained to Gladys what I knew about the bagel.

"Should we stop ordering them? Liability and all that. I can tell everyone from now on, only English muffins; they'll just scratch," said Gladys with great delight.

"Please find out what her real last name is."

"I told you Miss ..."

"Enough, already."

"Quisling. That's the name everyone calls her," said Gladys.

"That can't be her real name. Just keep digging."

"How is she doing?"

"The doctors gave her an NCV, which was bad, but the Bubinski was good."

"Oh, the Bubinski. Whatever the hell that is. And don't forget to expense the flowers you brought her."

"How did you know I brought her flowers?"

"C'mon, I'm still trying to find out how come you didn't know about Candy? Be careful. There's someone or someone's trying to hide this from you to make you look bad."

"OK. But call the police and have them start an investigation."

"You shouldn't do that."

"Why?"

"First, no one likes her. Second, it's not a criminal matter."

"It is a criminal matter. She was assaulted and now she's paralyzed."

"This is New York, There must some sort of bagel exclusion. A bagel is not a deadly weapon. And if you start an investigation, it will make you seem like a hard ass."

"See what you can find out about the guy who threw the bagel?"

"He already has the admiration of untold thousands. You should find him and give him a huge bonus."

"OK, we can discuss that when I get back. Thanks again for the information."

"Don't forget the Presidents Meeting tomorrow."

"What Presidents Meeting? You'll clue me in later."

When I returned to the hospital room, I surreptitiously tried to read Candace's last name on the medical chart and wristband, but the HIPAA rules got in the way. I noticed the cheap lithographs of flowers, the pastels of Paris, and boats hanging askew in her room. Surely a study existed that indicated that innocuous art made the surroundings more serene and salubrious, but the poor reproductions, in the glare of the hospital lights, only left me agitated.

"Look, she's writing you a note with her toes," said Alice.

The rest of Candace's body did not stir as she scratched herself to life. Alice slowly sounded out each word as it was laboriously formed. "I can still do my bob."

"I think she means job. She's new at this foot writing. Of course, she can do her job, even if she's paralyzed from the waist up. After all, she is the head of marketing," said her mother.

"Call me Candy," she wrote.

"I think she just invented the American Foot Language," said her mother.

The thought of calling someone like Candace "Candy" was like calling Stalin "Joey."

Funerals, weddings, and hospital visits were extreme tests of one's social skills. But at the hospital, you could not excuse yourself to freshen your drink or speak to Cousin Tootsie whom you had not seen in years. There were some who were comfortable in these situations and came armed with an arsenal of clichés, recited in alphabetical order, including reasons to leave. But now, clichés and excuses could be used as the foundation of a lawsuit. I did not realize that my new job would make me a hostage to bromides.

"That is very brave of you Candace ... Candy. But right now, your job is to get well," I said.

"Anyone else from the office come to see her?"

"Sir Reginald."

A nurse entered, trailed by what seemed like a machine used to induce a confession. "If you'll both excuse us, I must attend to Ms. Quisling."

"Quisling. I didn't know you were Norwegian," I said.

Waiting in my office when I returned, with a broad shit-eating smile, sat Frank Collins, also known as "The Thermometer," the head of Domestic Business. Buried deep in the *kishkes* of this 5'5", 335-pound bowling ball dwelled an indicator of his choler. Just the way a church celebrated the rise in donations for some project by filling in a thermometer with a red marker, Collins' blood surged skyward whenever he became agitated or flummoxed. First, the rings of his neck filled, then his ears and nose, all racing to his crown of his skull, where it planted a scarlet flag. Almost everyone froze when the blood rushed to his head and depending upon their opinion of him, they wondered whether they should dial 911 or not. Someone created a betting pool "Red to the Head" as to who could cause Collins to react the highest and fastest. Bonus points for fainting and death.

"That was a piss-poor performance on that TV show. Did you hear me smirking?" asked Collins.

"It's good to see you, Mike."

"I'm not Mike. I'm Frank."

I always confused the two of them and today, it seemed to work to my advantage.

"I'm not going to eat a fucking piece of paper, no matter what you say. I spit on new ideas," were the first words from Collins' mouth. Clearly, he had spoken with Mike Tompkins.

Although I continued to say nothing, Collins added without provocation, "If you bastards want me to stop smoking, I'll sue for discrimination against a fat man. I'll tell them I smoke for health reasons. I'm sure I could bribe some schmuck doctor to write that. Medical nicotine or some shit like that."

"Here, have a piece of paper, Frank."

A cult figure in the company, Collins openly displayed his disdain for humans and their conventions. He sported his heft like a championship wrestling belt. One of the last of the three-martini lunch breed, a company president without a college degree, Collins could pull himself together for 30 minutes of a perfect sales presentation. His teeth were a sallow yellow, a memory of his thousands of cigars. Collins flaunted laws and regulations, displayed an overflowing ashtray in the middle of his desk, and kept a rarely used spray bottle of air-freshener in a drawer. He also had a hookah off to one side with a nearby stash of mu'assel.

Collins stared at the paper and stuck it in his mouth, "Not bad. You got more?"

I gave him two more little sheets.

"Congratulations, Frank. I heard you're getting married."

"I'm marrying someone from one of the Stans, Afghanistan, Pakistan, could be fucking newsstand as far I as concerned. Some such shithole country."

"She sounds lovely, like love at first mail order."

"I think there's a 90-day return policy. But I'm lucky she wants to screw an old fat fuck like me. She thinks if she marries me, she automatically becomes a citizen."

"Does she know that she doesn't become an immediate citizen if she marries you?"

"Well, I'm not the one who's going to tell her and neither are you. And if you do, I'll fuck you over."

"She thinks her choice is sleep with you or be deported? Maybe you should write your Senator and ask for the *Dream Act* to include that provision."

"Not a bad idea, Stone. But you'd better not tell her she has a choice."

"If I did, it would strictly be as part of a greater humanitarian effort."

We went over his numbers for the quarter and projections for the year. "I see your sales are down."

"Nothing is better for bad sales than a good lay. Try it."

"I'm not in sales."

"Oh yes you are, sonny boy. If you're in this company, you're in sales."

The guiding principle of the company under Spaulding was, no matter how successful an individual, division, region, or country, he would not hesitate to appoint someone else who he thought could do it better. This demoralized some, but most became inured. So far, we never heard that anyone ever petitioned for a change.

In the short period since I occupied my new office, I developed a devious ploy of practiced disinterest when needed. I would stare over the shoulder of a guest, out the window, and across the Hudson River to check the time on the mammoth Colgate clock in Jersey City and use it as my wristwatch.

"It's almost 5:30," I said.

"I never liked you," said Collins.

"How can you say that? We just met."

"I don't like your type."

"What type is that?"

"The type I don't like."

"How is your division going to do better?"

"Well, in order to do better, we want to expand into the U.S. Muslim communities. I already spoke to Tompkins about it. He does business in Saudi Arabia and the UAE, and he knows all about Sharia Law and Takaful Insurance."

Collins, Tompkins, and a few other survivors started in the company together as young men and outlasted almost everyone else. Insurance roaches. When they acted brutally toward one another, they acknowledged the behavior as part of their tribal behavior. If one of them fell into disfavor, someone would hide them somewhere until the problem mattered less. In business, they would use something against you if they wanted to or needed to. Otherwise, forgiveness forged alliances both strong and suspicious.

"I'm not familiar with the specifics of Sharia law. And what's the other one?" I asked.

"Takaful Insurance. Muslims are not allowed to gamble, and regular insurance is considered gambling. And they don't like something called al-gharar."

"What's al-gharar?"

"I'm uncertain, but I'll find out. I do know that Takaful Insurance is more like a mutual company with dots on their head."

"Those are Sikhs, a religious group from India. They're not Muslims. And with that attitude, I'm sure you'll do well."

"Fuck 'em. I just want their money. I'll send a salesman who looks like them and isn't on the no-fly list."

"If you really want me to approve this, you're going to have to be more respectful and knowledgeable about Muslims and their beliefs."

"I piss respect. But once the world knows we are considering this, we can be screwed in different ways. If we do it, the people who don't know fuck about Sharia Law will still be against it and try to screw us over. And if we don't do it, liberals will think we're fucking bigots for not doing it."

"Sounds like you've thought about the important issues."

"Just remember: I'm richer than you. So, I know more."

"Unfortunately for you, the poorer of the two of us has the final say. And if you don't learn the specifics, we aren't doing to do it."

The Thermometer then lived up to his reputation as I watched the blood course through his body reaching the top of Everest without a sherpa.

His shit-eating grin returned, even bigger, and he said, "Too bad you didn't know about Quisling until this morning. We wouldn't want the new CEO to look like he doesn't know what's going on in his shop."

"You set up the bagel hit on Quisling. You made sure that I didn't know for days. You hurt that poor woman just to get at me."

"Maybe. Maybe it was a bonus when she was paralyzed, not just embarrassed. But don't think for a moment 'poor Candy.'" With that, Collins walked out of the office and said to Gladys, "The guy's a friggin' idiot."

I followed him out as he left and said, "I'm not sure what I'm going to do about him."

"Collins has been here forever. You just got here," said Gladys. "Believe me, you're not going to out-nasty and outsmart a guy who boils children in oil and serves them with hot sauce for his July 4th barbeque. That's the rumor anyway."

"That's a very specific rumor."

"Before you ask, I did sleep with him. But just once, when he was a sleek 245."

"You know, I wasn't going to ask and please do not tell me the details."

"If you're lucky, you'll figure out a way to get even with him. If you are lucky."

As I was leaving the building, someone grabbed my sleeve from behind the same pillar as Gladys had that morning.

"Sorry, Guv, I didn't mean to startle you," said Sir Reginald. "Now that you know about Candace, we have something important to discuss. Come with me," he said, his fingers still clinging to my sleeve and took me to the same spot as Gladys.

"We can talk privately here."

"You know people can see us."

"Candy, Candace is working on a new Remora ad campaign with the slogan, 'Don't be paralyzed. Get Remora Insurance.'"

"Isn't that a bit personal?"

"She is paralyzed from the waist up."

"Unfortunate, indeed."

"Innit? She has another one. 'You've tried the rest, now try the best.'"

"I think she nicked that from a pizza take-away box," I said, using the little British slang I knew.

"My suggestion is we accept this slogan and limit our liability of her suing the company."

"Maybe you should run those past outside counsel."

"OK. I don't want to interfere with her creativity. She said she was looking forward to the challenge. You know she writes with her toes now on her laptop."

"Can it still be called a laptop if she uses her toes?"

"Good point."

"And that is why you dragged me to this corner?"

As part of Sir Reginald's Anglophilia, he presented himself like an Oxbridge civil servant who applauded the Raj and justified striking insolent Indians with a crop. Since returning from the UK, he continued his across-the-pond look by growing a Terry-Thomas mustache and a gap between his two front teeth.

"Yes, the real reason I'm here. Candace needs an experimental operation to regain her old form. Not that she is doing badly now."

"What is this operation supposed to do?"

"Make her the same woman she once was. A couple of cuts and threads and Bob's her uncle. But the operation costs 150,000 quid and healthcare won't pay for it because it's experimental. Maybe Remora could pay for it?"

"Your accent is changing. It sounds a bit more Celtic."

"What do you think?"

"That's better, more Brit. Won't paying for it set a bad precedent?"

"It shows we care. I thought you were supposed to be a new type of progressive leader."

"Progressive, not stupid. What are the dangers?"

"It could pop her clogs."

"Pop her clogs?"

"Kill her."

"That's a serious side effect. Although that could solve a couple of other problems at once."

"Please think about it and when you decide, just give me a tinkle on the blower."

"Could you use another phrase? Let me think about it. But if I agree, mums the word about who paid for it."

"I won't tell anyone about anything."

"How did you know about this spot?"

"Gladys told me you always come here."

Chapter 5
The Presidents Meeting

Dramatis Personae

- *Frank Collins*—President of Domestic Operations
- *Dom Oleoso*—Head of Surety Bonds
- *Harvey Knoll*—Chief Claims Adjustor
- *Mimi Lee*—General Counsel
- *Candy Quisling*—Head of Marketing
- *Sir Reginald Pigot-Smythe*—Head of HR
- *Bob Stront*—Business Hit Man
- *Doug Friedman*—President of External Relationships
- *Mike Tompkins*—President of the International Division
- IT guy—IT guy
- *The Ghost of A.J. Spaulding*
- *Me*

The smell of tuna fish sandwiches and testosterone filled the air. Almost everyone in the room, save one or two people, thought they deserved to be CEO. Some rightly so. To make matters worse, I had never attended a Presidents Meeting before and did not know all the players, the unwritten rules, or what past words or events would ignite a fury.

On the kalends of every month, various leaders of Remora, including the divisional chiefs, General Counsel, HR Director, and the heads of claims and marketing, gathered for a lunch meeting. Pads of lined paper replaced place mats, accompanied by a pen and a bottle of room temperature water. Everyone was well-prepared for a sudden drought or random thought. Even the IT guy had a pad. People who were paid in varying degrees of six figures, positioned themselves around the luncheon platters in order to grab their favorite sandwich half. Cauldrons of macaroni salad and coleslaw protected the flanks. Yet, despite their corporate status, only cheap plastic forks and knives were available to slop on the mustard or more mayonnaise, or to use on each other. The call of free food at work might be stronger than sex and money. You could put up a sign by the office coffee machine—"FREE. Dog Shit."—and it would be gone by 9:05.

Like any well-trained waitperson, I did not start to talk to them until their mouths were full.

"Good afternoon. Gladys gave me the lowdown on what happens at a typical Spaulding meeting. But I would like to change things a little. I knew Spaulding liked to see who made their sales quota, but we will dispense with that from now on."

"Why change what Spaulding did? He treated us like family," said Bob Stront.

"Yes, Richard III's family," said Doug Friedman.

"You can't change things just because you say so," said Frank Collins.

"I think that's the way business works, Frank," said Mimi Lee. "It's a structured dictatorship with a designated hierarchy governed by some minor and severe restrictions imposed by the SEC laws of 1933 and 1934, the Attorney General of New York, and, unfortunately, the laws of nature."

"If you want to change things, that's on your head," said Stront. "But you're not going to change the opening prayer. Spaulding always started these meetings with a prayer."

"A prayer? What kind of prayer?" I asked. I did not want the meeting derailed by a debate about whether prayer was allowed or not. Or worse, to embroil the company in some Constitutional issue. "Mimi, is this OK?"

Lee just shifted her eyebrows, scrunched her lips, and waved her fingers. "Does it matter?"

"In honor of A.J. Spaulding, I would like to lead us today in prayer, something I always wanted to do. All together now," Stront continued. "Thank you, dear Lord, for allowing us at Remora to seek unfair advantages. And dear Lord, one new plea: no more bullshit like negative space."

Most responded, "Amen."

"Spaulding used to go around the room and ask how everyone was doing with their quota," said a persistent Stront.

"I think our time would be best spent discussing other things, while we're all together."

"But that is unfair to those of us who did make quota. Big sales, big dick; small sales, small dick. Sorry Mimi," said Collins.

"No, you're not," said Lee.

Lee wore her law degree squarely on her Joan Crawford shoulders. She rowed on the Radcliffe Heavyweight Crew as a walk-on when the only other women on the water at that time were sirens and the Xiang River goddesses. Even in the middle of winter, Lee wore sleeveless dresses to show her well-developed guns. She used impeccable logic supported by well-grounded legal arguments as a means of intimidation. Lee perfected the accentuated raised eyebrow, daring you to criticize her or proffer a counter argument. She had navigated her way to this position through a white male world by ignoring their norms and creating her own. On occasion, she would raise her voice, but never cursed. Even when cursed at.

"Your numbers are always unreliable, Collins," said Harvey

Knoll. "You always use paper towel math. Two rolls equal six, six rolls cover a room. No premium means reaching your quota. No one knows exactly what you're talking about. Nobody knows the truth but you, and even fewer people care." Knoll made Collins' thermometer rise to just under his lip. Level two.

"And without numbers, how can we humiliate someone publicly?" asked Stront.

"Ladies and Gentlemen, we must consider our external shareholders and partners," said Friedman.

"What the fuck has that to do with anything?" asked Tompkins.

"Did you know the Babylonians invented the insurance called bottomry?" said Dom Oleoso. "We wouldn't be here if it wasn't for bottomry."

"I knew there had to be some reason for us being here."

Oleoso continued, "Bottomry is how merchants got loans to ship their goods. If a ship sank and the goods were lost, the merchant didn't have to pay back the loan."

"You say that at every meeting," said Knoll. "And then remind us that Robert Hoover's grandmother's name was Remora."

"I didn't know that. That's an unusual name; what kind of name is that?" I asked.

"His grandmother's."

"Dom makes this shit up."

"It must be true; he's not clever enough to make it up."

"Who gives a flying fuck? I mean, a sailing fuck," said Tompkins. Stront and he were the only ones who laughed. And Stront laughed because he thought he had to.

"Today, it's called a respondentia bond," said Oleoso. He was the oddest of all savants, a surety bond savant. He knew little else about the world. He sat at the end of the conference table with the hope he would not be called upon. Unsure about human relationships, he smiled until someone turned off the lights or the food was taken away. His mustache twitched as he crawled along the baseboard, hoping his presence would not be noticed.

"Are you done, Dom?"

"Spaulding thought humiliation was a great motivator and I agree with him," said Stront.

"It wasn't humiliating, if you made quota," said Tompkins.

"It didn't matter anyway. If you made your quotas, Spaulding would just raise it," said Oleoso.

"Let's try to keep public humiliation to a minimum," I said. "Even self-inflicted humiliation. We're trying to do things differently now."

"You're not going to give us any of that airy-fairy bullshit like you did on that TV show, are you?"

"No more quota talk, I'm instituting the 'Dog Rule,'" I said.

"'The Dog Rule'? What's the 'The Dog Rule'?"

"When my wife walks the dog, she only allows him to sniff at a place once. Once he moves on, there's no going back to sniff again. Otherwise, it would take forever. Same here. Once an idea has been sniffed, it's over. We will not discuss it again unless there's a very good reason. A life and death reason. This includes quotas. And anyone can yell 'Dog Rule,' not just me."

"That's asinine."

"Not asinine, canine," said Knoll.

"Sometimes things have to be discussed over and over again," said Stront.

"Most of us understand things the first time," said Knoll.

"I thought we would discuss serious and future concerns like climate change, what an ageing population will mean to the world, advances in technology, sovereign wealth funds, and the privatization of water. Just to name a few."

"A few?"

"It's simple. We discuss these issues here. Then you decide how that will affect your business and your clients," I said.

"Maybe we can offer incentives to our insureds to be more ecologically conscious, especially in our D & O policies," said Knoll.

"Do you know what a D & O policy is, Mr. CEO?" asked Collins.

"D & O stands for Directors and Officers, which insures against specific suits brought against the executives of a corporation and protects their personal assets with regard to an action brought against the company," I said.

"How do you know this shit? Weren't you the guy who just put together those newsletters that nobody reads?"

"Sometimes, I actually read what was in the newsletter. Other times, it was a form of self-defense," I said.

"But none of us are prepared to discuss this."

"Fuck the future. If we don't do well for the next quarter, then we won't be around for next year," said Stront.

I looked closely at Stront and inspired by Gladys, I thought:

What an exquisite tie for a two-for-one suit.
A gift, a mistake, a wife? Museum shop?
Not a Klee or a da Vinci flapping its wings but
A shimmering pattern with collaborative colors
A new Olympic dive—a Triple Windsor with a
Degree of difficulty of every weekday morning
A pull-cord that releases drips of civility with a hope
Of a flood of money and a mote of recognition
There must be a stain somewhere.

"I don't believe in that bullshit climate change anyway," said Collins.

"It doesn't matter what you believe. What matters is what's happening and what the scientists believe and what the courts conclude."

"They're all full of shit."

"Collins, what is your scientific background?"

"Same as yours."

"Do you listen to your proctologist? For you, it's the same as climate change," said Knoll.

"Spaulding ruled with an iron fist. He would've never let this meeting get out of hand."

"Ladies and gentlemen, we must consider our external shareholders and partners," said Friedman.

"If you're so concerned about people outside the company, maybe we can trade you to another company. Lee, can we trade an employee, like baseball?" asked Stront.

"We can't do that," said Sir Reginald.

"Why? Is there a law against it? They trade ball players all the time."

"But there must be a law against trading insurance employees," said Sir Reginald.

"If it's acceptable and common among baseball players, why can't we do it? Right, Lee?"

"I will have to check," said Lee. "But if it's acceptable in one field, it might be acceptable in another."

"Even if they sign contracts?" asked Sir Reginald.

"A contract can be considered unenforceable if it is contrary to public policy," said Lee. "But on first blush, I don't see why that wouldn't would be the case here."

"Can we get back to the matters at hand? There are many at this table who are underestimating the consequences of climate change, both human and economic," I said.

"The art guy is making a good point," said Knoll. "While you guys carry on like little whiney babies, I've seen the consequences of climate change. So, before I start screwing around with your loss ratios, you'd better listen to him."

"This is not Russia. When you make a mistake, you don't have to stay away from open windows," I said.

All claims people see themselves sitting on a rocker on a porch spitting tobacco and wisdom in equal parts. They spout their brand of logic and cynicism, just waiting for someone to say something stupid. Especially Knoll. It is the rare claims person who ever went to a prestigious college. They always started with the assumption that everything was a fraud and everyone was cheating, including the 93-year-old granny with a terminal illness who died in a commercial plane crash. The resentment is mutual between claims and the businesspeople.

"If you change the loss ratios, let me know," said the IT guy.

"You don't have loss reserves; you're the IT guy."

"I write the algorithms for them. Very important."

"Why the fuck is the IT guy here anyway? Years ago, we didn't have the guy who ordered the typewriters or pencils come to the Presidents Meeting," said Stront. He threw his pen down in such frustration, it bounced back up and hit Sir Reginald in the head.

"Doesn't anyone care if I'm hurt?" asked Sir Reginald, who now had an extra little eyebrow.

"I've been here thirty-three years. How come I didn't get to be CEO?" asked Collins.

"Because that doesn't smell like coffee on your breath, Frank," said Knoll.

"Most of your lack the self-awareness to realize that your ambitions are greater than your talents," said Lee.

Most of the men at the table were the ones always chosen last in sports when young. In baseball, they were then stuck in right field until a left-handed hitter batted and then they were moved to left field. In basketball, they were instructed never to shoot, even when open. Now, they talked about golf as if it were a contact sport and sought retribution in whatever form available from a society that kept them a virgin way past their teens. A long-standing and broadly circulated rumor purported that most of the Presidents had a club where they scored points for screwing women in the company. Somewhere in my youth, I'm sure I helped create some of those leaders.

"Here's an example of the problems we face in the future," I said, "Take ageing and the birth replacement rates of some countries. For example, by 2050, Japan will have 25% less people and it will have more people over the age of 85 than under the age of 9. What will that do to their economy? What about the actuarial tables? Their military?"

"It's going to be a problem," said Knoll.

Support just from the General Counsel and the claims guy could work against me.

"Who gives a shit about that stuff? What people want are low premiums and their claims paid. Period. End of story."

"Why are you assholes so afraid of reality?" asked Knoll.

"I'm going to sue your stupid ass, Dom, you stupid bastard," said Stront.

People who were not paying attention lifted their heads.

"You stole the Vel-Com account," said Stront, lifting his plastic skull mug that he brought to all meetings with the hope of intimidating others.

"It is not Vel-Com, it is Wel-Com," said Oleoso.

"I don't care how you fucking pronounce it; you stole it. I've hired a lawyer and I'm

suing you," said Stront.

"You're not suing anybody without my approval," said Lee, "No one is suing any other division while I'm GC."

Oleoso and Stront went back and forth some more until I said, "Both you kids, stop right now and drop it."

"You stay out of this, you MaKissMyAss puppet," said Stront.

"Make sure Dom gets credit for the premium," I said.

"Congratulations, Dom. You have Picasso to protect you now."

Why did everyone invoke the names of Picasso and Rembrandt when they needed an artist's name, especially for an insult? There were plenty of other artists from different eras and genres to choose from. You would think these types of guys might have heard of Damien Hirst.

"By the way, we just closed a deal with a large manufacturer of disposable diapers. I've been chasing them for years," said Collins.

"Congratulations," said Friedman, "I have an idea."

"Dog Rule, Dog Rule," said Knoll.

"You don't even know what I'm going to say," said Friedman.

"That's right. But I just don't want to hear it."

"That's not what the Dog Rule is for," said Friedman. "The company should support the anti-abortion movement, so people will have more babies and buy more diapers. That way we can show them Remora is a great partner."

"See? I was right," said Knoll.

"That is nuts. We can't do that," I said.

"You're just a bleeding-heart liberal," said Stront.

"Well, at least I don't get my information from *paranoidfruitcake-dot-com*."

"Let me give my legal opinion here," said Lee. "There is no way in hell you are doing that."

"I think it's a great idea," said Collins. "It's business and business has nothing to do with morality or politics. Or anything else."

A strange noise in the corridor grew louder and interrupted the conversation until the door of the conference room squeaked open.

"Sorry, we're late, but Candy wanted to come," said Sir Reginald.

"What is that?" asked someone.

Quisling appeared strapped to a baronial chair worthy of an altar. Her feet moved quickly in small steps like a gerbil to propel her along.

Usually when Candy attended a meeting, her roller bag trailed behind her like an obedient dog and she held her coffee cup near her head at cocktail party height, all of which screamed, "I'm important." But not today.

"Well, you all remember Candy had a bit of an accident, but she's chuffed to be back here today. So, let's welcome her back warmly." Even Tompkins and Collins greeted her with applause.

"I just visited you in the hospital the other day," I said.

"As some of you have heard, Candy is paralyzed from the waist up. And yet, in spite of that, she wanted to be here today," said Sir Reginald.

"I never heard of such a thing, paralyzed from the waist up," said someone for everyone.

"Well, that should not stop her from doing her job," said Sir Reginald.

"Of course not. She's the Head of Marketing," said Lee.

"We are hopeful that it's temporary. The doctors are exploring the possibility of experimental surgery," said Sir Reginald. He unstrapped her and he raised her bare feet so that they sat on the table. He placed a pen between her first two toes.

"She now writes with her feet. It's a true talent. She's right-footed. And she is trying to master the laptop."

"Candace worked on new slogans for the company while in the hospital," said Sir Reginald. Quisling started to scribble with her toes. Sir Reginald peeked over and read aloud, "Our motto is our motto."

"What does that mean?"

"I think it's brilliant," said Sir Reginald, a reaction to his fear of lawsuits.

"I hope it's trademarked or copywritten, so we can't use it," said Lee.

Quisling scribbled again and Sir Reginald read, "We do it. You do it. We all do it."

"Isn't that a toilet paper reference or something?" asked Tompkins.

"We also should start TV ads. All the big insurance companies have them. But we would need an animal that could be identified with Remora," said Sir Reginald.

"Who says Americans don't get irony?" said Knoll.

"All insurance companies have animals."

"Yes, but all the good animals are taken."

"How about a fucking baboon?" said Tompkins. "Hey Dom, isn't your goomah a baboon?"

"Come up with a business plan for a TV ad campaign. And may I suggest a remora as the company mascot," I said.

"You can't do that. That was Hoover's grandmother."

"Thank you, we'll work on a plan," said Sir Reginald. "Candy had another suggestion, 'Remora will not give you skid marks.'"

"What the hell does that mean?" asked Stront.

"It's a nice way of saying that if you buy our insurance, you won't shite your pants," said Sir Reginald, whispering the last line.

"Very elegant," said Lee.

"One more thing. I think we need modesty panels for men," said Sir Reginald.

"What the fuck is a modesty panel?" asked Collins.

"It's an attachment to a desk that originally prevented men from looking at a woman's naughty bits."

"They haven't invented a piece of wood that will stop men from doing that."

"We need it to maintain equality among the sexes and the new gender identities," said Sir Reginald.

"Excellent idea," wrote Candy.

"Candy is a tad knackered," said Sir Reginald. With that he flipped Candy right side up again, strapped her in, and started to wheel her out.

"Wait a second, Ladies and gentlemen. Homework for next meeting. I want to know what would make things better for the workers at Remora."

"What kind of Communist bullshit is that?"

"We depend on them to make the company function."

"We do? I thought we were the reason the company succeeded."

"How many words?" asked Oleoso. "Double-spaced?"

"This is not a sixth-grade book report, Dom. Whatever you want."

As Sir Reginald pushed Candy out the door, the others paused to pick over the carcasses of the uneaten fare. They ate them even if they weren't particularly hungry or liked it. Others put brownies in folded napkins to conceal their theft.

I intentionally omitted the "thank you" from, "See you next

month. Don't forget your homework assignment. If there is a next month."

"You eating that?" asked Tompkins.

"How the hell did you become CEO?" Stront asked me.

"I guess they looked at the competition and made the easy decision," I said. "Let me ask you a question. When you were a little boy, did you think to yourself, 'When I grow up, I want to work in a corporate insurance office'? Well, neither did I."

Chapter 6

Short Form CV

As the Number 7 train snaked through Queens, we measured other neighborhoods' buildings and streets against ours. When the train slowed down, we peeked into their windows, partially as a cheap sociological study, but mainly as voyeurism. It all looked vaguely familiar.

"I'm sure we took this train twenty-five years ago to the 1939 Fair," said Unkle Traktor.

"This train didn't even exist twenty-five years ago," said my father.

"If I didn't exist, how come we're on it now?" asked Unkle Traktor. "You and your metaphysical bullshit. They had another train then but they ripped it down after the '39 Fair."

"You sure? I'm positive we took this train."

My mother pointed to the splotches of grease on our brown paper bags that held her homemade salami sandwiches. "Don't get it on your clothes. You don't want others to think that people from Brooklyn are pigs."

"How'd they know we're from Brooklyn?"

"Don't you worry, Bobby. They know."

To leave our neighborhood, we first took the F train, the immigrant's cheap tour of Brooklyn. You were first surrounded by the pungent aroma of garlic and onions, then strangled by cabbage, and for dessert, you inhaled the perfume of cinnamon and nutmeg. All mixed with car fumes and shadows from below the El on McDonald Avenue.

I sat between Aunt Georgia and Unkle Traktor, two old Trotskyists who rarely roamed beyond the walls of Brooklyn. They thrived in a constant snit against Robert Moses, the "tyrannical anti-Semite bastard" who single-handedly built the World's Fair and whose other nefarious projects bisected poor neighborhoods and razed perfectly good housing. And worse, he forced the Brooklyn Dodgers to move to Los Angeles. Yet, for some reason, they wanted to see Moses' miniaturized and discounted version of the planet.

Our salami now created little puffs of fat and spice. This prompted my father to say, "My sandwich smells really strong, like Ben-Gay. Why didn't you make something less smelly?"

"Like what? Chicken salad? The mayo would get hot and go bad. Then we'd all die. Is that what you want?" asked my mother.

"Why are the subway cars painted blue?" I asked. "I've never seen blue subway cars before."

"They're special for this World's Fair," said my father.

"Because they were designed by a *faygala*," added my mother.

"What's a *faygala*?" I asked Aunt Georgia.

"A designer, dear, a designer." In reality, it was a derogatory term in Yiddish for a gay man that literally meant a little bird.

When the doors of the Number 7 subway finally opened at the Willets Point station, the crowd poured out and pretended to know in which direction to run. To our backs, rose the recently completed Shea Stadium. The seats, the scoreboard, and the excitement of the new stadium partially obscured a nearby third world city of Quonset huts and junkyards ringed by sagging chain-linked fences. Along those streets of mud, they sold second-hand car parts. There were no addresses or sewers. We hurried along with the crowd in the other direction, toward an imagined future.

Upon entering the fairgrounds, we unfolded and flipped our maps in various directions to understand just where we were, and to lay claim to what we wanted to see. Our neighborhood in Brooklyn was defined by its narrow sidewalks, cast bronze streetlamps, and concrete traffic stanchions in the middle of heavily trafficked streets that gave rise to weekly accidents. Here, the Fair creators believed our future lay in wide boulevards with oddly colored and multi-box shaped street lights. It left us temporarily disoriented. But one of us made a decision and said, "That way," and we all followed.

"I want to see the *Pietà* at the Vatican," said my mother.

"Do you know what a *Pietà* is?" asked Unkle Traktor.

"I know that I want to see it."

"Let's eat first."

With blind obeisance, and under the assumption we were always hungry, we found benches where we could lay out our salami sandwiches and eat sideways. The family always sat. If wars could be won by sitting and eating, we would be a dynasty.

"I want to see *It's a Small World*," I said. "It's in the Pepsi building. And then we can go on the GM and Ford rides."

"Listen to him. Pepsi. GM. Ford. They're brainwashing our children. This isn't a World's Fair. It's all big business. And the little singing bastards are in the UNICEF Building, not the Pepsi Building. UNICEF does good things, unlike those big business bastards. Pepsi rips your stomach lining apart," said Unkle Traktor.

"So. Why'd you come today? Just to complain?"

"I like to know what's going on, see what the enemy is doing. Reconnaissance. Recon by subway. The proletariat way."

"What does that mean? You don't want to see anything in particular?"

"I'll know what I want to see, when I see it."

"Like some definition of Commie pornography," said my father.

"What's pornography?" I asked my Aunt Georgia.

"A form of design, dear," she said staring into the distance.

We wandered the avenues and cross streets of the Fair. Some places we passed at least twice, if not three times. Finally, we entered the Vatican exhibition, where we waited patiently to see the *Pietà*.

"You know, this is the first time this thing has left Rome," said my father.

"Maybe they were afraid they'd drop it. It's just made of old stone," said my mother.

"Marble, not stone," said my father.

"Like the rye bread?"

Three tiers of moving walkways carried us and millions of others past the *Pietà*. Our heads rotated for our first and final views. We wondered, "Is this way you see the Pope and the other treasures in the real Vatican?"

I worried what they would do if they found out we were Jewish. We learned in Hebrew school that the word ghetto was from the time when the Jews were forced to live in a restricted area in Venice.

"What are you doing?" my mother asked.

"Nothing."

"You just crossed yourself."

"No, I didn't."

"Yes, you did."

"Well, Vinnie does it every time we pass a church. This way, we'll fit in here."

"Well, just stop it. Do you know, if you do that one more time, you'll be Catholic for the rest of your life? Is that what you want?"

Once outside, my father asked my mother what she thought of it.

"I'm disappointed," said my mother. "I thought it would look smarter."

"Smarter? It's a statue."

"Yeah, but it's Michelangelo. Isn't it supposed to look smart?"

"How can it look smart? It's religious art," said Unkle Traktor. "It's a piece of marble designed to make you weep and fall to your knees. They want you to surrender to religion."

"It looked smart to me. And smooth too," I said.

From there, we headed for *It's a Small World*, where Unkle Traktor and Aunt Georgia decided to camp outside. Cramped into tiny boats, we passed hundreds of little creatures that sang at us as we floated by. The insidious song rolled around in my head for hours afterwards. I tried to shake it out by using the same techniques you used to get water out of your ear after swimming. I hopped on one foot with my head tilted toward the ground. I tried to create a vacuum by pressing the palms of my hands over my ears to allow the song to spring from my head. Nothing worked.

"I love that song," said my mother, humming the tune.

When we emerged from the exhibition, Aunt Georgia and Unkle Traktor were nowhere to be found. This left us with mixed emotions. We were worried they were missing, but now, we did not have to abide by their wishes or listen to any more of Unkle Traktor's screeds.

We again walked about without direction, until we happened upon a group of about 150 people in front of the Spanish Pavilion. We could hear Unkle Traktor's voice above the others.

"You, the men with the patent leather hats and the souls of patent leather, leave free people alone." Unkle Traktor stole Garcia Lorca's description of the dreaded Guardia Civil. Generalissimo Franco imported the Guardia to protect his pavilion of deceit filled with riches from one of the poorest and most repressive countries in Western Europe at that time.

That morning, the Guardia stood upright in their indigo uniforms and black tri-cornered hats in front of the Pavilion. They watched Unkle Traktor and the others with narrowed eyes. We now understood Unkle Traktor's true mission for that day.

Unkle Traktor approached the Guardia. He knew none of them understood English but said anyway, "You know who you're talking to? Someone from the Abraham Lincoln Brigade. That's who." Being part of the Abraham Lincoln Brigade, one of the international groups of leftists who fought against Franco during the Spanish Civil War, was a source of great pride to Unkle Traktor. He often wielded it as a weapon of piety during political arguments.

One of the Guardia strutted over and said, "*Señor, por favor, silencio.*"

A fellow protestor gave Unkle Traktor and Aunt Georgia buttons that read "Amnesty for All Political Prisoners in Spain." He whispered to them, "It's a court ruling. At the World's Fair, it's legal to wear these buttons, but not legal to yell things."

"You're *Fascistas*. Fascistas for that Fascista pig, Franco," yelled Aunt Georgia.

"*Silencio, Señora, silencio,*" said one of the Guardia. In Spain, they were feared and would have arrested my Aunt and Unkle just for existing.

"Peace through understanding," yelled a passerby, the motto of the Fair. But apparently the Guardia had informed the New York Police Department about the protest. As soon as the cops showed up, they arrested Unkle Traktor and Aunt Georgia.

"What are we going to do?" asked my father.

"They've been arrested before. They know their way home," said my mother.

"I hope they have tokens," I said.

My mother grabbed my wrist as if I were three and dragged me into the Spanish pavilion. Intent on getting away from the protestors and so angry at my Aunt and Unkle, she willingly paid the 25-cent general admission and the additional 50-cent fee for the art galleries, without complaint.

We stopped in front of a display of some of Spain's most revered artifacts, including El Cid's sword and the Treasure of Guarrazar. My father looked at Queen Isabella's crown. He puckered his lips like a giant grouper and made a dry, spitting noise, "PUH. She's the one who threw the Jews out of Spain. And the

Muslims. And then it was all downhill from there. Serves her right."

"*Sha*," said my mother, "They can hear you."

"Who's they?"

"The men with the hats that look like their shoes."

It was incumbent upon every child to be separated from their parents at the World's Fair. My parents did not notice that I had stopped to stare at the works of Velazquez, Picasso, El Greco, Miró, Dali, and Goya. Until that moment, I did not know their names nor the names of their paintings. Here my attention was not limited by the descriptions of my art teachers or the two-dimensional depictions in a book. I was at once confused and elated by the profusion of shapes, colors, perspectives, and subjects. I had not known that art could be done in so many ways. I didn't know such freedom existed. And the body parts. Elongated. Detached. Normal. And the nudes. The nudes brought on an early onset of puberty.

I hurried to find my mother and father and tell them about my new discoveries. I found them in a replica of a typical Spanish tavern where I peppered them with questions. "Why are there two Majas? A naked one and one with clothes? What is a Maja anyway?" I pronounced maja with a hard "J."

"Maybe, I'll be an artist some day and paint majas."

I tried to express my newfound enthusiasm for the centuries of Spanish art, for all art, but my parents were exhausted. They were suspicious of the tapas. "Who serves such little food on such little plates?" They thought they were being shortchanged until the waiter explained *tapas* was a celebrated Spanish form of eating. At once, they felt sophisticated and exotic. They bought a few bottles of Sangria to share with friends back in Brooklyn. My parents knew that none of their friends had ever heard of Sangria, let alone tasted it. And at that moment, they felt even more sophisticated and exotic. As did I.

Soon after the World's Fair, I started to paint and draw with all the skill and subtlety of someone my age. I watched the last years of John Nagy's art lessons on television and my parents even bought his instruction kit for me. They continued their loud encouragement for my interest in the arts with the hope that I would abandon it all and become a doctor or lawyer.

Somewhere in college, I learned that the Guardia Civil I saw at the 1964 World's Fair would sooner destroy the art than protect it, if so ordered. In high school, most of the art teachers formed a different garrison of the Guardia Civil. Although a few instructors wanted us to express a greater freedom, they made sure no one produced anything offensive to anyone, insuring mediocrity. In college, the Ivory Tower afforded us a greater freedom to create whatever we wanted, as long as we adhered to the confinements of the assignment and satisfied the instructor's aesthetic. And in the workplace, they again wanted the innocuous, but this time on glossy paper. So, if I wanted to protect my new position, I was not going to hang Andres Serrano's photograph *Piss Christ* in the lobby of the Remora Building.

I claimed a small space of Spaulding's office and hung a faded and crudely assembled framed memento from the World's Fair of six postcards pasted on colored construction paper background. Five of the images were Spanish paintings, including Goya's *La maja vestida*, El Greco's *El caballero de la mano en el pecho*, and Zubaran's *Santa Dorotea*. And another was of the little creatures singing *"It's a Small World."*

Chapter 7

Stretchpants, OK

IN BUSINESS, most sound decisions are based on some combination of logic, financial reward, or foresight. But if all corporate decisions were sound, we would not need Chapters 7 and 11. Besides abject failures and corruption, there were still many inexplicable actions, for which no one could remember the original impetus or thinking. These mysteries were labeled institutional knowledge. Somewhere, someone might recall how certain events became mythical, but no one wanted to stop them for fear of retribution from the grave or fear of being exposed as someone who did not recall why they existed. And if the mistake was repeated often enough, it became tradition. Such was Spaulding's annual trek to Stretchpants, Oklahoma.

No one ever unearthed any documents explaining why Spaulding established a distant outpost in Stretchpants, OK, rather than Tulsa or Oklahoma City. Let alone explained why it became a yearly pilgrimage. No one remembered the real name of the town, so everyone in New York called it Stretchpants and everyone in Stretchpants called New York Godless.

Harvey Knoll and one of his youthful assistants, Phil Dent, accompanied me on the trip in the corporate jet to the nearest airport they could find to the local Remora office. Knoll, about one round trip from retirement, filled his plush seat and cabin with *The World According to Knoll.*

"Thanks for backing me at the Presidents Meeting the other day," I said to Knoll.

"You're welcome but it really had nothing to do with you. Those schmucks sold their souls, and they could give a shit about the hundred-year floods or the Cat 5 hurricanes that seem to be happening weekly now."

"Climate change is one of the reasons I was chosen for the job."

"Well then, do something about it."

"Is this your first business trip?" I asked Phil, who needed the pink innocence washed from his cheeks.

Knoll answered for him. "He's a travel virgin. He's here to lose his cherry. Sorry, we're not supposed to talk like that anymore about our subordinates." I half expected Knoll's voice to crack the airplane windows, sucking us all out.

I realized this was not only my first business trip, but my first time on a private jet. Why would an insurance company send a graphic designer anywhere? Maybe, I thought, an admission like that might make me appear more folksy, more approachable, but then I decided against it. It might create a crisis in confidence.

"I've never been to Oklahoma either," I said, "But I am looking forward to it." Playing the assuasive uncle did not come naturally.

"I've been to Oklahoma many times. It's a snap. You threaten to close their shop if they make a mistake and then you leave," said Knoll.

"Isn't it easier just to call?" asked Phil.

"Sure, but not as much fun as seeing the look on their faces when you say it. Basically, business travel is doing the same thing as usual but in a different place with better meals. Except in Stretchpants."

"I read your report about the office there. There's a Louella Sample who has an extraordinary record of claims adjustments."

"Yes, Louella does, and when we get there, you'll know why," said Knoll. Our small talk got smaller and smaller until Knoll said, "Usually, I only get called to the CEO's office when there's a major fuck-up. But this is great. I feel like a rat in the sunlight. You know what claims does? I'll tell you what claims does. Did you ever see the guy at the circus who follows the elephant with a shovel and cleans up their shit? That's us. We clean up other people's shit. And the more experience you get, the smaller the shovel and the bigger the pile of shit. That's me."

"Remind me not to use the men's room after you."

"You didn't mention any of that during my job interview," said Phil.

"If I had said that, who would have been the bigger idiot if you took the job? And, Phil, do you know what insurance is designed to do?" Knoll asked.

Phil was smart enough not to answer. He knew whatever he said would be wrong.

"Insurance lets us protect schmucks from themselves. It's for all the know-it-alls who think they're too smart to make mistakes. But then, 'Whoops, I didn't think that would kill anybody.' No offense, Rob. You're a know-it-all now, too."

"I'm sure there's something I don't know."

But as I listened to Knoll, I knew his stories and opinions had been repeated countless times at bars, going away parties, BBQs, and funerals. Like any good raconteur, he tried to make them sound fresh each time. If written, these tales would have been yellowed and wrinkled.

"We get separate rooms, right?" asked Phil.

"Afraid of my bullshit? Of course, we get separate rooms. But once you see the shithole we stay at, you might be more afraid of other things than me and want a shotgun as a roommate."

I did not know if he was preying on the kid's fear or voicing an honest opinion.

"We have to talk about Rooderman," said Knoll.

"What's Rooderman?" I asked.

"Rooderman publishes science textbooks for schools. Apparently, they didn't mention that aliens might've created the Nazca lines in Peru. Now, some rich nutjob, douchebag is suing Rooderman saying that this omission is defaming aliens and repressing their First Amendment rights."

"Defamation and repression of the aliens' rights? I like that. What about the courts?"

"It seems the guy contributes a lot of money to local candidates, including judges. The wackier the candidate, the more money he gives."

"Why don't we just settle?"

"You can't settle. You know why the government rarely settles suits brought by prisoners?"

"Why?"

"Because they would tell other prisoners and then all the inmates would sue just to try to make a couple of bucks. I'm sure there's a whack-a-do grapevine on the internet for people like the Rooderman nut job, where they goad each other and share information about aliens as if it came directly from other aliens."

"Hey Phil, what is that thing, ComicCon? Where they dress up like creatures and then I'm not sure what they do."

Before Phil could answer, Knoll continued, "I'm sure the human aliens have a college called Shitforbrains.edu. If we settled, we would be overwhelmed with space suits and weirdos wearing aluminum beanies with propellers. The most important thing for them is a forum where they can spew their bullshit."

"Can't we settle and keep it quiet?"

"Not advisable at all."

As soon as the private jet landed, a car picked us up. No pushing in the aisles. No elbowing at the luggage carousel. I could not tell anyone but Cassia about this guiltiest of pleasures.

"You guys know anything about Oklahoma or Stretchpants?"

It did not matter what we said. Knoll was going to tell us anyway.

"Stretchpants, OK, is near Fort Supply, the home of the first state-operated mental institution in Oklahoma. Besides that, Native Americans east of I-35 will tell you that you shouldn't conduct business with Native Americans west of I-35. Native Americans west of I-35 call their brethren unworthy because they would not share their newfound wealth. They're probably both right."

"We'll be there in an hour or so."

"Which side of I-35 are we on now?" Phil asked.

"We go right down the middle."

Larry Evans, the office manager, greeted at us the door of a small modern building which resembled a green-eyed insect. The building was surrounded on three sides by Oklahoma brush and wildflowers known as forbs with a parking lot on the fourth side.

"Hello Harvey. Good to see you again. And you must be Rob Stone."

"I am."

Phil just trailed behind us, unnoticed.

"Welcome to our little corner of Oklahoma."

The cheapest chairs, desks, and supplies that Remora could find filled the office. They made the standard company computers look as out of place as a chocolate fountain at a yoga retreat. Oklahoma University banners and stickers prominently covered the walls and cube partitions. People sat on Sooner pillows. They pasted the OU football schedule in the break room next to the Heimlich maneuver poster on which someone had scribbled the letters "UT DNR" on the choking victim's shirt. "I guess they don't like the University of Texas here," said Phil.

"Rob, I want you to meet Louella Sample."

Sample, a smallish woman in her 40s, wore a neat skirt and blouse and carried a pistol on her hip. Her shoes matched her embroidered holster.

"Louella's the best claims adjuster in the entire company, not just in Oklahoma. I don't know how she does it. She has an excellent Expected Loss/Actual Loss ratio."

"Maybe it's the fucking gun she carries", I thought. Are assassinations big out here? Besides Louella's gun, everyone was dressed appropriately for the office. They were blue-collar workers in a white-collar setting, their version of the Stockholm Syndrome. Rural vs. urban. Tornados vs. hurricanes. Pick-up truck vs. crosstown bus. College football vs. corporate seats. All these contradictions created both distance and the need to impress.

"Nice to meet you," I said, not sure of the expression on my face.

"Nice to meet you, too," said Louella.

"This is where it all happens. Here's where we decide who's a fool, a victim, or a fraud."

"I'm sure that it's not as simple as it sounds," I said. She has a fucking gun. I kept staring at her gun. I half-expected her to say, "Hey buddy, my eyes are up here."

"And let's not forget the rest of the crew who aggregate the premiums for the region," said Evans. A small band of women waved with the most timid of wrists.

I shook everyone's hands and would have kissed their babies if any had been present. Evans and his staff had prepared a spreadsheet of their numbers. I pored over the data like I knew what I was reading. I pretended to be interested in whatever they showed me.

Evans corralled the lot and herded us all to the break room. Some who knew the drill and wheeled in their own desk chairs to sit. One of the women, Gabbie, said, "Enjoy the fried pies, folks. I made them specially for the occasion."

"She makes the best. Harvey here doesn't like them, but Harvey doesn't like anything," said Evans.

Phil didn't hesitate. "These are really good," he said and ate a second and then a third.

It was incumbent upon the person in charge to say something regardless of the situation or their knowledge. I met the minimal requirements with a terse but sincere platitudinous speech. But when speaking to only eight people, you sounded like a delusional dictator, pretending to address thousands.

"Any questions?" I concluded.

Louella asked, "I don't mean to start trouble or nothing, but are you here to close the office?"

Every satellite branch hated and distrusted the home office and with good reason.

"You're not starting trouble. Of course, I didn't come here to shut the office." I almost added that I didn't know why I was here in the first place but caught myself. "But I did come here to take everyone out for a late lunch. Where would you like to go?"

"Jimmy Jenx."

"Yeah, The Handle."

"It's the same place, 'Jimmy Jenx All You Can Handle.' We call it The Handle," said Evans.

Class warfare broke out when we entered the all-you-can-eat restaurant. Phil sat next to Louella and the other local workers, while Evans asked Knoll and myself to join him at a separate table. Otherwise, The Handle was filled with large people with large families sitting in large booths eating large portions.

There were no lines or rushing for more. There was a calmness. Everyone knew an empty tray would be filled quickly. It was expected at The Handle. The only thing that interrupted their meal were Phil, Knoll, and myself. Although we entered with amiable smiles and were accompanied by identifiable locals, our clothes, glasses, belts, shoes, and mien declared the fancies had landed. It did not help when Knoll said in a loud stage whisper, "This is only place in the world where people can call me Slim."

A fortress of steamer trays dominated the center of the restaurant protected only by sneeze guards. Evans circled the food just to check if anything new had been added when he had not been looking. We made it our business to make a show of eating the local favorites. Knoll had fried chicken, fries, and mac and cheese. I had the ribs and the mashed. When we sat back down, Evans said, "When Mr. Spaulding visited, he ate here like death was waiting at the motel."

"What did he eat?"

"Lamb fries."

"Lamb fries?"

"Lamb fries are someone's balls," said Knoll, "Just dunk 'em in hot sauce or something, anything and you'll think you're eating something else."

"It's part of the tradition when visiting here to eat lamb fries," said Evans.

Cassia and I had traveled enough to understand the weight of local customs. This was no time to fuss or cavil. In Stretchpants, OK, this was a test of machismo and hospitality. "Show me where they are," I said and brought some back for Knoll.

"I'm not eating them again. I paid my dues," said Knoll. "And don't tell anyone back in New York you had them. It's not a gay thing. You just don't want them to know what you ate."

"What do you think prompted the first person to try them?"

"I guess someone was really hungry. May I ask you a question?"

"Sure."

"You're a Hebrew, right? Do you ever think about the lost tribes of Israel?"

This is like the moment when a cop asks, "Do you know why I pulled you over?" Ignorance was better than a confession and American Jews rarely referred to themselves as Hebrews.

"Why? Have you thought about them?" I asked.

"As a matter of fact, I think I know where at least one lost tribe of Israel is."

"And where might that be?"

"Hawaii."

"Hawaii?"

"Hawaii."

I knew what was coming. One fact had been put on a potter's wheel and spun into an unprovable theory. It was an affliction that usually only struck men—pseudo exceptionalism. They found a lonely idea dangling on a thread, proffered in one book, the internet, or some half-ass documentary and then it became a concept they thought they created. They then became the sole repository of esoterica and the truth on that subject. They were deadly at Thanksgiving. Their obsessions invariably dealt in war, assassinations, religion, or aliens; it was never flower arrangements or origami.

Agreement encourages recruitment of a co-conspirator. One person is not a conspiracy, just a lonely nutjob. So, finding even one fellow soldier is emboldening.

"The main reason why I think at least one lost tribe is in Hawaii is because how close two certain words are," said Evans.

"Two words?"

"Yes, two words—*shalom* and *aloha*. They both mean hello, good-bye, and shalom also means peace. While aloha also means compassion and sympathy, which is a form of peace. See, they're also identical."

"How did the Jews get to Hawaii? They didn't have package tours then."

"Well, you know the explorer, Thor Heyerdahl, built a raft and crossed the Pacific; the Hebrews could have done the same."

"The Jews were stowaways on a Norwegian raft?"

"No, they probably built their own."

Vocal disagreement only led to an extended conversation, complete with fractured logic and tortured facts. Usually, I remained silent and slowly shook my head up and down, covering my upper lip with the lower one. I kept the Socratic Method nearby and never did state my opinion. But sometimes I couldn't contain myself.

"Have you considered the similarity between the Hawaiian *lei* and Jewish prayer shawl, called a *tallit*? Both go around the neck and have significance to each group."

"I never heard of the tallit before, but I think you're catching my drift. You should join me. A Hebrew and Christian, we could help one another and maybe solve some ancient problems."

"That's a thought. But I really have a busy schedule these days."

This was almost benign anti-Semitism. No harm intended, in fact; the intent was to build a greater bond by this revelation of a non-Jew.

He did not know that the best way to persuade a Jew of anything was not through intellectual contortions, religious exorcism, or an epiphany but through food, especially potatoes, bread, and meats soaking in a brine. Certainly not lamb fries.

"Do you know about the Maasai Warriors of Africa? There are some who consider them a lost tribe of Israel," I said.

"Thanks, I didn't know that. Be sure to give Doris the waitress a big tip; she's good people."

The motel in Stretchpants, OK, was everything that Knoll described and could have been used as location for a true crime TV show. You could feel the rumble of the semis zooming past on the nearby interstate. The rooms smelled from gas and musty vents. The ice machine doubled as an alarm clock.

In the morning, Knoll waited for me in the communal breakfast area. Most of the offerings were wrapped in cellophane. A baffled Knoll studied a machine that looked like a cow.

"Do you know what this thing is for or how to operate it?"

Some guest at a nearby table said, "You just pull the big udder for the batter, the little udder for the syrup. That thing over there is the waffle-maker. City folk."

"Where's Phil?" I asked.

"I don't know. I haven't seen him since The Handle last night."

"For some reason, I forgot to tell you something. You know your 'Asshole of the Month' idea? Shitcan it. I think it's funny, but it's caused a lot of grumbling. And if I don't like something like that, it's a loser."

"Thanks for the heads up. I'll see what I can do."

About fifteen minutes later, Sladka burst into the breakfast area. He pushed Phil in front of him, much to the astonishment of all, including a couple of seniors muddling through breakfast.

"Where the hell have you've been? Who is this guy? He looks familiar," said Knoll.

"That's Sladka. He works security for us. He didn't say he was coming to Oklahoma. In fact, he doesn't say anything."

"Sladka? I've seen him a million times. I didn't know he had a name."

Sladka shrugged.

"Maybe he can transfer to claims. He can become the Louella Sample of New York. He can scare the shit out of the constipated," said Knoll.

"He doesn't talk," said Phil.

"And where were you? We called your room. We were looking for you."

Phil looked sheepish, "Out."

"All night?"

"Where did you find him, Sladka?"

Sladka took the phone out of his pocket and typed in the answer, "He was with Louella Sample."

"Louella?"

"She really knows claims and I'm just starting out. She was helping me. And she's beautiful and sophisticated," said Phil.

The three older men immediately knew our young Phil Dent was smitten and nothing we could say could change that, even though Knoll, being Knoll, had to try.

"You're a lucky lad. Louella's one of the best in the company. But even though her numbers are good, don't let her break your heart."

"Last night, after The Handle," said Phil, "We went out for drinks. Lou said I could expense it and I should speak to someone named Gladys when I got back to New York. And then we went back to her place. She's remarkable."

Sladka punctuated the statement by raising his eyebrows.

"That explains the imprint of her holster on your forehead," I said.

Phil, not realizing it was a joke, quickly touched his face and then turned a whiter shade of talcum.

"Can I come back next year?" asked Phil.

Chapter 8

St. Petersburg, Petrograd, Leningrad, Remora

AN OFFICE TEMP sat at Glady's desk. Every year Gladys and her sister Mary spent three weeks in a turquoise-stained guesthouse on A1A in Fort Lauderdale. Gladys could afford better hotels, but Mary liked to stay where the other guests were mostly Québécois. It allowed her to dust off her high school French and call herself Marie, an affectation the Canadians never acknowledged and a slight that Gladys ignored. The guesthouse had a little kitchenette reserved for heating restaurant leftovers and separate beds. Its aquamarine walls and ceiling made them feel like they were sleeping on the beach. At least once a visit, they would make their way into Miami to dine at a restaurant which claimed to be "The World's Most Famous Cuban Restaurant." Just the slogan made Mary feel worldly.

In the past, Gladys would insinuate herself into the more glamorous corporate boondoggles, including trips to Las Vegas or Hawaii, and once even to Paris. After the Chairman, she was the most powerful person in the company. No one wanted to alienate Gladys. While she had seen and done far more than her sister, and her world had always been larger, she gladly acceded to Mary's request for simpler accommodations.

Office temps in New York came in various sizes and shapes.

Among the most common were actors, singers, and writers who did not like waiting on tables. There were obsequious wallflowers who had trouble fitting in for long periods of time. There were those akin to substitute teachers who would not tolerate some kid calling himself Dick Hertz. And those who had seen it all and could not wait for five o'clock. Glady's replacement, Tiffany, a young woman of good intentions, seemed to defy these ready categories. She appeared at the door of my office and announced, "Barry the Beneficial Nematode is here."

"Why did you call him The Beneficial Nematode?"

"Ms. Pierson left a long list of instructions. One of them said that if Barry Belette came, let Mr. Stone know by saying, 'The Beneficial Nematode is here.'"

"You are the Nematode, right?" she politely asked before escorting Belette into my office.

"That's right. Thank you, Tiffany," I said.

"I had to come and tell you what's going on with The Caf. You won't believe how many weddings and bar mitzvahs we're booked for already."

"How could that be? We just discussed this only a few weeks ago."

"We went viral."

"Good viral or bad viral?"

"Good, of course. After we discussed it, I got cracking on it right away. I heard about two Remora employees who wanted to get married and I cut them a deal. You know Ken Shapiro from Property and Linda Wong from Accounting? They got married. It was my great experiment."

"The Wong-Shapiro wedding? Their kid should be automatically accepted at Cal Tech."

"Well now, we're booked for months. I put a notice in the corporate newsletter, although it's not as good as it used to be since you left." Barry handed me a copy.

"Look what I wrote. 'Have your wedding, bar mitzvah, or special occasion at *Tray Chic*, a special setting.' I am not sure what

Tray Chic means, but your friend Lindsay Ackerman likes it. And I know she's your lunch buddy, so I thought the name change would be OK."

"Do they use The Caf's food trays at the weddings?"

"Yes. Isn't it exciting? The guests queue up, that's a Sir Reginald word. They queue up behind the stainless-steel railing, take a plastic tray and then plop food on their tray. Cool, isn't it? And that means we also save on waiters."

"Then it should be Tray SHEEK, not tray chick. SHEEK."

"OK, I'll try to remember that."

"How come the wedding took place so fast?"

"Something to do with Chinese numerology. Either that or she was pregnant."

"And what did you serve?"

"We served Chinese and Jewish food. In the steamer trays, we served a fish which sounds like the word surplus in Cantonese. I don't remember how to pronounce it, but it's supposed to bring good luck. And you're Jewish, right? We also had something called *kishka*."

"That's cow's intestines stuffed with matzo meal and, usually, ground meat. And if my mother didn't make it, it also included various spices," I told him.

"I'm glad no one knew that. And they also offered the usual cafeteria favorites, like mac and cheese and those cellophane-wrapped individual pizzas."

"A something for everybody and nobody affair."

"I think it'll catch on. People had a great time. And we had a DJ. The DJs used a little folded stage that they set up in the corner of Tray Chic. We'll use it for future events. We made $10,000 even, even after I installed a disco ball."

"You put a disco ball in the cafeteria?"

"Sure, where else would I put it? That's where the parties are."

Belette was an accidental storyteller. Rarely was his descriptions of an event as interesting as the event itself. He told his story flush with excitement but without the least bit of irony or adornment. I hadn't realized that Barry's insecurities suited him perfectly for this task. It was a classic example of someone doing something better than what he was originally hired for. Frightened of failure, he created something no sane person would. And now Remora had the only corporate cafeteria with a disco ball.

"We gave out industrial snoods as door prizes."

"Snoods?"

"Do you know what snoods are?"

"Snoods and roods. I do crossword puzzles."

"They're really just hairnets."

"Your idea?"

"No, one of the cafeteria staff. We already had them in stock. Sold them to us cheap."

"And now everyone wants them for their wedding. I came up with the slogan, 'Don't be Snoody.'"

"Did Lindsay like that?"

"I didn't tell her. But you know how each table has four chairs?"

"Yes."

"It seems the number 4 is an unlucky number with the Chinese, so people started moving chairs around. Threes and fives. Maybe we should have shoved some tables together for the bride and groom and their whatevers."

"And the orange trays clashed with the bride's second dress, a red one to symbolize good luck. How was I supposed to know that a bride would wear two dresses?"

"At different times, I assume. Well, you are new to the catering business."

"Did you know that a roast suckling pig means that a Chinese bride is a virgin? You would think the opposite, wouldn't you? But there you go."

"Maybe you need a paid advisor on the different traditions, foods, rites, and customs of those who book Tray Chic?"

"Well, I never heard of Kosher style until Saturday night.

Someone said it's Kosher Lite. But then, the roast suckling pig didn't even fit the description and didn't seem to sit well with some of Shapiro's older relatives. Now the PC police jumped on it and it's all over the internet."

"That's not good," I said.

"No, it's great. A lot of people videoed everything with their cell phones, including the chair problem. The yelling. The mixed food. The Chinese bride/pig thing. And now we're getting all sorts of people asking to have their party in ..." Belette paused dramatically, "Tray Chic."

"Tray Sheek. Tray Sheek."

"And, if you're wondering about problems in the future, I'm going to get them to sign a hold harmless agreement in the future and avoid these teensy errors."

"Teensy?"

"The next event is a *Quinceañera*."

"Quinceañera? Do you know what a Quinceañera is?"

"It's a Mexican Sweet Sixteen but the girl is fifteen. They wear big dresses. It's a big deal."

"Make sure someone explains the nuances of Quinceañeras to you, so we don't alienate most of the Western Hemisphere also."

"Changing subjects to another of your projects: we're going to have to stop the 'Asshole of the Month' campaign. It's not getting the right reaction," I said.

"It's too late to do anything this month."

"I heard rumblings that it's really pissing off people. So, play it down, stop the publicity. People are rarely fired because they're incompetent; they get fired because they're assholes. They can't get along with their bosses, co-workers, or anybody. But we have to stop this anyway. Right idea, but I was wrong to suggest it."

"Never say you're wrong, when you're the boss."

Although in Florida, I could hear Gladys say, "'Asshole of the Month' is your stupidest idea yet. Funny yes, but still stupid. People are very anxious and this only makes them more anxious. They wonder if they'll be next."

"Barry, we have to stop it. How is the meritocracy idea going?"

"I'll let you know in a few months."

"Let's try for sooner."

"People don't know how to act now or what to do. Before this, people knew who the backstabbers were. Who stole your work. Who got unfair promotions. Who made a mistake but kept making them, so that no one would know about the first mistake. Who came in late. Left early. Took two-hour lunches. Who spread gossip. But now you want them measured on what they actually do and what they actually know. So, they don't know who to trust."

"Sounds like you know a lot about this."

"Pure research."

"Tell people gossip is OK, but the other stuff isn't. And keep pushing the meritocracy."

"I'll make sure that happens. I have my own idea about this. How about bringing in dog trainers to modify behavior? I watch those shows all the time and those trainers are very good," said Belette. "You know the guy who goes 'psst' to make a dog sit?"

"I do. But we don't want people walking around making 'psst' sounds at everyone. We already have the 'Dog Rule.'"

"I like the 'Dog Rule' but maybe we can call ours 'The Employee Whisperers.' That whisperer thing is also very popular these days."

One thing was certain in business, the higher the office, the segues of the day were rarely smooth, or required the same logic or amount of attention.

Mike Tompkins walked into the office as fast as he could walk. He was followed closely by Sir Reginald and Mimi Lee. All three ignored Belette as if he were the drapes.

"Ivan Petrov's been poisoned."

"Who's Ivan Petrov?" I asked.

"He's in our St. Petersburg office."

"St. Petersburg. I didn't realize we had an office in St. Petersburg. Why are we still in St. Petersburg?" I asked.

"Someone has to keep an eye on those Rooskies."

"What does that mean?"

"The Company has been using Remora as a front for years," said Tompkins.

"What Company?" I asked.

"That's what we call the CIA around here, the Company. No one told you?" Tompkins said to me.

"This is more than an oversight."

"You haven't been cleared yet, but you had to know about this. The Company has been using Remora as a front for decades and Petrov is CIA. And now, there's been an assassination attempt on him."

"Are you CIA?" I asked Tomkins.

"No, D & O."

"He's been poisoned, Guv," Sir Reginald whispered. "But before we say anything else, has this room been swept for bugs?"

"I don't know."

Sladka's head suddenly appeared at the doorway and nodded yes and then disappeared again.

"Petrov was KGB before he became FSB and then he turned CIA."

"The KGB is now called FSB?" I asked.

"Marketing. They changed their name because nobody liked or trusted the KGB. Remember when Ozark changed its named to USAir? Same thing," said Tompkins.

"Not really marketing. More like rebranding, Guv," said Sir Reginald.

"True, they rebranded the KGB to FSB. KGB was too closely associated with murder, torture, and Stalin."

"Don't they still torture and murder?"

"They do, but not as much as they did under Stalin."

"There's a low standard," said Lee.

"Don't forget the other branch of the KGB, the SVR."

"It's almost like a wholly owned subsidiary. They do the spying outside Russia."

"Remember, Google was rebranded from Backrub and Paypal was once known as Confinity."

"I must say, although he worked primarily for the CIA, Petrov was an excellent insurance salesman," said Tompkins.

"Similar skillsets, Guv," said Sir Reginald.

"Insurance is the perfect front for the CIA and Mossad," said Lee.

"And MI6, don't forget MI6, the British Secret Service," said Sir Reginald.

Tompkins explained that reporters and academics were once a common front for the CIA, as their job was to gain information, but that became somewhat too obvious. Insurance people were in the perfect position for espionage.

"First, almost every individual and company can benefit from some sort of insurance. Salespeople ask harmless questions that might lead to more substantive questions and answers in the future. And if they do buy insurance, they end up giving all sorts of additional details to the underwriter. If it is a factory, the underwriter might want to look around."

"Even a factory that makes what seems to be innocuous parts for tanks or missiles, might offer vital information," said Sir Reginald.

"Do you know why an army installation can't even divulge how many spoons it has? Because then you would know how many soldiers were located there. Something as simple as the number of spoons can be useful. Spoon math. That can apply to many things. It can be helpful if you know how to apply it," said Tompkins.

"Besides insurance and reporters, other common covers are airlines, voluntary groups, big pharma, and big agriculture," said Lee.

"Did you say airlines and voluntary groups?"

"Yeah."

"I worked as an airline reservationist while in college and later in the mountains of Jamaica teaching after college," I said.

"The Russians aren't interested in you."

"And I didn't tell the consultants that because it made me sound more detached than being an artist."

"The consultants knew anyway. Believe me," said Lee.

"The Russians could think I've been spying all my life."

"Calm down, Guv," said Sir Reginald.

I felt slightly humiliated, that I had to be told to calm down by Sir Reginald, of all people.

I kept thinking about airlines, teaching, Remora. They all seemed innocent on the surface, deadly at the execution level. I was not just the head of a large company, I was in charge of a world-wide spy ring. But I could not be seen acting like a paranoid lunatic. There were certain situations for which life did not prepare you and managing an overseas spy assassination was high on that list.

"I don't want to die because of insurance. You're supposed to die and then get the insurance. You remember I said at the last Presidents Meeting that Remora isn't Russia. If you make a mistake, you don't have to stay away from open windows. You think they heard?"

"What that the cause?"

"They poisoned him; they didn't defenestrate him."

"This is the greatest day of my life," said Belette, still sitting in the office listening to all these revelations. "I've never been part of such insider information before. And especially assassinations and spy stuff. Wow, this stuff is great."

And then Belette realized, when every head turned in his direction, that he should not have said a word. Tiffany, who was just outside the office door listening but not able to observe the reactions, added, "Me too. This is the greatest day of my life. Spies. Poison. Wait till I tell my mother. Wait till I tell the other temps."

No one had to tell Sladka what to do. He slipped outside to

confer with Tiffany, to calm her down and explain the consequences.

"We should have thrown you out on your ass at the beginning," said Tompkins to Belette.

"I'll be quiet. I won't repeat a word of this to anybody. Never. Even if I'm tortured. Promise," said Belette.

Tompkins knew the cat was already out of the bag, "You'd better. Otherwise, I know who to call." At the moment, Belette did not know who to fear more.

"Should I fear for my life?" I asked.

"They don't care about you, Rob. And tell the consultants when they hear about this, that they have nothing to worry about, too. The Russians don't think frat boys are worthy of assassination," said Lee.

"First, we don't know if Petrov is dead, and this bunch doesn't use gulags in Siberia."

"Who do you think grassed him up?" asked Sir Reginald.

"What?"

"Oh sorry. I forgot not everyone knows Brit slang. Did someone ratted him out?"

Sladka handed me a note. "Novichuk."

"What's Novichuk?"

"That's the poison they think they gave Petrov. It's a very popular poison among a certain class of Russians."

"Isn't anyone concerned for me?" I asked. "I have a wife and I often thought about having kids."

Tiffany yelled, "Is there a Mike Tompkins here? Phone call."

"Petrov's been medevacked to Charité Hospital in Berlin," said Tompkins, putting down the phone.

"What the hell is going on here?" I said. "Do I need a bulletproof vest to work here?"

"Just be careful of someone with an umbrella. Especially when it isn't raining."

"I quit," I said.

"Don't be such a drama queen. The Russians aren't interested in you."

"Why not?"

"I can't tell you anything under the British Official Secrets Act," said Sir Reginald.

"Bullshit. Your father was the zookeeper at the monkey house at The Bronx Zoo. You're not covered under The Secrets Act," said Tompkins.

"I asked you not to say that in front of anyone. That's not proper. Besides, as a self-proclaimed anglophile, the British Official Secrets Act applies to me," said Sir Reginald.

"Isn't anyone afraid?" I asked.

"They got who they wanted. They made their point. They don't want to start trouble on American soil," said Sir Reginald. "Should I call the headhunters or the CIA for a replacement for Petrov?"

"I think they already know," said Tompkins.

"I'm going home," I said.

Sladka interrupted his admonition of Tiffany and came back into the office. "No, you're not," wrote Sladka and aimed the palms of his hands at me.

"Why don't you calm down and have lunch with Sladka?" Lee said to me.

"I'll go get my lunch," said Belette.

"That's alright; my day can't get much worse."

A noxious smell suddenly filled the office. Tiffany came in with a sheepish look on her face. "Ms. Pierson sent an overnight package, and I accidentally opened it."

Tiffany brought in plastic containers packaged in Styrofoam and ice packs, with a note, "Enjoy Cuban Mojos from sunny Florida."

"Get back in here, Barry. As the head of Tray Chic, you're going to share this with me," I said.

"Would you like to join us?" I asked the others.

There was a chorus of replies. "No, no thanks." "Another

time. I have things to take care of." "We'll keep you posted on Petrov. Thanks anyway."

Tompkins and Lee took the opportunity to slip out.

"I don't like mojo," said Belette.

"It's Spanish, so it's pronounced mo-ho. You never had it right," I said, "It's just fish in a garlic sauce."

"Mojo sounds cooler. Maybe I shouldn't eat something I don't know how to pronounce," said Belette.

Sladka came in with his own lunch and wrote, "Shkembe chorba."

"What's shkembe chorba?" I asked.

"Tripe soup. Can I have some? My mother used to make it," said Tiffany from the other room.

When Sladka heard Tiffany ask for a taste, he made the sound of a moose in heat.

"Come on in, Tiffany," I said, trying to be a matchmaker of the oddest proportions.

"I brought Banista. Maybe we can split it." Tiffany opened up some tinfoil to reveal a baked square.

Sladka almost spoke.

Belette stared at the Banista as if it needed to be disarmed.

"Banista's just phyllo dough pie with feta. It's street food usually eaten for breakfast. But I like it for lunch too," said Tiffany.

"Isn't Tiffany an unusual name for someone who eats Banista?" I tried to be clever without asking her ethnicity outright.

"Yes, I was born here but my parents called me Bisera, which means pearl in Bulgarian. The kids at school made fun of me. So, I took one of those Internet quizzes. It said pick your favorite hooker name and your favorite candy and that will be your new American name. Tiffany is my favorite hooker name. And Turkish Delight is my favorite candy and you're supposed to combine them. Tiffany Delight. But I only use Tiffany because most Bulgarians don't like the Turks because of something that happened a long time ago. Maybe hundreds of years ago."

I almost had to put Sladka in a separate pen, even though Tiffany was twenty years younger. They exchanged written messages as if Sladka was deaf too. I ate my fish out of deference to Gladys's efforts.

Belette stared at Tiffany and Sladka and the fish and asked, "Hey Boss, is it OK if I slip out for a burger?"

"What happened to the greatest day of your life?"

"I have to get to work on that meritocracy thing."

Chapter 9

No Tedium for the Weary

THE NEXT MORNING, we learned that Ivan Petrov survived his attack. Of course, I was relieved, even though he was someone I did not know about until yesterday and would probably never meet. For a fellow for whom I only had indirect responsibility, he created a new form of life-threatening anxiety through a tiny reenactment of the Cold War.

When I accepted this position, I thought if I could move the plodding and outwardly stodgy world of Remora an inch forward, I would have achieved a minor victory. Nothing in the company newsletters, which I had helped style, had prepared me for this job.

I wanted a day of tedium. I needed a day of tedium. A day when I could yawn and not feel guilty. A day when I could stare at the Colgate clock across the Hudson with the hope that it was 5:00 PM when it was only 9:20 AM. I could leave for lunch at exactly noon and come back at 2:00 PM. I could call Cassia about nothing. Even the bomb squad must wait patiently for its next death-defying assignment.

I asked Tiffany to reshuffle the parade of good and evil Dewars which would give me time to sign documents and consider ideas, both new and old, in a rare period of quiet and

Success Is Not An Option

calmness. Every job has needless and monotonous tasks, but seldom were they appreciated and welcomed. After a mere fifteen minutes of such reverie, an apologetic Tiffany popped her head in and said, "I tried to stop them."

Mimi Lee and a man I did not recognize pushed her aside.

"Are you here to tell me something new about Ivan Petrov?" I asked.

"No," said Lee. "This is Joe Greegan. He's in charge of our Fraud Prevention and Investigation Unit. In fact, he is the Investigation Unit."

"Don't know this Petrov fella. We're here to talk about a couple of crimes that are going on under your nose," said Greegan.

"A couple?"

I could tell Greegan was an ex-NYPD detective by his balls first, side-to-side walk like a gunfighter but with a paunch. He wore a sports coat, a requirement from his old job which also helped conceal his weapon. When he was an active cop, his clothes had to be cheap, not fancy threads that would raise suspicions about corruption, if not taste. Why should that change now?

Before Greegan retired, he probably wore a clip-on tie, so he could not be hanged by his own wardrobe during an arrest. Now he wore a real tie, pulled up to a closed collar. This indicated he felt safer among our white-collar criminals. In fact, I doubted he now wore his bullet-proof vest. An ironic role reversal for both of us.

"How many years were you on the job?" I asked, trying to flaunt my knowledge of New York cop lingo.

"27 years. I worked Financial Crimes Task Force, but I was close to the Chief of Ds."

"Sure, Chief of Detectives. Welcome to the 3-7," I said.

"What's the 3-7?" asked Lee.

"We're on the 37th floor, so this is the 3-7."

I got the usual New York look from Greegan and now from Lee. "Not funny. You're wasting our time."

"Let's get to the business at hand. We need to discuss two serious crimes," said Greegan.

"There's been some skimming of premiums and the falsifying of information on the current 10-Q. Which one would you like to discuss first?" said Lee.

"Neither but go ahead."

"The premium skimming is hard to prevent but easy to solve," said Greegan. He explained how outside brokers issued insurance policies with fake numbers. That way the policy looked legitimate to the client but the broker pocketed the premium, never filing the proper information with the home office. The broker told the client to call him if they had claim. But sometimes the client filed a claim directly with the home office and they couldn't locate the policy.

"And *voil*a! A *fugazi*. A fraud," said Greegan. "And with everything being electronic these days, it's become easier and easier to issue a fugazi. Usually, there's also an inside man.

"Right now, the number of fraudulent policies is unknown and the FBI has been notified 'cause it's interstate crime."

"The documents will be housed in my office and we'll go through suspected policies to ascertain the extent of the crime," said Lee.

I was a bit embarrassed when I realized how easily I understood the scheme. I thought every employee of every company thought of ways to steal. But cowardice, law enforcement, industry standards, and even honesty acted as preventative measures. A large mortgage could be both a deterrent or an incentive to commit a felony.

"How can we stop it in the future?" I asked.

"You'd have a revolution if you tried to stop it and lose a lot of legitimate business," said Lee. "Some experienced brokers are given what is called 'The pen.' That means they can write policies under a certain policy limit amount without getting approval from the higher-ups. It's an indication of success and freedom. Any effort to change that could result in all sorts of problems.

"I'll liaise with the FBI. Even though they are self-important pricks," said Greegan. But he quickly added, "Pardon my French. I still have some old bad habits I have to fix. I meant to say that the FBI are problem solvers." He stretched out the last two words.

As a one-man band and the only person who did what he did, Greegan could not get a promotion. At the same time, he didn't have to maintain the persona of a businessperson. He sported a gaudy pinky ring which attracted a different type of attention at Remora than on the street. In a company where money was everything, outward displays of success were unacceptable.

"Do you have any idea who the culprits may be?

"We do. The inside guy probably works in Frank Collins' area."

"OK, keep me posted. You said you had two things. What's the other worse thing that is going to ruin my life?" I asked.

"How'd you know it could ruin your life?" asked Greegan.

"It's not going to ruin your life," said Lee, interrupting Greegan. "But the SEC thinks there were inconsistencies in the latest 10-Q we filed. Since you signed it, in the eyes of the SEC you are culpable. Oddly enough, they rarely scrutinize a 10-Q closely."

"Me? I don't know a damn thing about them. The 10-Q is some kind of financial report, right? People tell me to sign stuff, I sign. I don't even know the right questions to ask to see if it's OK." It immediately became clear, even tedium could be a source of trouble.

"'I know nothing' is not a good excuse for the SEC. And they're words the media and Wall Street does not want to hear."

"You said it's unusual for the SEC to audit these things?"

"Right. They rarely audit the quarterly reports," said Lee. "I'll liaise with the SEC and get outside counsel, if necessary."

"Sounds like you're being set up from the inside, Boss. Looks like someone intentionally included bogus info and then ratted you out to the SEC," said Greegan. "But we'll find the culprit and bring them to justice."

"I've watched enough detective shows to know that you're not supposed to promise you'll find the guilty party."

"That's murder, but this is just fraud."

"The incorrect data could have come from Collins' area," said Lee.

"The same guy who set up the bagel hit on Quisling," I said.

"You want me to look into the hit?" asked Greegan.

"No. *Mio consigliere* Gladys, told me to let it lie."

As Lee and Greegan got up to leave, Mimi said, "I'll talk to Collins. And you should too. If you find out anything, let us know."

Again, I tried to calm my nerves by working on mindless tasks. I reviewed and signed forms with a newfound wariness. Collins soon appeared and I immediately asked, "Do you know anything about the premium skimming scam?"

"Not personally, but it happens on occasion. 'The pen' is just part of the price of doing business."

"Are you looking into it?'

"Not me. I can't be responsible for everyone. But I'm cooperating with the authorities. I also have to maintain our relationships with outside brokers. They're our lifeline."

"Do you know anything about the problem with the 10-Q?"

In a very bad Jewish accent, Collins said, "You're velcome. Get it? '10-Q,' You're velcome, 10-Q." He wore that same shit-eating grin as when he told me who was responsible for the hit on Quisling.

"Did you have a hand in the 10-Q problem?"

"I want to 10-Q for making time to see me."

"I'm going to call the SEC and explain the fraud."

"Go ahead and call. But don't forget: this company needs me much more than it needs you. I make the company money. Not you. Me. Lotsa money. You lose money."

"It's still fraud. Did you know about the premium skimming beforehand?"

"Sure, but I'll deny it. I will destroy you and your whole fucking family, you little airy-fairy MaKissMe ass-licker."

"You're fired," I said, not knowing if I had the authority, grounds, or the three layers of warnings required by HR and witnessed by choir boys and rabbis before someone was actually and truly fired.

Collins stood up. "Try it, you little bastard." His eyes dilated and his bulbous nose became redder and wider. His whole body was probably crimson. If I had entered the Collins "Red in the Head" pool, I might have won.

"I'm going to kill you, you worthless piece of shit," he yelled with spit punctuating a much longer rant.

"Go right ahead. Try it, you flying asshole," I said, not my finest HR moment.

At that moment, Sladka appeared from nowhere and frightened Collins.

"And the horse you rode in on," said Collins, pointing at Sladka.

Sladka made one step toward Collins, who lost his balance, waved his arms to help gain his equilibrium, and fell backwards through one of the plate-glass windows. There were a series of discordant sounds.

First, the impact of Collins against the glass. Then shattered glass. Followed by a gust of wind through the jagged hole, a few moments of silence before a muted thud from the street below. Sladka and I looked at each other in shocked disbelief. Images that would always be remembered. Collins trying to keep his balance. Then the biggest insect on record squished against the windshield. And finally, an unobstructed view of Jersey through the hole.

Tiffany came running in. "What was that?"

"Collins just fell through the glass, Tiffany. Don't go anywhere near the window."

"I'll call Mimi Lee. You call the police and an ambulance."

People rushed in and out of my office. Lee and Greegan reappeared, this time along with Sir Reginald. There were a few people I never saw before, all asking the same questions.

The police evacuated everyone from my office when they arrived. They spread their arms and said, "Crime scene. Please leave the crime scene."

"I'm Detective Simmons; this is Detective D'Angelo."

Sladka, without coaxing, presented his private detective license, New York assault weapons gun permits which had to be registered before January 15, 2014, his Class D operator's license, which allowed him to drive a tow truck and a truck with a GVWR of 26,000 lbs. or less, a security guard license, Federal Firearms Act of 1938, something called the Bail Enforcement Agent and Watch, Guard and Patrol License, and his receipt from that morning's breakfast of *mekitsa* and *popara*. When Tiffany saw that, she fell in love again.

Sladka wrote a note and handed it to the detectives. "Mr. Stone innocent. Me too."

Mimi Lee jumped in. "I'm the General Counsel of Remora. Mr. Stone is innocent and is clearly not guilty of defenestration."

"Who said anything about a fence? And who said he was guilty?" asked Simmons.

Greegan asked, "Hey, are you Simmons from the 4-5? I'm Joe Greegan. I used to work in the Financial Crimes Task Force. I was close to Jimmy Dempsey, the Chief of Ds. Jimmy Dee, Chief of Ds. The CDs. A little financial joke. Get it?"

"How long have you been off the job?"

"A little over four years."

"Dempsey hasn't been Chief of Ds for three years," said Simmons.

"In fact, Dempsey had a heart attack two years ago and died," added D'Angelo.

"Sorry to hear that. We've been out of touch. Please send my condolences to Agnes."

When Greegan eased himself away, Simmons said to D'Angelo, "I didn't know Dempsey died."

"He didn't. I just wanted to see his reaction."

"Yeah, those old guys love to gossip more than we do."

D'Angelo introduced himself to me and said, "Hey, aren't you that guy that talks about things that don't make sense on TV? My wife watches you all the time."

"I was on TV once."

"Hey, Mike, this is the guy on TV who doesn't make sense."

"Should be a great witness."

"What's your name again?"

"Rob Stone."

"Nice to meet you, Rob Stone. Wait 'til I tell the missus. By the way, why'd you kill Frank Collins?"

"I didn't kill anyone, especially Frank Collins."

"Why was Mr. Collins up here?"

"He's a company President. We were discussing many things. He's been here before. We talked about some problems in his area."

"Problems? What kind of problems?"

Greegan insinuated himself into the conversation. "We have a rampant premium skimming problem and found some misinformation on some SEC filings. I've been looking into it."

"Hey, who's paying you now, Greegan?" I thought.

"Nice insurance company you run here. What kind of fraud?"

"An outside broker sells a policy but pockets the premium. It's a little more complicated than that," I said.

"Is that why you killed him?"

"What? No, I didn't kill him. He lost his balance. He flailed his arms like one of those inflatable tube men in front of a used-car lot, then fell backwards through the window."

"Did he kill him?" asked D'Angelo, pointing at Sladka.

"No, and by the way, he doesn't have a tongue, so he can't speak."

"What did you and Collins talk about today?"

"They talked about the premium skimming because it was in

Collins' division. And the misinformation on the SEC thing could send Mr. Stone to jail," interrupted Greegan.

"That sounds like a motive for murder to me," said Simmons.

I wanted to tell Greegan to stand closer to the hole.

Greegan said, "Premium skimming. Easy crime to commit; easy crime to solve. Hard crime to prevent."

D'Angelo and Simmons acted like they knew what Greegan was talking about.

"But you were in the room when he went through the glass, right?" Simmons asked me.

"Yes."

"What were the last words you said to him?"

"I asked him if he had anything to do with the misinformation on the 10-Q," I said. Lee tried to shush me. I then added, "Just before he fell, he almost admitted he had fixed the 10-Q report to make me look like a crook."

"That's convenient. Although, it's a little hard to corroborate that story now."

"What were Mr. Collins last words before he went through the window?"

"OHHHHHHHHH shit." I omitted that Collins screamed he was going to kill me. That surely would have complicated the matter.

Tiffany called to the detectives, "I heard Mr. Collins say to Mr. Stone that he was going to kill him."

"Tell us your version now Mr. Stone and make everyone's life easier. Sounds like self-defense," said Simmons.

Between Petrov, the underwriter fraud, the SEC fraud, and Collins going through the skin of the building, I wondered what kind of job I had accepted. Ecology initiatives, in-house daycare, and a meritocracy now seemed stupid and insignificant. It was one thing for greed and ambition to simmer under the surface at any company, but do it on someone else's time.

"Form 10-Q shall be used for quarterly reports under Section 13 or 15(d) of the Securities Exchange Act of 1934 (15 U.S.C.

78m or 78o(d)), filed pursuant to Rule 13a-13," recited Lee without being asked, as if she had studied it that morning.

"Is that the reason you killed him? Legal mumbo-jumbo?"

"I didn't kill him. I just became CEO a short time ago. That guy wanted to kill me."

"So, it was self-defense."

"No. His whole head turned red when he got excited. He lost his balance and went through the glass. He weighed over 300 pounds."

"Being overweight is not a reason to murder someone, sir."

My office become a scene of forensic ferrets sniffing about complete with gruesome selfies, feather-dusting, and the little yellow numbered crime sandwich signs. Even the Medical Examiner came to the floor, although the body lay elsewhere.

"I am Sir Reginald Pigot-Smythe, head of HR. And murder is not in Mr. Stone's job description," as if that would exonerate me.

"So, you're English."

"I am an anglophile."

"No, you're the official tight ass."

"What was your relationship with Collins?"

"Not much really. Mr. Collins was also known as 'The Thermometer.' He was called 'The Thermometer' because he turned different shades of red when he was brassed off. Good family man though. Long-time employee. A tad overweight."

"So, Mr. Mustard did it with the pipe in the library? Is that what you are saying, Mr. Pigot?"

"Sir Pigot-Smythe. We weren't mates and had limited bants."

"If you don't stop talking like that, I'm going to run you in for being anglophile."

"That's not against the law."

"I know, but I am not sure the inmates at Rikers do."

"People always said that they wanted to kill Collins, but that was standard business jargon," said Sir Reginald.

"Did you ever hear Mr. Stone say that?"

"No, he's new at the job."

"He's new?"

"He's been with the company a long time but took over this position when A.J. Spaulding died."

"Did Stone have anything to do with Spaulding's death?"

"No, he just helped with the obituary."

"When Spaulding was in charge, this floor was known as Mt. Cyanide because few survived. People would say, 'Turn down all promotions. Never become Icarus. Never get too close to the sun,'" said Sir Reginald.

"Or the windows," added D'Angelo.

Lee stood next me, "This wasn't defenestration. I was a history major as an undergrad. Defenestration is the act of throwing someone out of a window. The first recorded instance was at the Prague Castle in 1419. Later incidences of defenestration in Prague led to religious wars including the 30 Years War. Technically, Collins was not a case of defenestration. He went through the glass, not an open window. Just saying."

I watched the cops from the civilian side of the crime scene tape take apart Spaulding artifacts and hoped they would not find anything incriminating in what he or I left behind. I wanted to call Cassia to avoid her asking the most mundane question, "How was your day?" And if she had already heard something on the news, she wouldn't be concerned.

"We'll be back after Forensics and the Medical Examiner issue their findings. I hope they don't find your fingerprints on the deceased's clothes," said D'Angelo, the Torquemada of the two.

Sir Reginald and Lee conferred. Then Lee told me, "I think we can keep this from the press, but only for a day or two."

An Executive VP from a nearby office who I did not know eased over. "Nice going, boss. Collins was dangerous. Very dangerous. Everyone called him 'ipso fatso.' We all wanted to do what you did, but no one had the balls. I think you'll get some respect now."

I simply thanked him. Whatever else I would add could wrongly be construed.

My personal cell phone rang.
"It's Bob Stront."
"How did you get this number?" I asked.
"It doesn't matter. I heard Collins died."
"Yes, he did. The police are here now."
"I know we don't always get along," said Stront, "But you know, Collins controlled the corporate Knick tickets, right? Do you know if he had tonight's tickets on him? If not, can I use them? For business purposes of course."
"I don't know. I'll check with the Coroner and get back to you."
"Well, if not tonight, keep me in mind. There's a steak dinner in it for you."

Chapter 10

Name a Famous Business Speech

WITH THE POLICE forbidding entry to my office, I moved down the hall to another space. Its finest amenities were full panes of glass, a shorter walk to the executive bathroom, and freedom from Spaulding's gallimaufry of overpriced tchotchkes and gewgaws. Death, crime, and an assassination attempt wreaked havoc with my schedule for days. Not that I minded. These complications and the relocation created a horde outside my door. They resembled the hungry crowds who anxiously waited outside a store on Black Friday, eager to trample on other humans just to buy a pair of discounted socks. Unassuming Tiffany did not know how to manage this swarm. While Gladys would have had the crowd weeping and prostrate on the ground, Tiffany needed to enlist the imposing mien of Sladka. He stood crossarmed, like a cartoon genie, sans *scimitar*, in front of my office, daring all to pass.

I asked to speak to the consultants first. This was more a cost-effective maneuver than the value I placed on their advice. The consultants, like a waiting taxi, charged for idling. The MaKissMe consultancy pod entered the temporary office and immediately asked if I needed a grief counselor.

"I didn't think I did until you asked that question," I said.

"This was a shocking event. You don't have to hide behind your flippancy."

"What did the police ask and what did you say?"

"The police told me not to leave town. They made it sound like I was taking the next stagecoach to Newark."

"Have they reached any conclusions?"

"None that they shared with me. It was an accident, pure and simple. The guy lost his balance and fell backwards through the glass."

"Don't they have building codes for that? You can lead the charge for a new building code regulation for stronger glass panes and position it as empathy," said Quinn.

"This is one of the problems with business," I said, "Something happens once, whether by accident or intentionally, and a new procedure is instituted so that the improbable would never happen again."

"We believe you should present this as a suicide story. Your image will benefit. We can even make you into a sympathetic character. He did it before your eyes."

"For consistency and to avoid perjury and jail, I'll stick with the accident story. By the way, how did you keep Collins' death from getting a lot of press coverage?"

"We positioned it as a suspected suicide. Just another faceless businessman committing suicide in New York. Not as sexy as a weird accident or homicide. A weird accident would lead to a lot of questions and we didn't want to have the word 'unknown' bandied about. That would have caused all sorts of speculation. The media is quiet except for that pesky local news station that shows his body covered in a white sheet on the sidewalk every 20 minutes."

"Aren't you afraid that some will think that working at Remora induced his suicide?"

"Certainly not. And there is always opportunity in tragedy."

"Are you also selling numbered and signed shards of glass from Collins' fall?"

"No. We think you should give a speech about the health of the company."

"There's no way in hell I'm giving a speech."

"Peabody said that you can give the speech on his show."

"Speaking of shards of glass, are you three planning my future without including me?"

"Before yesterday, you were becoming known as an independent thinker, now we can make you into a cult hero."

"Don't say that. Mao was a cult hero and he murdered 25 million."

"People really like your artsy answers."

"They liked it because they didn't know what I was talking about. I understand people like freak shows, so I'm not doing it."

"A speech will raise morale. You should give a speech everyone will remember."

"Tell me one business speech that people remember? Politics, sports, military, the arts, people remember, but memorable business speeches?" I asked.

"TED talks."

"Steve Jobs' death speech."

"Boo-yah."

"Sheryl Sandberg."

"Michael Douglas in *Wall Street*, 'Greed is good.'"

"Those are not speeches, those are epigrams," I said. "All people remember from any speech is one line anyway. The one line makes the speech special. The rest is fluff and clichés and you hope that one line doesn't gets lost. 'Ask not what your country can do for you, blah, blah, blah.' Nobody remembers anything else from the speech."

"So, we'll write one good line," said Fiona.

"How many motivational posters, books, and speakers do you need to realize they ain't taking?"

"You're too cynical."

"No business speech is important," I said, "Because they all have making-money as the end result. It's not about uplifting lives like 'I Had A Dream.' Or the irony of having a terminal illness and Lou Gehrig saying, 'Today, I consider myself the luckiest man on the face of the earth' speech. Business speeches are all about money. Business is necessary for the world to move ahead, but not particularly noble. Most think 'Free at last. Free at last.' You three think: $400 an hour plus expenses."

"OK, then give a speech that no one remembers. They remembered your speech you gave on "Estrogen and Tonic," said Fiona.

"Those were random words and events. They remember things that had nothing to do with business."

"Maybe if we put the speech to music. People remember lyrics like ads," said Quinn.

At that moment, Lindsay walked in. I welcomed her entrance, knowing a stranger's abrupt appearance would stop Mommy and Daddy from arguing. "Here's Remora's formal press release about Collins, carefully neutered by everyone, including inside and outside counsel and the *gonifs* in the lobby who overcharge for breath mints and stale candy."

"*Remora Property and Casualty has lost of one its most experienced and valued leaders, Francis X. C. Collins. The entire Remora family sends their heartfelt condolences to Mr. Collins' family and friends.*"

"Thank you," I said. "That is wonderfully innocuous."

"Are you sure you can just add an apostrophe after his name and not an apostrophe 's' on Collins?" asked Fiona.

"It's acceptable either way," said Lindsay. "Because of the nature of his death and size, I wanted to add 'Funeral services will be held on Thursday, Friday, and Saturday,' but even I have my limits."

"Thank you, Lindsay." I stretched my eyebrows in her direction, meaning "thank you" and "I'll call you later."

She did not leave immediately. We both knew she wanted to stay to see what mattered to the nuclear triad but neither of us could think of a reason for her to stay. "I'll leave the door open, in case Rob wants to make a quick getaway," said Lindsay.

"She must be a friend of yours."

"My oldest friend here."

"Despite this week's events, the Remora stock is soaring."

"And better take credit for the rise, because you'll be blamed when it goes down, whether you had anything to do with or not."

"Why'd it go up?" I asked.

"The EPS exceeded the experts' prediction by a penny."

"Just because of a penny? What's the ESP again?" I asked.

"E-P-S. Earnings per share. The experts predicted the EPS should be $1.28, while the actual amount was $1.29, and the market went crazy."

"All because of the ESP?"

"EPS. Financial professionals predict what the EPS will be based on various factors."

"Impatient lot. Why don't they just wait for the real one to come out and stop guessing what the ESP will be?"

"They want to give themselves and their costumers an edge."

"So, they create a mystique."

"Just like you do with art terms."

"Nice going, Quinn. Protecting your allies in illusion. Artists often create their own illusions, so maybe we have more in common than I thought."

"In any event, people believe you're doing a great job leading the company," said Quinn.

"When do we get around to the important issues like climate change, creating a meritocracy, privatization of water, and ageing?"

"You've made great strides and established an excellent first step in building a foundation and trust. You must show that you know the rules before you can break them."

"Around here, laws aren't broken, they're ignored," I said.

"Before we go. Sir Reginald is worried about litigation from Quisling."

"Maybe we can make the bagel maker a joint tortfeasor to share the blame. Sir Reginald is always worried about litigation. He's like a hypochondriac; one day he'll be right," I said.

"How do you know what a joint tortfeasor is?" asked Fiona.

"It was the name of my band."

"Flippancy. Flippancy."

It is hard to believe that these people were once babies. Although, you can imagine them as teenagers. Pimples were not allowed, and they would never go near the bad crowd or even the cool kids, as they might be drawn into the vortex of middling grades and the freedom that surrounded a lack of ambition. In college, high grades were as important as the right haircut.

Although Gladys was not supposed to return for another week, I thought I heard her voice in the hallway. The antidote to death and those who wanted to profit from it. Her years of experience, intimidation, and unfiltered thought created a distinct tone. I peeked my head out the door and walked toward her, trailed by the consultants and Tiffany.

"Why is this stuff still up? Do you think little yellow strips are going to stop me? No more of this *Law & Order* crap," said Gladys as she ripped through the yellow crime scene tape pasted on my office door jamb like a blowtorch on a cobweb.

"The police haven't given us permission to take it down," I said. "What are you doing back?"

"When I heard about the Fat Man falling out the window, I knew you needed my help. While we were still in Florida, I called an old friend in the New York City Police Department and told him that you are incapable of killing someone. Boring them to death, yes. Killing someone by throwing him out a window, no. Sorry, I couldn't have been here to see that," said Gladys.

"Thanks guys, for stopping by," I said to the consultants. "If someone goes through the glass again, I know where to find you."

"I assume they're still investigating," said Gladys.

"Yes, but it was an accident. Wasn't your sister with you? Where is she now?"

"She's on a tour to Disney."

"I hope she skips the 'It's a Small World' exhibit for your sake."

"She will; she thinks she is a wrinkled Cinderella. Then they'll put her on a plane for New York. That took a couple of days to arrange. Otherwise, I would have been here sooner."

A few weeks away invigorated Gladys.

"I called your mother every night. Boy, she told me stuff she shouldn't have. We're old friends now. What does she mean about you two have *tsuris* in the below-the-belt department?" Gladys captured my mother's tone and words.

"It's a Yiddish word," I said without telling her it meant trouble.

"Well, she did tell me some things that were embarrassing, too. I may keep them to myself, unless I need them. And I also spoke to Cassia. She's very nice and very smart. Smart enough not to tell me the really juicy stuff about you."

Tiffany stood to the side, as useful as the first murder victim in a horror movie. Too overwhelmed to learn or take notes, she said, "I can stay an extra day or two and catch Ms. Pierson up on what happened." She, of course, was the only person who did not know that Gladys needed no advice.

"I called him a flying asshole before he went through the glass."

"I've never been more proud of you," said Gladys.

"I appreciate that for all the wrong reasons."

"Jr. Jr. will probably take over for Collins."

"Who's Jr. Jr.?"

"He's one of Spaulding's sons. We think. Believe it or not, even I don't know much more. Everything about him has always been hush hush. I don't even know who the mother is. I don't know where or when. It was when people cared too much about these things. Today, you can have a bastard naming party. People celebrate all sorts of shit."

Success Is Not An Option

"Try to be more delicate. The PC police are more dangerous than the Homicide Squad."

"Sorry, it's been building up for weeks. But Jr. Jr. is a like a floater. No one knows what he does or who he reports to. I don't think he has a permanent position. And now that the old man is gone, who knows what will happen?"

"I never heard of him."

"Because he was never in your precious newsletter. And then there is Sir Schmuck fucking Quisling upside down and backwards."

"I didn't know that."

"How blind are you?"

"I try to concentrate on business issues."

"Well, that's stupid. If you really want to know about the company, you have to know what the people are doing."

"That's none of my business."

"You naïve child. There are two types of people at any company—pricks and pockets."

"OK, please tell me who are the pricks and who are the pockets?"

I ordinarily did not speak this way. Not that I was a prude or priggish, but I was polite. Yet for this 86-year-old woman, it was a form of currency.

"Pockets are interested in money; pricks are interested in sex or abuse of power."

"What are the people who just want to do their job and go home?"

"Pockets."

"Collins?"

"Prick."

"Stront?"

"Major prick. More abuse than sex."

"Quisling?"

"I'll have to work on that."

"Me?"

"Neither. That's what frightens people about you."

"Sir Reginald?"

"He's the most frightened adult I know. He's so scared, I'm surprised Sir Schmuck is screwing Quisling. It's so out of character. He must think it'll somehow stop her from suing the company."

Gladys pulled a box out of her bag and gave me a gift.

"Thank you. I didn't know they still made these things. Are they legal?"

"How the hell do I know? Someone sold it; I bought it."

I had not seen a stuffed alligator in decades. They always seemed to have a wry smile and generated a fear that if you turned your back, they would bite you on the ass. I did not check for dust as if it might have been hanging around the Pierson household and this was the perfect opportunity to dump it.

"You don't have to put it on your desk. Although, it might help your image."

"By the way, my desk drawer doesn't open. The cops must have done something when they were looking for clues to frame me. Please call maintenance."

A few minutes later Gladys came back in.

"Maintenance is working from home. They'll set up a teleconference and explain to you how to fix your desk."

"Maintenance can't work from home. How do you fix something over the phone?"

"Teleconference."

"What can we do about it?"

"Do you want to start a war with maintenance? By the way, how did that girl Tiffany work out?"

"Stop calling them girls."

"I was a girl for almost 50 years until it became illegal. Now, I'm a senior and I still can't even call myself what I want."

"I think she and Sladka got to know each other very well."

Gladys finally got someone from maintenance to teleconference with me and explain how to fix the desk drawer as she could not find a maintenance person in the building.

"Hi, my name is Rob and I'm having trouble opening my desk drawer."

"Aren't you the guy in charge now?"

"Some days."

"That's not good; people in charge never know what they are doing."

"So, if I had this problem months ago, I would know what to do?"

"Probably. Do you have a long something, because we have to jiggle the doo-hickey. You mind tilting your computer, so I can see what you're doing? No, a little more. Good."

"What kind of long thing. What's your name?"

"Joe. Do you have a flathead screwdriver or a letter opener."

"I have an X-Acto knife."

"Too short. Can you jiggle the drawer back and forth and loosen whatever is stuck?"

I did as Joe instructed with no success.

"Let's try one more thing. Does the drawer open enough to stick your fingers in?"

"No, it doesn't open at all."

"Yeah, that's not going to work. I'm in on Tuesdays."

"I'm on the 37th floor."

"Go to our website and make a formal request."

"How come you work from home?"

"COVID."

"COVID is basically over."

"You never know when it could come back."

"Do you think it could return this week?"

"It could."

"What if this is an emergency?"

"How many desk emergencies are there?"

"And what if it was a leak?"

"Call a plumber."

I felt uncomfortable for a variety of reasons being back in my office. Although the NYPD had allowed the broken pane of glass to be replaced, the tint did not exactly match. Maybe the old windows were weathered or the proper hue was unavailable or someone was simply complacent. It was not like I took out my Pantone color wheel to determine the differences, but it became a daily reminder not only of Collins' death, but of the difference a few shades made and how I used to think.

Without warning, Detectives D'Angelo and Simmons appeared at my door. "Who ripped down the crime scene tape? And why are you sitting in here?"

Gladys came over. "I tore it down. I called Eddie Fox, the old Brooklyn Borough Chief, and I told him Mr. Stone was innocent."

"Everybody knows somebody. Sorry madam, this is a crime scene, and you can't interfere with an ongoing investigation. And what is your name?"

"Gladys Pierson, old biddy personified. And I'm not a madam. Not anymore."

Everyone knew Gladys should not have torn down the crime scene tape, but she just did not care. She then argued with the cops. They fought like children about who would first lick the spoon with the chocolate cake mix.

I interrupted. "Hey. Any of you guys know how to unjam my desk drawer?"

"You gotta be kidding," said D'Angelo.

"It was OK before Forensics did whatever they did."

Simmons put his hand under the drawer. "Sometimes, these old desks have a secret latch underneath. There ya go." And the drawer popped open.

"Thanks."

"See," said Gladys. "He couldn't kill anyone; he can't even fix his own drawers."

Lee, Sir Reginald, and Greegan ran in from the elevator and joined us. They were out of breath. "We heard the police were here and came right over." I half expected Reggie to appear with a magnifying glass, a pipe, a deerstalker, and a tweed frock.

"Don't say anything, Rob," said Lee.

"Do you have any new evidence?" asked Greegan.

"As a matter of fact, we do. But first, we have a few more questions," said Simmons.

"Does anyone want to change their original statement? Any of you?"

Everyone murmured, "No, no."

"The Medical Examiner found that Mr. Collins did not sustain any injuries previous to the fall. Nor were there signs of a struggle or defensive wounds. And Forensics did not find any of Mr. Stone's fingerprints or traces of fabric from the clothes the victim was wearing. So right now, the DA does not have cause to indict. But that doesn't mean we won't find something in the future."

Everyone cheered and clapped.

"I knew it would be hard to prove nothing," I said.

"What does that mean?" said Simmons.

"It means you can't prove something that doesn't exist."

"Are you hiding something?"

"No, it means thank you."

"I told you he was boring," said Gladys.

As soon as the elevator door closed on the cops, Gladys yelled, "Let's celebrate. For better or worse, Rob's not going to jail." She retrieved a key from her desk that unlocked a small refrigerator filled with booze. "This was Spaulding's secret stash."

"What's the most expensive?" asked Lee.

"What about this one?" said Gladys. "Moët & Chandon Dom Pérignon Charles and Diana 1961. Look it up on the Internet."

"Holy shit," I said. "This was drunk at Diana's and Charles's wedding and there wasn't supposed to be any bottles in existence."

Reggie looked at the screen. "That bugger's worth over 4,000 quid. That's a heap of dosh. May the Princess rest in peace."

"Let's drink to Collins, the bastard."

"Good-bye, you old salad dodger," said Reg.

We invited Tiffany and Sladka to join us. Those two fell in love quicker than you could say "shkembe chorba." Unfortunately, I heard Tiffany bragging on the phone, more than once, about Sladka's sexual prowess in giddy detail. You cannot yell, "I heard that." Nor could you forget minutiae you wish you had not had in the first place.

Spaulding only had a few heavy cut crystal glasses, but we found some paper cups and divided the champagne, I said, "A toast. Let us lift our cups. Here's to Frank Collins, may he rest in pieces. And to me, for not killing him." This sentiment was greeted warmly.

When all the champagne was drunk and everybody left, Gladys said to me, "Sorry I couldn't have been here to see you throw Collins through the window. But I wrote a poem about him on the flight back from Miami." She took out a crumpled napkin. "Would you like to hear it?"

"Of course," I said. Would I also deny a child with an axe?

"You remember how I wrote a poem *Barry the Beneficial Nematode*? This is another one."

Good-bye you big fat fuck,
You couldn't have been a bigger schmuck
You were a lying sack of shit
And now you are paying for it.
I hope you drop dead once more
So, I can set you on fire and make a s'more.

"What beautiful imagery. I'm almost teary eyed."

"Don't forget, tomorrow's the Presidents Meeting."

"Gee Mom, can you write me a note that I'm sick?"

Chapter 11

Death as an Opportunity

Dramatis Personae

- ~~Frank Collins—President of Domestic Operation~~
- *Dom Oleoso*—Head of Surety Bonds
- *Harvey Knoll*—Chief Claims Adjustor
- *Mimi Lee*—General Counsel
- *Candy Quisling*—Head of Marketing
- ~~*Doug Friedman*—Director of External Relationships~~
- *Isla White*—New Director of External Relationships
- *Sir Reginald Pigot-Smythe*—Head of HR
- *Bob Stront*—Business Hit Man
- *Mike Tompkins*—President of the International Division
- *IT guy*—IT guy
- *A.J. Spaulding Jr. Jr.*—President of Domestic Operations
- *Carlos*—the delivery guy
- *Me*

There was probably nothing as useless as a meeting, but we persisted. I persisted. I did not want to appear dictatorial or neglectful. After all, people thought merely showing their faces was helpful, while quite the opposite was often the case.

I was sure some business school professor knew the origins of the business meeting but not knowing the exact history suited my purposes. Meetings, of course, took different forms. The ancient Greeks were known for their agoras, democratic meetings, yet women, slaves, and foreigners could not vote. Up to 6,000 Athenians would assemble on Pnyx Hill to discuss whatever Athenians discussed. Much later and elsewhere, Caesar was assassinated in the Roman Senate. Slight progress there. But at our meetings, we didn't even vote on matters, as if that would have mattered. And we wisely ate with cheap plastic forks and knives that broke under the pressure of cutting lettuce, making it more difficult to stab one another.

Business meetings could look like many things—Passover Seders, a gathering of mob bosses hosted by Marlon Brando to make peace with the other families over drugs, or King Arthur and the Round Table. King Arthur and the Round Table began as an aspirational myth. It epitomized democracy and chivalry for a round table assumed no leader. There were no substantial penalties for the violation of the code of chivalry, as any transgression signified shame enough.

King Arthur left a seat vacant, the *Siege Perilous*, the Perilous Seat, for the Knight who found the Holy Grail. No matter how hypocritical, I thought I needed to do something to recognize the recent death.

"Today, in honor of Mike Tompkins, we have left one chair unoccupied."

"You trying to be funny? Is that a threat? You gonna throw me out the window too?" said Tompkins.

"Sorry, Mike. Sometimes I get you guys confused. That's not a good apology. Sorry, Mike, I meant Frank Collins was dead, not you."

"How dare you get me confused with that fat bastard."

"Which one?" said Lee.

"Harvey Knoll is away on business, but he'll be on the speaker phone," I said.

"You mean that dumbass thing that looks like a UFO?"

Everyone stared at the phone in the middle of conference table as if it were Knoll himself.

"How come he isn't visible on some computer screen?"

"Can I stay and watch?" asked Carlos, the deli delivery guy.

"Why?' asked Stront.

"I'm studying business at night and I want to learn the practical aspects."

"Gladys learned all about business at night," said Tompkins. Only the older guys laughed.

"He's going to steal our trade secrets," said Oleoso.

"The only secret here is how you lasted so long, Dom," said Knoll.

"Sure, have a seat over there, Carlos," I said.

Carlos placed the sandwiches within reach of the people with the shortest arms. He dealt out the napkins and neatly arranged the oversized spoons in the plastic vats of side dishes before sitting on the window ledge with the vents for the HVAC system.

"You think you going to learn something here?"

"Listen carefully and do the opposite."

"No eulogies. Nobody liked Collins, the bastard," said the disembodied voice of Harvey Knoll.

"Don't get me wrong. I wasn't going to say anything nice. More like a clarification of what happened," I said.

"He's dead. Don't care."

"Ah, a Hallmark card?"

"I'll miss him," said Bob Stront. "Even though he was an asshole, he owes me big time. I wonder if he covered that in his will? Does he have a widow?"

At that moment, A.J. Spaulding Jr. Jr. glided into the conference room and assumed Frank Collins' chair as if born to the throne. As far as I knew, no one had contacted him requesting him to appear or appointed him as a replacement. I slipped out and called the consultants who feigned ignorance. Jr. Jr., as he liked to be called, had elevated himself to the position of President of Domestic Operations, apparently without authority and fanfare. The others did not question his presence either. Completely flummoxed as to how to handle an impostor, an impostor who I assumed, as did the others, held more shares than the rest of the room combined and more secrets than Gladys, we simply acquiesced.

"The prayer, the prayer," said Stront. "All together now. Thank you, dear Lord, for allowing us at Remora to seek unfair advantages. And, dear Lord, one additional plea: may you treat Frank Collins the way he treated us."

Everyone responded, "Amen."

"Can I give a half 'Amen?'" I asked.

"Dom, why the hell are you wearing a hockey mask?"

"Last meeting, Stront hit me in the head with a pen," said Oleoso.

"I just threw it on the table and your head got in the way."

"Dog Rule."

"Dog Rule doesn't apply to this, right, Stone? It only works if somebody keeps on repeating himself and not when someone just doesn't give a shit."

But I liked this permutation on the "Dog Rule" if it could indiscriminately stop a host of bad behavior.

"Before we start," Stront interrupted me. "Since we're no longer saying aloud how our budgets are doing, I think we should start with a stare-down like those ultimate fighters."

"How come they don't start laughing at each other?"

"I don't think practiced and artless macho nonsense should have a greater place in business than it already does, do you?" asked Lee.

"Where's Doug Friedman?"

"He was traded. This is Isla White; she'll be taking over Doug's duties," said Lee.

"Hello all. I'm Isla White and I hope I bring new perspective to Remora."

"Where's Doug?"

"He's with Entimos Insurance now."

"Hi, Isla. Welcome. Where are you from?"

"I'm from Entimos."

A silence fell for a moment. Consternation fell over most faces as Lee arched one brow.

"Isla, were you traded for Doug Friedman?" asked Tompkins.

"Not traded, exchanged," said Lee.

"You mean like a prisoner exchange in the fog on a bridge?"

"What's the difference?"

"An exchange is voluntary. A trade implies lack of consent," said Lee.

"Did we at least get a draft choice?"

"Holy shit. She was traded for Friedman. Who ever heard of a man being traded for a woman?" said Stront.

"I think they used to do that in Shakespeare's time."

"And what firm was he with?"

"I would like to discuss plant-based insurance," said White from behind her bamboo bangs and oversized glasses. A respectable tattoo peeked out from under her shirt sleeve.

"No wonder they didn't want you."

"There is no enthusiasm for plant-based insurance in this room."

"You don't know what it is."

"Right, but we already have Crop/Hail insurance in the farming states. And in case you don't know what it is, it's basically financial protection against losses like drought, damaging freezes, hail, wind, disease, and price fluctuations."

"Carlos, where are the packets of mayonnaise? You know, I represent the Mayonnaise Institute," said Stront.

"No one uses them."

"I use them" said Stront.

"I think I have some," said Carlos.

Stront ripped the mayonnaise packet open with his teeth and put some on his tuna salad sandwich.

"What the hell is the Mayonnaise Institute anyway?"

"They're a client of this company who pays your mortgage. The Mayonnaise Institute is for the advancement, use, and product safety of yolk and non-yolk type products, including mayonnaise and other creamy preparations."

"You have some Institute on your chin."

"Would you like a napkin?" asked Carlos.

"In fact, when this meeting is over, I have a conference call on how to celebrate this year's International Mayonnaise Appreciation Day."

"I tried to sell medical malpractice to the Mayo Clinic."

"My family's from County Mayo."

"Can we get back to the matters at hand?"

At that moment, the now familiar clang of Candy's portable throne coming down the corridor heightened as it approached the door. Sir Reginald held the door open with one foot as he carefully pushed Candy to her rightful position at the table. Sir Reginald said, "I'm chuffed to announce Candy's experimental surgery was a brilliant success. And future procedures should make it perfect. Ta to the medical staff. As you recall, her condition, being paralyzed from the waist up, is the first in the annals of medicine."

"You mean to say that she had an operation and it failed?"

"What's experimental about it? Does that mean it wasn't covered by medical?"

"I hope Remora didn't pay for an experimental operation."

Then Candy spoke. A muffled sound arose from what seemed like the back of her skirt.

"What did she say?"

She repeated her words but with the same muzzled tone.

"Wait, wait," said Sir Reginald. He unstrapped her and

flipped Candy over so her ass stuck up in the air to face the conference table.

"Thank you for welcoming me back. There is much to discuss," said Candy.

"She's talking out of her ass!" said Tompkins. "She's talking out of her ass!"

"Well, she is the Head of Marketing," said Lee.

"Until the next operation, this is the only way I can speak."

"Out of your ass?"

Jr. Jr. rose and left the room. As soon as the door closed, Oleoso said, "He has the same bladder problem as his father."

"How do you know this?"

"Stall talk."

"What the hell is stall talk?"

"You know."

"No, I don't know. That's why I asked."

"In the men's room, there are partitions."

"Like horses."

"So, people talk when they're doing their business."

"Like I said, stall talk."

"I also heard Jr. Jr. drives to work in one car and goes home in another."

"Well, how does the other car get home?"

"Ask Dom if they eat urinal cakes for dessert."

At that point, Jr. Jr. returned to an air that reeked of gossip.

"You know, once you sit in that chair you have to sit there the rest of your life," said the IT Guy.

"You just want to be near power," said Stront.

Yet no one knew Jr. Jr.'s true power. No one knew what he would say or do or even if a secret family agreement existed. Without any evidence, no one wanted to confront him. Or if someone did challenge him, and he did have the proper power, no one knew what their future in the company may be.

"I know that is true with home poker games. Once you sit

somewhere, that is where you have to sit from then on, no matter what happens. Even after you die," said Tompkins.

"I know you'll do a great job, Jr. Jr.," said Oleoso.

"You're just a *tuchus* licker, Dom. If I wanted you to read a memo, I would have stuck it up Spaulding's ass. Sorry Jr. Jr. Your father's ass, not yours. Dom, you've raised 'groveltas' to a new level."

"'Groveltas'. What's that? There's no such word as 'groveltas,'" said Oleoso.

"Yes, there is. 'Groveltas' is the opposite of gravitas. It means you have no fucking shame and there's no bottom to how low you would go at a given moment to keep your job."

"Is that bad?"

"That must be a word used on this side of the pond. We use wanker or tosser," said Sir Reginald, who realized suddenly that his vulgar form of Anglophilia contributed to a hostile work environment. "We would only use that, of course, at our local."

"If you guys do not improve the quality of these meetings, I'm going to ply you with liquids and not let you go to the bathroom. Or make you stand the entire meeting. Or turn up the heat in summer and the A/C in winter. Or invite your mothers to attend," I said.

"Mimi, is there something against my mother coming to these meetings?" asked Tompkins.

"Nothing I can think of."

"We have a huge agenda, so let's jump in."

"Have you changed your mind about going around the room and asking how's everybody's budget doing? It's tradition," said Tompkins.

"Tradition is a mistake made twice," I said.

"Tradition usually arises from the need for communal comfort and a unifying common experience. And I believe that comfort and a unifying common experience are not specifically permitted under the Remora by-laws," said Lee.

"Thank you, Ms. Ivy League lawyer," said Tompkins.

"But humiliation works. It's a tried-and-true motivator," said Stront.

"How's your individual effort to build a meritocracy going? I'm sure you have all spoken with Barry Belette about it. No more nepotism, cronyism, and quid pro quos."

"If old man Spaulding is dead, how could it be nepotism for him to appoint Jr. Jr.? Don't you have to be alive to say something? Unless he specified something in his will," said Oleoso.

Jr. Jr continued to say nothing, unnerving many at the table.

"That wasn't fair to sic Barry Belette on us with that meritocracy thing."

"Sic semper tyrannis," said Lee.

"I hope you're not saying anything nice about Belette," said Tompkins.

"You know, Jr. Jr., Collins wanted to start a domestic Muslim practice at Remora," said Tompkins.

"Muslims consider insurance gambling. Their laws don't permit interest either," added Knoll.

"Insurance isn't gambling."

"Collins just wanted to fuck Stone over with Sharia and Takaful laws. If Stone opposed it, he is anti-Muslim; if he's for it, he's anti-American."

"Well, I for one don't want to be ruled by Sharia law," said Oleoso.

"I can assure you," said Jr. Jr., "I have no evil intent. Just money. As you can see, I'm the raisin in the milk and I can do and say things you cannot. I believe that is my dominion of control now."

"I have the slogan, 'A dollar for Allah.' Or how about, 'It's a slam with Islam'?" said Quisling.

"See what I mean. I've been telling you over and over that insurance started in Babylonia about 5,000 years ago. An obvious connection," said Oleoso.

"Your timeframe doesn't make sense. The Babylonians existed about 4,000 years ago and Islam is about 1,400 years," said Lee.

"Dog Rule."

"Double Dog Rule."

"Many of our policies talk about 'Acts of God' but they never specify which God."

"Can we get back to the agenda?"

"What about your campaign to improve morale and your 'Asshole of the Month' contest, Stone? Isn't that company-wide humiliation? Do you need a shovel for that too?"

"Yes, people are complaining about being targeted."

"I have reconsidered that campaign and I think we should cancel it," I said.

"Too late; they're already posting pictures for this month's winner."

"OK, we'll take them down."

"We can't," said Lee, "That means we made a mistake."

"Who was the winner anyway?"

"One of the guys in accounting that makes people beg to have their travel expenses covered."

"I hate that guy."

"Me too."

"Me too."

"Me too."

"That bastard deserves it."

"See, nobody likes him, so the process worked. We all agreed he merited the choice. But we still have to stop it," I said.

"We could exclude accountants from the 'Asshole of the Month' in the future. That would widen the field. And not too many people know our lawyers, right Mimi?" said Knoll.

"Or claims adjustors."

"I want Remora to buy a healthcare company," said Stront.

"That's not on the agenda."

"You didn't ask me if I wanted to add something."

"I got the slogan already," said Quisling. "A claim denied is not a death sentence."

"That should draw them in."

"Almost poetic," said Sir Reginald.

"I really don't think that slogan will work, Candy," said Stront with the sudden realization of her situation. Proper etiquette and good communications skills require that you look someone in the eye when you speak to them. But what do you do when you are arguing with someone's ass? Modern medicine has created many new questions founded in ethics, but what of those questions arising from etiquette?

"Everyone else is running away from heath care because of the uncertainty," said Lee.

"Exactly. Maybe we can pick up something at a bargain basement price."

"How about this for a slogan for a healthcare company? 'Big Pharma, Good Karma?'" said Quisling.

"Bring us numbers and a business plan next time," I said to Stront. I knew extra work for him would stop his project immediately.

"Yes, like a CPM," said Oleoso.

"And what the fuck is a CPM?"

"It is the Critical Path Method used in construction. Things must be done in a logical order. You can't put on the toilet seat until the toilet is installed," said Oleoso.

"And you can't wipe your ass until you shit," said Tompkins

"Another Hallmark card."

"You must have a solid business plan, before we can discuss it."

"How about 'Don't get sick, unless you really have to?'" said Quisling.

"I think that's brilliant," said Sir Reginald.

"There's a rumor that the SEC is conducting an investigation here. Is that true?"

"No comment," said Lee.

"What's that about? Who's involved?"

"The next one who asks a question about it, I'm going to report them to the SEC," said Lee.

"Let's discuss something on the agenda. Climate change. Here's a very brief summary of the UN's latest report on the climate crisis."

"That's on your agenda. Here's the other side," said Stront. He handed out his version.

Lee looked at Stront's pages. "You didn't even delete the search words 'Bogus Climate Change Claims' from your handout. OK, Bob, summarize what this says," she said in her best prosecutorial tone.

Stront fumbled through his printout.

"Bob, this nonsense was discredited years ago," said Lee.

"Then why is it still on the Internet?"

"What I handed out has something for everyone's business." I sounded like my father, if my father was in insurance. Until a few months ago, I was a graphic artist working for an insurance company and now I'm in insurance. Many Americans define themselves by what they do for money.

I continued, "Besides the usual lines of insurance …"

"'Books of business,' not 'lines of insurance.' That's the way our businesspeople refer to it."

"Climate change is important and if you idiots don't pay attention, your claims will skyrocket in the near future," said the telephone.

"We'll worry about it when it happens."

"It's here."

"Let's brainstorm a little and see how this affects you and the company."

"Gladys called it braingusting as it never seemed to rise to the level of a storm," I said.

"Let's discuss how climate change will affect your policies, reserves, capacity, reinsurance, and claims." Knoll spoke about how the claims adjustors had seen a huge increase in property damage, commercial and residential, and how responsible companies are concerned.

"I got it," said Quisling, "We'll help you reach a climate."

"What about Isla's idea about plant-based insurance?" asked Sir Reginald.

"We should sell at least $3 of that."

"What is that?" I asked.

"I thought you would know. You're the liberal," said Sir Reginald.

"Groveltas."

"Dog Rule."

"It can't be the Dog Rule; it's the first time it's been brought up."

"I'm expanding the Dog Rule to include things that are fucking stupid," said Stront.

"I got another idea: DIY cremations," said White.

"What does that have to with insurance or anything for that matter?"

"We can offer it as a rider to life policies."

"I think it's brilliant and I will form a committee to suss it out. We might have to ringfence it though," said Sir Reginald.

"Thank you, ladies and gentlemen. This has been most informative," I said to conclude the meeting.

"Why don't you start an innovation team and work on new business ideas like the DIY Cremation?"

"I want to thank you for letting me listen," said Carlos.

"What did you learn?"

"Well, they don't teach us this stuff in the books."

There are numerous reasons for the death of chivalry and knights. One can cite the ability of crossbow to pierce armor or some disastrous crusades, but those are inconsequential compared to the rise of mercantilism. The burgeoning middle class destroyed The Round Table as they usurped the powers of the nobles and killed courtliness. Despite the virtues of knighthood, the merchants, in the name of business, eroded the myths and realities of knighthood despite their virtues.

The poetry of honor was replaced by the self-imposed sobriety of business. Of course, the Arthurian myth was also filled with death, murder, incest, thievery, and treachery. But so was insurance.

As people departed, Stront lingered and asked to speak with me. I did have my pocketknife. At first, he was evasive. Long had there been rumors around the company that a small group of men in upper management tallied points whenever they had sexual encounters with women who were not their wives. Spaulding and Collins were thought to be charter members.

"On behalf of the committee, and against the better judgement of some, I am extending membership to you to join our exclusive club."

"Do you have a clubhouse? Do you have bake sales to raise money for your club?"

"Don't get cute with me. I'm just the messenger. And it wasn't my idea to invite you," said Stront.

Chapter 12
Seder at Mt. Taygetus

Dramatis Personae

- *Cassia*—Rob's wife
- *Mom*— Rob's mother
- *Tanta Gee*
- *Unkle Traktor*
- *Cousin Hippolyta*
- *Ortal and Pomegranate*—Hippolyta's children
- *Eli*—the waiter
- *Cousin Heshie*
- *Assorted children*
- *Me*

Until her semi-unexpected death, we held our Seders at Aunt Georgia's. Although the family missed her, no one missed looking for parking in her neighborhood, or her scratchy bargain brand of toilet paper, and her cooking that left life-long emotional and physical scars. My father said, "She was an alchemist. She turned perfectly good food into shit." People should not be frightened of food.

The task of finding a new place for the Seder fell to my mother and her sister, Tanta Gee. While they understood that grieving was an individual matter, they also understood that no one particularly liked their cooking either.

"Let's create new memories," said Tanta Gee Gee.

"You can't just say 'poof' and create new memories," my mother said.

"Why not? If I say there will be new memories, then there'll be new memories. How about making new traditions then?"

"People keep the old ways because they're too lazy to think of something new."

"Perfect. We'll make traditions then."

No matter what my mother and Tanta Gee Gee told the others, they chose Mt. Taygetus because they were spellbound by the overgrown pies and thousand-layer cakes that sang, danced, and shimmied in the spinning dessert carousel by the front door. "It's a like a Broadway show with bananas," said Tanta Gee Gee.

Cassia and I were already seated when we saw Cousin Heshie snaking his way between the tables of the Mt. Taygetus Diner. With his coat collar taut around his ears, his chin sunk deep into his chest, and his head buried under the widest brimmed hat he owned, he thought no one would recognize him, even if they knew exactly who he was.

"I hope no one saw me enter this place," said Cousin Heshie. He wheeled a heavy suitcase behind him, which kept nicking other diners.

"Like who? Someone from your sect? If they do, they shouldn't be here either," said Unkle Traktor. "And in the highly unlikely event that one of your fellow cult members would acknowledge your presence, what would happen to you?"

"I would be shunned. Shunned," said Cousin Heshie.

"Doesn't seem that bad. At least you'll have Saturdays free."

Unkle Traktor lived in his own self-imposed haze of history. At times, he posed as a Bolshevik or a Communist, a Trotskyist or a Marxist, or the fellow in front of you at the ATM, who couldn't remember his own PIN but yelled at you for not being patient, although you hadn't said a word. He called talk radio shows making up names and voices, even though the producers recognized his phone number. Unkle Traktor would do anything that would irk someone else. It made him feel alive.

My mother and Aunt could not have chosen a less appropriate place for our Passover Seder than the diner. The Jewish dietary laws are confusing enough but, when you add the layers of Passover rules and regs on top of that, they become as bewildering as French numbers past sixty-nine. For Passover, observant Jews must scrub every inch of the kitchen to rid it of *chametz* (any products made from wheat, oats, barley, spelt, or rye). Super observant Jews clean the kitchen plus give the equivalency of a power wash to the rest of the house to ensure not a crumb of chametz remains.

"Coming here just proves we are more middle class than Jewish. Except for you, Cousin Heshie. You make up for all of us," I said.

"We do love Mt. Taygetus," said Tanta Gee Gee.

"Did you know the Spartans left the elderly and sickly children to die on the real Mt. Taygetus?" said Unkle Traktor.

"Well, aren't you Mount Pleasant? Why don't you tell us about ancient pus and urine too?"

"We get it, Ma."

Unzipping his old misshapen suitcase, Heshie said, "In keeping with our pious Jewish traditions and what is righteous, I have brought my own *matzo, k'arah* (Seder plate). And the proper kosher for Passover dinnerware and silverware."

"Did you take the subway or rent a U-Haul to get that here?" asked Unkle Traktor.

Orthodox Jews have four sets of plates, one set each for meat and dairy for daily use and a second set of meat and dairy for Passover. Mt. Taygetus, like all diners, had one set of plates that they used until a new busboy dropped them.

Cousin Heshie's tarnished silver k'arah did not have separate sections for the symbolic foods as modern ones do. "My k'arah has a provenance that includes Israel and Spain, and many important Rabbis."

"Remember when we went to provenance on that tour to Paris?" my mother asked Tanta Gee Gee.

As a reflection of her modern Judaism, and a justification for purchasing a kiln, Cousin Hippolyta removed from her hand-knitted bag, a hand-crafted ceramic Seder plate. The wavering thickness of the edges and the unsteady letters created an asymmetrical authenticity.

Because things quieted down for a few moments, Unkle Traktor said, "We really shouldn't have our Seder in a diner. Why didn't we have it somewhere else? Is this your idea, Cassia? Do you know the owner?"

"You think because she's Greek, she knows every Greek?" said my mother. No one was going to attack her daughter-in-law. That was her job. "Do you know every Jew?" my mother asked Unkle Traktor.

"As a matter of fact, I do know every Jew," said Unkle Traktor.

Cassia created the most extraordinary architectural models of buildings, parks, and other structures. These were the miniatures you saw in exhibits and museums but hers made the cardboard people and the foam and cork buildings seem alive. We no longer tried to explain to my mother and aunt what she did, and I had not bragged about her ability in decades.

My mother and Tanta Gee Gee had specifically requested Eli as the waiter for the occasion. They looked upon him as their friend and personal servant. Eli appeared obsequent, gentle, slow, not very smart, with a body welded from spare parts. His lips parted long before he spoke, as if his words needed time to gather in his throat first. Most importantly, he never got an order wrong and he always served the food hot.

"Hello Eli. How are you?"

He shrugged his shoulders without saying, "It's Tuesday."

Success Is Not An Option

Eli started to take the empty chair away from the table. "No, no. Leave it there. It's Pesach. It's for Elijah, who isn't coming."

"It's a good thing you're seated, Eleni. The hostess doesn't like to seat incomplete parties," said Eli.

Eli was, at once, the hardest working and the laziest person I knew. He worked 14-hour days, seven days a week for six months. Then he went back to Greece and did nothing for the other six months; he simply idled. His entire life was planned around doing nothing. I searched on my phone and the word sabbatical came from the Greek word *sabatikos*, meaning day of the sabbath. Would a hiatus or sabbatical work at Remora? Would the employees return clear-headed and rested or anxious and uncertain? How could someone be absent for so long? Teachers went on sabbatical.

"So, Eli, you are having a *sabatikos*?" I asked.

"Sounds good. I'll have the sabatikos too, but without the feta," said Hippolyta.

"What is a sabatikos?" asked Eli.

"That is what you do for six month in Greece a sabbatical."

"No, I don't do anything."

"And you, Mr. *Ganztzeh Knacker* (Big Shot), how come we don't see you anymore, now that you're so so important?" Tanta Gee Gee asked me.

"Oh, c'mon. Even in the past, you never saw me that often. We saw you once a year at these Seders, even when I wasn't important," I said.

"Mr. Ganztzeh Knacker has an answer for everything."

No one can say with certainty when the first Seder occurred. It is one of the few major religious rites that doesn't take place in a temple but in the home. Accordingly, there are countless familial, geographical, and inexplicable variations of the Seder. Cousin Heshie, of course, chose the most traditional approach, while Hippolyta chose a modern dance interpretation. Ironically, the literal translation of Seder is order.

For the *Maror*, both used horseradish. That and *Charozet* are reminders of the harshness of slavery. Their *Charozet* was a mixture of apples, pears, wine, and nuts, which signified the mortar used by the slaves. You could not, however, discern different ingredients in either of them. For their Charozet, each placed romaine lettuce next to a separate cup of salt water. Hippolyta let it be known her organic lettuce stood above the others. Cousin Heshie took some lettuce and horseradish and put it between two small pieces of matzo for a *korech* sandwich. But before he took a bite, he washed his hands, explaining over his shoulder, "The Talmud says that 'Any food that is dipped into a liquid requires washing of the hands before it is eaten.'"

"He never washed his hands before," said Unkle Traktor.

Zeroa represents the sacrificial lamb slaughtered on the eve of the exodus. Cousin Heshie plopped down an oversized shank bone of a lamb that overshadowed his Seder plate; for Hippolyta, a bone from a kosher chicken served duty.

The roasted egg symbolized a desire for redemption The Aramaic word for egg is *bei'ah*, similar to the Aramaic word for desire.

Karpas symbolizes the backbreaking work. Cousin Heshie used a sprig of parsley. Hippolyta a potato.

Although not part of the Seder plate, matzo remains the omnipresent food of Passover. Matzo is the symbolic unleavened bread that the Jews took with them when they fled Egypt, since the bread did not have enough time for the yeast to rise. Cousin Heshie's matzo was a familiar and accessible brand. Hippolyta bought her matzo from a kibbutz, manufactured by descendants of the first tuba player in the Israeli symphony. Hippolyta then took a small piece of bread and dropped it on her Seder plate. Everyone froze, then gasped.

"That's chametz."

"Everything here is chametz," said Cousin Heshie. He felt, as the most observant member of the family, his opinion on all matters religious was the most meaningful.

"What is that?" someone asked Hippolyta.

"When I was in college, we proudly put a piece of bread on the Seder plate because there's as much room for a lesbian in Judaism as there is for a crust of bread on Passover."

"I didn't know she was a lesbian."

"I didn't know she went to college."

"Take that off right now."

"No."

"Stop being different. Just for a minute. Especially in public places. It's annoying and a *shonde* (public embarrassment)."

"There are gay rabbis and gay shuls now."

Hippolyta removed the bread with a quick swipe, like a hawk pouncing on a rodent. Cousin Heshie then reached into his bottomless bag and distributed *Haggadahs*, which contains the text for the Seder ceremony. Tanta Gee Gee pulled out her tattered and stained Maxwell House Haggadah from her purse.

"We can't have different Haggadahs. It will be impossible for all of us to follow along together," said Cousin Heshie.

"They say the same things, but on different pages. And Maxwell House is my favorite," said Tanta Gee Gee.

Both Cousin Heshie and Unkle Traktor tried to argue with her, to no avail.

"Did you know that Maxwell House is named after the hotel in Nashville where they had the first International KKK meeting?" asked Unkle Traktor.

"You say that every year."

"That doesn't change the facts."

Tanta Gee Gee pursed her lips and said with a long satisfying sigh, "Good to the last drop!"

"What's that got to do with the Jews and Pesach?" asked Cousin Heshie.

"I've been using them all my life, maybe longer. The Maxwell people were nice to make them free for the Jews. Name another goy who makes Haggadahs?"

"Put that away and take a real Haggadah."

"Don't shit on my Haggadah." said Tanta Gee Gee.

Eventually, every Seder lands on the question, "Who is the youngest?" The youngest must recite the Four Questions while an adult must provide the answers and explain each symbolic food on the Seder plate.

"What about Hippolyta's little ones? What are their names again? Moist and Fruit Fly?" asked my mother.

"Ortal, which means morning dew glow in Hebrew, and Pomegranate. A pomegranate has 613 seeds, the same number as the number of commandments in the Torah."

"That's why you're divorced Hippolyta; you named your children after fruit and nuts," said Unkle Traktor.

"Cassia, you're beautiful. How come you and Mr. Ganztzeh Knacker don't have children yet?"

Cassia has been in the family long enough to know that any sentence that began in a compliment ended in an insult. She learned the essential Yiddish insults years ago, as well as the subtleties between proper etiquette and self-defense. The Yiddish words she did not know, she divined by the volume and inflection. Yiddish speakers seemingly have captions under their chins.

"Leave them alone. Obviously, they have *tsuris* in the below-the-waist department," said my mother.

"Let the children ask the questions, already."

"Before we start, I want to do one thing," said Hippolyta. She held her Seder plate high over Unkle Traktor's head and chanted, *"Bi heelu Yatsanu."* Then she sidled over to Cousin Heshie and chanted again.

"What the hell are you doing?"

"This is a Moroccan tradition. The words mean, 'We had to leave Egypt in a hurry.'"

"Well, hurry up now."

"We're not Sephardic, we're Ashkenazi. And stop dancing. We're in a well-respected diner."

"Watch it. You're getting horseradish on my head," said Tanta Gee Gee.

"Enough about impotence and Moroccan strip teases; it's time to humiliate the children," said Unkle Traktor.

"Hippolyta's kids are the youngest."

"It is a source of both pride and embarrassment for the child to read," I said.

"If my children mispronounce a word or read too slowly, your rude and uncalled for comments will scar them for life."

"Which one is younger: the fruit or the nut?"

"You see, you upset them already." Hippolyta sat down and refused to budge.

"So that means Cassia is the youngest. Read the Four Questions, Cassia."

"She doesn't know Hebrew."

"I'll read the English transliteration," said Cassia.

"That is the exact reason they do not have children. She had a transliteration."

"That's right. Hebrew is written in the wrong direction."

"I'll do it," I said and began, "*Mah nishtanah, ha-laylah hazeh, mi-kol ha-leylot?* Why is this night different from all other nights?"

"Well, for one thing we're in a friggin' Greek diner," said Unkle Traktor.

Heshie answered all the questions with great equanimity as I stumbled through the Hebrew. Unkle Traktor laughed, and my mother acted as if I was the star of the fifth-grade play. I agreed with Unkle Traktor. I knew these few minutes would be used against me now and long after my death.

"We're ready to order, Eli."

"We didn't do the plagues."

"We've had plenty of plagues already."

"Eli, bring us your cheapest wine," said Uncle Traktor with a flourish in a terrible French accent.

You are supposed to take a sip of wine or grape juice after every plague.

"The wine must be kosher for *Pesach*." Cousin Heshie

reached into his bag yet again for the most Jewish of Jewish wines, a concord grape. It was so sweet, there was a possibility that your teeth would rot of out of your head before the Seder ended.

"Oh yes, we are ready. Eli, we're ready." He sidled closer to my mother.

"Eli, have you ever been part of a Seder?" His lower lip jutted out and he shook his head from right to left. His eyebrows seemed to have become part of the frontal region of his scalp.

"What do you think of the items on the Seder plates?"

Eli looked at all the symbolic foods, "They look like board game pieces."

Heshie began eating his Passover meal that he had brought from home—a sweet potato casserole with marshmallows, withered string beans, and most of a four-pound chicken. The chicken soup had already leaked onto his black pants.

Eli hovered over my mother.

"Don't order it," Tanta Gee Gee said to my mother.

"But it's my favorite."

"It's not kosher for Pesach."

"Everything's chametz. What difference does it make?" asked Cousin Heshie with a measure of disgust and resignation in his voice.

"It's a double shonde," said Tanta Gee Gee.

"You're the one who wanted to come here. I'll have the roast pork on the garlic bread with French fries. Don't forget the duck sauce," said my mother.

Roast pork on garlic bread is offered in many Greek diners in New York City. It is a dish that makes no sense. The pork is tinged by a red dye giving it a patina of Chinese origin, especially when accompanied by plastic packets of duck sauce. Duck sauce, invented in the United States, has nothing to do with ducks, of course. The Italian garlic bread cannot be found in Italy. And everyone knows that French fries are from Belgium while lettuce, tomato and pickle accompany everything in a diner except scrambled eggs.

Eli looked at her with one eyebrow arched just enough to make a statement, but not enough to expend too much energy.

"OK, plain matzo instead of my beloved garlic roll."

"I'll have the sole," said Cassia.

"But be careful. It was dry two weeks ago."

"I'll have the rotating gyro meat. I like to watch them cutting off pieces and catching them in a dustpan. It looks like a modern sacrificial lamb," said Tanta Gee Gee.

"I'll have the Turkey Club," I said.

Cassia looked at me, knowing that I had sneaked bacon into the meal.

Hippolyta ordered the organic vegetarian vegetation varied vegetable special for her and her children.

"Heshie, there's very little difference between you and Hippolyta except who decides the rules," said Unkle Traktor.

"Isn't this nice we're all together and no one has to wash the dishes?" said my mother.

"And we get those nice plastic clam box things to take home the leftovers, instead of one of Aunt Bessie's dusty mayonnaise jars left over from World War II."

"Where's Eli? It's time for dessert."

"But we didn't do the plagues." The plagues are a recitation in Hebrew and English of the disasters God brought upon Egypt. After each plague—blood, frogs, lice, flies, pestilence, boils, hail, locusts, darkness, and killing of the first born—the adults sprinkle some wine and children sprinkle grape juice.

"Another plague is listening to this," said Unkle Traktor.

"Then why do you come?"

"I wouldn't be a good Jew if I didn't come."

Eli said nothing; he instinctively knew it was time to bring his pad and pen and take the dessert orders.

"Wait. Before you order, I made Matzo-Almond Croccante with cayenne pepper," said Hippolyta.

"What the hell is a Croccante?" asked Unkle Traktor, "Sounds like a Dean Martin song."

"I'll have the banana cream pie," said my mother.

Tanta Gee Gee said, "Give me the strawberry shortcake. They make it so high here, you have to bring a ladder."

Soon after we ordered, Eli reappeared not with the orders but with a huge mound of red Jell-O. We stared in wonder.

"Where's my lemon meringue?"

Then from behind his back, Eli lifted a mammoth kitchen knife and with great force sliced the Jell-O into two. Most of us gasped.

Little Pomegranate leapt to her feet. "That's the parting of the red Jell-O?"

Eli's right eye lit up.

And then Ortal said, "Are those little pieces of fruit supposed to be Egyptian soldiers?"

Eli almost smiled and pointed to his nose.

"Eli, how did you know this?"

"Yes, Eli, how did you know this?"

Eli whispered, "The chef is Puerto Rican. He knows these things."

Eli then brought the requested desserts, but he also gave everyone a bit of the parted red Jell-O but with a dollop of whipped cream on top. He waved his hand to indicate the Jell-O was on the house. Mike, the owner, came over to our table. "Thank you for spending your Passover with us."

We all thanked him for a wonderful meal and his usual generous hospitality.

"Since you had your Passover here, do you think others might like to do it too?" asked Mike.

"Of course," said my mother and Tanta Gee Gee, an affirmation of their choice. Cousin Heshie looked horrified, Unkle Traktor laughed, and Hippolyta thought it over.

"Was it good?" asked Mike.

"Of course, it was good," said my mother.

"But it wasn't kosher," said Cousin Heshie.

"If it was good, then it's kosher," said Eli.

"You know, we are pioneers doing this. Let's see where it goes," I said.

Cassia thanked him in Greek, which he did not expect.

When Eli brought the bill, it migrated to me as the theoretically richest person at the table. I held the bill high and asked, "Who had the egg salad?"

"Pay it, you cheap bastard," said my mother, "So I can be proud of you."

As Cassia and I walked out, Cousin Heshie grabbed me by the arm. "You know, we didn't sing 'Dayenu.'"

"We'll sing it twice next year."

"We do everything right at our shul. Why don't you join my shul?"

"No, thanks. I would rather be an informal outsider than a heretic."

Chapter 13

When an Argument is Lost

Lee asked for a few minutes early in the day. She entered every office as if an army trailed behind her. Of course, she always stood alone. She did not need the paid affirmation of toadies. To her, sycophants were more of a nuisance than assistance. And if she needed another opinion, she sought that in private, as she would never render a half-ass legal decision in public. Mimi always honored her appointments promptly. She never mentioned anything personal, nor something that was not contained in my file which we had not discussed. And as was her wont, she immediately spoke to the matter at hand.

More sober than usual, Lee said, "We have a new emergency. It seems someone is product tampering and one of our biggest insureds is the target. We've tried to keep it out of the press, but we can't any longer."

"And what is it?"

"Exploding suppositories."

"Exploding suppositories?"

"Yes. They look genuine but then you insert them, and they go 'bang!'"

"Aren't they supposed to?"

"Not like that."

"I assume there is all sorts of protective, anti-tampering packaging."

"There is, but somehow, our suspect still manages to prime the charge."

"He's probably a proctologist or a plumber."

"He calls himself the Taint Terrorist and wrote the 'Taint Manifesto' which says he and many other people are neither here nor there. But it seems what he does is very here and there."

"He is a self-proclaimed terrorist, not a linguist."

"Announcements will be made this afternoon all over the country. The professionals say you must stay ahead of a PR crisis in the first 72 hours and actually do something like an effective recall."

"Keep me updated."

"Will do, Rob. But there must be a recall and we'll be on the hook for a lot of that."

"It's funny. In a way."

"Not to the victims."

"I'm glad I'm not on that bomb squad."

"Rob, stop it."

"They can write some great ads when this is over. In the background, they can play the '1812 Overture' with the slogan."

"Rob, pull yourself together and don't mention this to anyone before the recall."

Even if Lee thought of the funniest retort in history, she was not the person who would deliver it. I, at once, admired and resented such an ability.

"We have another problem. Did you know Sir Reginald has been firing and promoting people randomly?"

"No, I did not. Why?"

"It's apparently his way of getting more people back in the office and not working from home."

"That is the trend. Is there an HR or legal problem or official position about people working from home?"

"In tort law, there is a legal theory called respondeat superior.

It holds that an employer or principal is legally responsible for the wrongful acts of an employee or agent if such acts occur within the scope of the employment or agency. There is no national standard about responsibility to others when working from home, however. And there could be issues with cyber security."

"Sounds like it could get messy. What happens if someone's kid hurts himself or destroys office property?"

"It happens here every day. We'll see where that leads. But back to Reginald. He thinks that working remote is generally not good for the company and is discouraging it."

"OK, I'll bite. How is this discouraging it?"

"He thinks that if someone is indiscriminately fired or promoted, it will create paranoia among those working remote. The person working from home might think, 'Why were the others fired or promoted, and not me?' They're isolated at home in their underwear and hoodies so they can't just pop into someone's office to find out what's going on or gossip at lunch. And no one wants an e-mail chain and phone calls with others, especially when they don't know who is involved exactly. Thus, Reginald thinks they will return to the office, so they'll feel less isolated."

"Besides what's wrong with that, what's wrong with that?"

"There are at least two labor law theories; one is wrongful termination, which is self-explanatory, and constructive termination. Constructive termination, in general, is when the employer creates a situation where the employee quits on their own because of intolerable conditions created at work."

"What happened when you told Reg to stop?" I asked.

"He said he has already stopped, and I am getting a list of all those who were fired and promoted by him," said Lee.

"Do people work better or worse from home?"

"Studies are all over the place, but most think it's good, especially for working mothers.

Reggie always thinks he will be blamed for anything and everything, even though he creates a blame tree for every project before it begins. It is like a decision tree, but for blame, with candidates predetermined."

"What about the supervisors whose people he fired and promoted?"

"He mentions his J. Edgar file. Everyone thinks he has a personal dossier with a lot of dirt on them, so most of them bend."

"Does he have a J. Edgar file?"

"I would imagine on some, but it is the fear of them that matters and knowing he would use the information if needed. The only thing Reginald cares about is litigation because he might be named. And that is what I hold over him. Sometimes, I use weasel words to describe legal doctrines to keep him in line."

"People think Quisling has a similar file."

"Hers would be more like our exploding suppository problem," said Lee without an ounce of obvious joy or irony.

Even though I trusted Lee, that did not mean I told her what I thought of HR.

HR are the fundamentalists of business. If there is a harsh interpretation of the rules and a lenient one, they always go beyond the harshest. I could see HR rehab facilities or twelve step programs, in the future, for constant offenders. Or HR summer camps for the palest of students where they salute each other. They represent the company, the way fundamentalists represent God. If there were 21st century Nazis, they would not need bombs or soldiers, they would just contact HR and HR would ask "Would you like the employees lined up by height or in alphabetical order?"

"What are going to do about our Reginald?" I asked.

"Willful neglect is often seen as a resolution in business. It's cheaper and usually less fractious. But if he does it again, we'll have to do something," said Lee.

"Thank you, Mimi, for the explosions and the imploding Sir Reggie."

The next scheduled visitor was Isla White. Before this meeting, I tried to ascertain what she did, what Doug Friedman did before her, who hired her, and why. Nobody offered a concrete answer. How do you ask politely, "What the hell do you do and why are you needed?" It seemed like one of those modern positions that no one deemed necessary in the past or they changed the name of something that had been needed once but was no longer necessary. Yet there was Doug and now Isla at the Presidents Meetings.

This reminded me of an old saying in Yiddish. "With money in your pocket, you are wise and you are handsome. And you sing well, too." So it is with an elevated title.

When I first started, you may recall that the cavalcade of visitors disguised as well-wishers, professional assassins, posers, and entertainers was endless. Although I did not become smarter or stupider overnight when appointed CEO, I was forced to make decisions that I would not otherwise have made, let alone considered. I had not been on the job long enough to know who might provide altruistic or honest advice and information. At times, I was not sure I would even recognize valuable advice from the useless. It was both an advantage and a detriment to realize that people who you had not expected to be helpful could actually be helpful, even some of those with the narrowest of self-interests. And, of course, I found myself tethered to others who were rarely helpful but thought themselves otherwise.

There were also people in the company who had jobs I did not understand, even when explained. And I was afraid to get rid of them, because what if that job was actually needed? Such was Isla White.

"Some Goth, hipster, hip sister, I just made that up, is here to see you: Isla White. Is she the one who was traded from another company? You know Goth is very suburban and Staten Island."

White peered over Gladys' shoulder, surprised that this elderly woman would have a geo-sociological opinion about her looks.

"Thank you, Gladys. Show her in."

"Hello, Isla. Gladys has her own way of doing things. Happy to meet you in a more intimate setting."

"Hello, Rob. It's nice to sit down for some face time." That term "face time" always seemed to border on the vulgar.

"Have you adjusted to Remora? What projects are you working on?"

"Oh, didn't you read the summary I sent you of my projects? I was hoping you'd have an opportunity to read them before we met."

I was the one who is supposed to be conducting the meeting and asking the embarrassing questions. "Well, let's start with the projects you think are the most important."

"I'll need your help with some of the businesspeople because I am trying to create affinity groups. Did you know the most successful affinity is AARP, which started when an insurance company wanted to sell policies to seniors? But an affinity group can be any group with a common interest."

Actually, I did not know any of that. "Do you have a specific affinity group and a specific idea?"

"Well, my idea is to sell homeowners to faith-based groups."

"Why would faith-based groups be different than other homeowners?"

"Houses of worship lead to homes of worship. Those people take better care of their homes Thus they are better risks."

"Any statistical evidence of that?"

"Well, negative evidence. After all, how many church ladies have wild parties?"

"Fortunately, I can't speak to that either way. But did you find that our homeowners division is not interested?"

"They want me to bring a group to them and then they'll discuss the possibilities."

"Isn't that a reasonable approach?"

"Well, I don't really associate with any faith-based groups," said White.

"Perhaps then, you should work on that. Have you spoken to Tompkins about insurance for Muslim-Americans? I'm sure you two would get along. And what else are you working on?"

"I also think we should target Asian-Americans. They now comprise about 7% of the American population."

"That's like targeting European-Americans—who are, of course, of different cultures, religions, cuisines, economies, and some are historical enemies," I said.

"Then we'll be the ones to draw them together," said White.

"With insurance?"

"It is a common need."

I did not understand half the things White suggested. Ironically, that made me feel stupid. "OK, work up a business plan."

"I mentioned that I wanted Remora to be a leader in plant-based insurance."

"What does that mean exactly, or even loosely?"

"We're involved in many traditional lines and they may not be ecologically sound."

"Someone mentioned this at the Presidents Meeting. We already offer Crop/Hail Insurance."

"Crop/hail is a very literal example with a long history. I was talking about something different, something new."

"And yes, what might that be?"

"You're so negative. I had the same problem at the company that traded me to Remora. They just didn't understand my intent."

"Well, let's move on to your next idea."

"Why don't we offer DIY cremation?"

"Doesn't that seem a little morose?"

"We can offer it as a rider to life insurance. And auto, if something really goes wrong."

"Have you checked individual state laws, to see if they would allow it?"

"I assume the insurance departments would like something that would help their constituents."

"Sounds like something that needs to be investigated. Anything Doug Friedman left hanging?"

"Nothing that I saw. Did you know that many at the company think we are similar because we don't think like ordinary businesspeople?"

"That could be true for those who don't consider the subtle differences. Thank you for coming. Make an appointment with Gladys for three, four months from now and in the meantime, you can keep me appraised of your progress on the ideas we discussed today."

When White was done, Gladys popped her head into my office. "Boy, whatta whack-a-do."

"You know something, Gladys; that wore me out. But in this land of bullshit, Isla White actually believes in what she's saying. The details were not important to her." On any Sunday morning, I might find an Isla White knocking on my front door, like many proselytizers before her, filled with unshakable beliefs. And like other missionaries, her doctrine crumbled under logic and facts. But that would never deter any of them.

"So, trade her again. You know the old baseball insult? Trade her for a bag of balls or a broken-down bus."

Little time had passed after Isla left, when Gladys announced, "Sir Schmuck approaches."

"He can hear you. And so can everyone else," I said.

"That's the general idea, Einstein," said Gladys.

I then said to Sir Reginald, "There are many subjects I want to discuss with you."

Reg was an avoidant liar. They omit important facts in a way that will either make them look good or someone else appear poorly. If they are very talented, one omission will do both. The problem is, you have to guess what was omitted.

"I'm chuffed that you're seeing me. I don't get much face time with the gaffer. I know you have plenty of problems, but I have the solution," said Sir Reginald.

There are certain people who should teach classes in business survival, even if they border on the illegal. Their courses would include self-aggrandizement, backstabbing, stealing the work of others, appearances of success, false friendliness, obstructive bureaucracy, and sexual advantage (for both men and women). Of course, there are other personal favorites, but every list is arbitrary and incomplete. Sir Reginald could teach a master class in casting the blame elsewhere, "34 Ways To Say FU, When the Finger Is Pointed at You."

"If I may, here's how to handle your problems. Why don't you become a LGBT activist? That will give you protection. No one wants to attack a LGBT activist. And I daresay you would be the first in the insurance industry. I'm sure there are gays in the industry. AND since you are an artist, everyone will believe it."

"Not everyone in the arts is gay."

"Right," said Sir Reginald with a wink. "But then, why are they in the arts and not in business?"

"Isn't that a bit cynical, to use LGBT as a front?"

"Not at all. And this conversation stops with us."

"It certainly will because I'm not going to do it."

"Don't be quick to dismiss it. It's clever and creates its own protection."

"No."

"I have two more things for you. First, I would like you to marry us."

"Why? Who's getting married?"

"Me."

"Aren't you married?"

"I was. The divorce just came through."

"Well, congratulations. On your marriage, I mean, not the divorce. I never meant your first wife. She was your first wife, right?"

"And you happen to know the bride-to-be."

"Really? And who may that be?"

"Candy Quisling."

I must admit I was taken aback, but after careful consideration, I said, "Is this marriage to avoid litigation? As you know, a wife can't testify against her husband."

"And I thought you were a romantic. I'm barmy about her."

"No one can deny love. Does Candy know about this?"

"Of course. Do I sense some hesitation about my wedding?"

"It's sudden."

"And the wedding will be at Tray Chic. I already spoke to Barry."

"I hope you're paying full tilt."

"Barry has instituted employee discounts."

"Is the marriage of love or accommodation? Has Candy ever been married before?"

"No, so I am a lucky man. And ..."

"And what?"

"Candy and I would be chuffed if you officiated at the wedding. You can be certified by one of those Internet churches. Look in your e-mails. I sent you a URL."

"I'm what is called a secular Jew. Will they take me?"

"I don't think they'll do a background or financial check. They should be modern, not blinkered."

"I am honored but let me think about it," I said and thought I'd better ask Mimi; if I married them, could I be charged as an accessory in some sort of legal scheme?

"Before I go, I have another idea."

"And what might that be?"

"You know I am always looking for ways to help the employees and to improve the company ..."

"Go on."

"Well, we want to avoid employees getting into fights, so I developed a list of phrases ... Once they're stated by either party, the conversation is over, even if no conclusion has been reached."

"Don't you think that the company will be seen as a bit of a Big Brother?"

"No, I think of every employee as a punter, and we have to keep punters happy. Here's the list. It's called 'Lines that indicate the argument has been lost.' We truly want to avoid aggro. So here we go."

You're just like Hitler.
Look it up.
I know about these things.
I took a course in this once.
I know I'm right.
You know I'm right.
What do you know?
Look, I've been around.
Somebody who knows about this stuff told me.
I saw it on the Internet. Twice.
Do you think I make up these things?
You think you know everything.
I have a degree in that.
My daughter (son) is studying that, so I know
    about it.

"How are you going to initiate this? Or worse, enforce it?" I asked.

"I'm not. You are. Even if they're mere suggestions."

At least he asked. And on his way out, he said, "Think about marrying us. Bob's your uncle. Ta and Tata."

One of the great ironies of business is that business turns both responsible and irresponsible adults into children who need permission from others to do or say things. The ones granting permission may or may not how to do the job better but that, of course, matters little.

Chapter 14
Dog Eat Dog

IT SEEMS, every morning we need to fill a hole that did not exist yesterday.

The current mania is the automatic survey with its maddening degree of urgency and scrutiny to evaluate of what was just said or sold. Each penny spent needs to be assayed. While they do ask evaluators many questions about themselves, they never ask the essential question, "Are you nuts or what?" We do not know if those who respond are rational, knowledgeable, or a just a plain idiot or vengeful moron. On the other hand, that does reflect the general population. Nor do we know if they answer truthfully or not. With the increasing influence of the Internet, there is a growing number who simply want to be heard or are paid to be heard who equate a negative response with sophistication.

Then everything is reduced to stars or numbers. But this has been done with the annual business review have been around way longer than Internet self-gratification. I am sure some business school professor has researched the origins of the annual review, but I think it started with the gladiators and immediate feedback. Thumbs up, thumbs down. Immediate and specific feedback. It is to this that modern businesses pay lip service. No room for ambiguity. No time for retribution or redemption. No unintended consequences. While I am sure the emperor had his prejudices, both good and evil, immediate judgement with harsh consequences still remains part of the human condition.

There were different types of gladiators then who have modern counterparts. Like today's employees, some gladiators were slaves, while others wanted to improve their social status. The *Samnites* fought with a large oblong shield, a visor, a plumed helmet, and a short sword. Today, people with little swords are usually in sales.

The *Thracians* had a small round buckler and a dagger curved like a scythe; they often fought the *murmillones*, who were armed with a helmet, sword, and shield. Their modern business equivalents are accounting types fighting those with legitimate travel expenses.

The *retiarius* (net man) was matched with the *secutor* (pursuer); the former wore nothing but a short tunic or apron and sought to entangle their pursuer, who was fully armed. Young women and abusive has-been male executives are today's version.

The *andabatae* rode on horseback and wore helmets with closed visors—that is, they fought blindfolded. Your basic 9-5'er.

There were others including the *laquearius* (lasso men), who roped their opponent like a rodeo cowboy. Unfortunately, jousting with sharp instruments is currently frowned upon.

How did we know if today's emperors, the people who judge us, are honest and intuitive or just vengeful fucks? How did the next person who read the job review know how smart-stupid, nuts-sane, or prejudiced-objective the writer/manager was? Perhaps reviews should attach a copy of the manager's annual review or latest psychiatric report for reference?

Even though less than a year had passed, the consultants sought a review. Of course, they wanted me to enumerate my successes and failures, so it could be compared to theirs. This was like a child being asked what they wanted for dinner and then the mother giving them whatever she cooked anyway.

I had not seen the consultants in weeks, and it did not matter why. The two younger ones sat in my office. Bill appeared by electronic conveyance from the Maldives. Fiona tilted her laptop so we both could see Bill. He wore a colorful short-sleeve shirt that revealed his festive sunburnt mottled arm hair. Off screen, you could hear the clink of ice in a glass. It could have been either Mrs. Bill or a younger woman in a smaller bathing suit.

"Before we begin, I just want you to know, Rob, that we never give fives on our reviews, since everyone has room for improvement," said Bill. He donned his mask of sobriety, trying to obscure the beach behind him.

From one of my desk drawers, I took out drawing pencils and a pad of paper and started sketching Quinn. If I started with Fiona, the lack of context would have appeared sexist.

"So, you never give fives?" I asked.

"Correct. There's always room for improvement."

"All of you went to elite business schools. What would you have thought if your professors said that no matter how well you do, you will never get an A. You can produce the best projects, understand the curriculum perfectly, and even teach an undergrad course, but no matter what you do, you will not get an A. Would it strike you as a bit irrational and affect your attitude and motivation?" I asked.

They seemed startled, as did I, by my aggressive posture. "And what happens if someone in the future actually reads this and is unaware of your random predisposition?"

They stammered and mentioned historical and psychological precedents.

I continued, "And then you go out into the work world and compete against students who attended schools where true grades were given, or worse, where there is grade inflation." Their silence was broken only by the creak of Bill's chair while people ran into the ocean behind him as if they were being chased. My review had little to do with me and everything to do with their choice of me.

Secure in this knowledge, my words mattered little to their self-preservation.

"Why are you drawing?" asked Quinn.

"It's my way of recording this review session."

"Is it necessary?"

"Not really. Quinn, could you turn your head a little to the left? Thanks."

"Let's start," said Quinn, stretching his neck at an exaggerated angle. "What is your greatest achievement as CEO?"

"You know, when you sketch with pencils, the less pressure you exert, the lighter the color. And of course, the more pressure you apply, the opposite is also true."

"What do you think was your greatest failure as CEO?"

"Some days are boring and some days take my breath away. On the days when my breath is taken away, I am happy you chose me for this position. On the days that are boring, I do nothing I don't need to do. That way, I don't have to fear that I'll create a day that will take my breath away."

"What's he doing?" asked Bill.

"I'm sketching," I said. I turned Quinn's portrait around. "Do you like it?"

"Yes," said Bill, unsure how to answer. He could say no, but he did not want to either condemn or to condone my behavior.

"Can you tilt the computer a little, so I have a better angle to draw Bill," I said.

"Is that necessary?"

"It's necessary if I want to get the proportions correct."

Bill asked, "What are your six-month and 12- month goals?"

"There are people who speed sketch and others that take as much time as they think they need. Some want to catch a specific moment, while others are afraid they will forget the details. Bill, hold your head just like that. That's perfect."

They continued with their questionnaire, and I continued to pretend to answer them.

Success Is Not An Option

"Before we conclude, we just want you to take a personality test," said Fiona.

"You mean the one whose name sounds like a lawn mower?"

"You mean the Myers Briggs test?" asked Fiona.

"Yes, the Briggs Stanton lawnmower test?"

"No, it's not the Briggs Stanton lawn mower. It's the Myer Briggs test. It's the standard of almost every industry."

"Standardized tests yield standard people."

"It measures characteristics. Are you an introvert or an extrovert? How do you judge things? Are you a feeling or a thinking person?"

"And then, what do you do with the results?"

"We see if we can help with certain aspects of your management style."

"Has that ever worked? When was the last time you changed an adult's behavior to conform to a stereotype and made it worse?"

"The goal is positive change, of course."

"How come you didn't administer that test before you hired me?"

"We didn't want to be influenced by the results."

"What will be the result of this review?"

"We'll let you know the final result of the review."

"Not that it was decided before today."

A few hours later, the unmistakable but surprising sound of a dog's nails clicking on a bare tile floor filled the office. Sladka held one end of a leash and on the other was an elderly German Shepherd. Without being asked, Sladka wrote, *Profit Sniffing Dog.*

I have long heard rumors that Spaulding brandished a profit-sniffing dog to startle underwriters into greater sales. *Trained like DEA dog,* wrote Sladka. There were so many unfounded Spaulding legends, but only one had four legs and panted.

I take dog around to see about profits, wrote Sladka.

With the residue of antagonism remaining from the annual review session, I said, "Stop with the note writing. I know you have a tongue. I heard your girlfriend bragging about your sexual abilities."

Sladka slumped over. "I didn't like lying to you but didn't know how to stop."

"Gladys," I yelled, "Did you know Sladka could speak?"

"Of course, I knew he had a tongue. And no, not because of that. Good for you, Sladka," said Gladys.

Now I had to decide whether to unfold the tongue façade to the whole company or not. I did not want Sladka to lose his intimidating presence or for him to become an object of ridicule. A Spaulding era lie revealed, designed solely to menace others.

"OK, I won't make a formal statement. But from today on, no more notes."

Sladka started to write, *OK*, but crumpled up the paper.

I asked Sladka if we could walk around the company with the dog. When I worked in graphics, they never paraded the dog through there because we were considered a cost center. Nowhere could a profit be found, like legal, IT, accounting, regulatory, and a few others.

"Do you know the dog's name?"

"Spaulding called him Greed is Good. Just Greed usually," said Gladys.

"The DEA called him Pepsi because he was always looking for coke. Pretty funny, no? Pepsi, coke, get it?" said Sladka. His voice was thin and high-pitched, the type of tone that prevented some silent movie stars from moving to the talkies. His shoulders used up all his testosterone.

"We should change that. That's from another era. We can give him another name, even if he doesn't answer to it."

"We can name him after a prophet, like Hosea. Get it? Profit, prophet?" said Sladka.

I thought we should take the dog around to the underwriting offices and see the reactions. Their whole world was sales and loss ratios. A loss ratio is basically claims paid compared to revenues. The lower the loss ratio, the better. Some would think intimidation by dog was cruel but others would just pet the dog and think of it as therapy.

"Maybe we can train the underwriters like dogs. We can carry little treats in our pockets and when they do well, we give them one. Ruff, ruff," barked Sladka.

"Do you want to stalk the halls with me where the underwriters lurk?" I asked.

"Ruff, ruff," barked Sladka again. "How about if we give the dog a new name, like Find Dough?"

"I have an idea, Boss. Why doesn't Sladka keep his old secret a secret and you and I will be tight-lipped about it," said Gladys.

Gladys never used the word "Boss" before, signifying an extreme situation. The dam had been breached and the valley flooded. I was sure Sladka spoke when not at work, but I knew I had made a mistake by asking him to talk.

"Excellent idea, Gladys." To Sladka: "It's far too complicated to explain to everyone how you suddenly grew a tongue and could speak."

"So, you don't want me to talk at work again?"

"Yes. Don't speak ever again. At least not at work. It would just be too complicated to explain."

Sladka and I went to the underwriting floors with Find Dough. The dog was trained in deceit and trickery. He would sit every time he entered an office, similar to his previous existence finding drugs or other contraband. But here at Remora, it was a device that indicated that the underwriter was guilty of something and the crime did not matter.

Many of the offices were vacant. I was not sure if business was bad or if people were working from home. I thought of Sir Reggie's ham-handed solution of randomly firing or promoting people to discourage working at home.

"Hi, I'm Rob Stone. This is Sladka, and this is the profit-sniffing dog, Find Dough."

"Nice to meet you. I'm Bruce Mallory and I'm glad to see that the dog was paper-trained. Here, let me pet him so you can go and try to trick someone else."

Old-timers like Mallory knew the charade and either petted the dog or suffered from cynophobia. The new underwriters did not want to appear either cynical or naive.

"Hi, I'm Rob Stone. This is Sladka, and this is the company's profit sniffing dog, Find Dough."

"Hi, I'm Mike Fletcher. How does a dog sniff out profits? I just started a few weeks ago and I'm trying my best."

"I'm sure you are. What makes him special is he used to be a DEA drug-sniffing dog, and now he is retrained and working for us."

The young underwriter stared at the dog as if it were endowed with special powers. The dog just wagged its tail, content in his second career. Like many ex-cops, the dog had a pension and new gig that gave him some extra cash.

We continued making our rounds and came upon the office of Hal Wick. Although no smell of incense filled the room, nor odd trinkets dangled from the ceiling, nor cryptic religious/philosophical samplers hung on the walls, a strange aura engulfed the room. Wick looked like a Dickens character, if a Dickens character could use their nose as a pen or lead pencil. His hair remained in the same position as when he woke that morning and his glasses had not been cleaned since 1957. In fact, I think his glasses were glass. I am sure every company with more than 50 employees has a Hal Wick.

"Hi, I'm Rob Stone. This is Sladka, and this is our profit sniffing dog, Find Dough."

Wick introduced himself and asked, "How can I help?"

"We're making our rounds; the dog sniffs out unrealized profits."

"That is a Deutscher Schäferhund, a breed originally developed by Max von Stephanitz in the late 1880s. Today, there's an issue in the UK with some German Shepherds developed by Max von Stephanitz, as breeding has caused a problem with their extremely roached topline. It can cause a poor gait in the hind legs."

"Huh, an expert. Do you own or breed Shepherds?"

"No, I just read about them."

"What do you do here?"

"I do QC at Remora. It's on my business card." He handed each human a card, not the dog. "I do QC on the underwriters' proposals. So, I don't make profits as much as try to limit losses."

"And how do you get the proposals?"

"The underwriters been sending them to me for years. Now, they just repeat what they've been doing."

"Who's your boss?"

Wick hesitated. "I don't know."

"When you have a problem, what do you do?"

"Solve it myself."

"Who does your review?"

"No one."

"What about raises?"

"I don't get them, because then I would find out who my boss is. And then whomever it is, would probably make changes that I wouldn't like. I regard it as a fair trade off."

He and Isla White must work for the same person. How could someone exist in a company without a known boss? Even the CEO answered to the Board. I was perplexed what to do next.

"You're Sladka. You're supposed to have a nuclear device in that satchel and no tongue. But your cheek just bulged. So, either you have some weird disease, or you do have a tongue."

"No nuclear device. No tongue," I said.

"Sure, OK. But it looks like he has a tongue."

There are just some people who know how to outsmart the system, even if just for themselves. It cannot be transferred, explained, or learned. I let Wick continue doing whatever he did and assumed one day, when he retired, he would simply walk out the door without telling anyone.

Chapter 15
Reviews of Another Kind

A RAGTAG BUNCH of Remora business casuals gathered outside my door. At first, I could not discern their shouting. I guessed the volume was more important than the actual words. But as their voices tired, I was able to distinguish their chants, "Free Frequents Now" and "No Ferretocracy."

Approximately twenty-five unruly men, who in the past would have complained over extra drinks at lunch about their wretched positions, now jeopardized their jobs. This neatly dressed, off-off-Broadway version of *Les Misérables*, wearing polo shirts with collars, necessary to distinguish them from ordinary tee-shirts, and shoes that matched their belts, shouted their wants.

My loyal defenders, Sladka and Gladys, appeared immediately. They pointed their most lethal weapons—their narrow-eyed glares—directly into the crowd but were ignored. Either the mob did not know who they were or did not care.

"Free Frequents now!"

"No ferretocracy!" shouted another.

"I'm sorry. I don't know what any of you are yelling about," I said.

"You know."

"Don't act dumb. Spaulding told you everything about our frequent flyers."

"And we don't want the new work rules you proposed either," yelled someone else.

Rebellion in business is almost always quiet and stealthy. But this level of distrust needed time to foment into cabals in the warren of cubes and at copiers where fingers blackened from changing the toner. "You bums better back off before I smack someone," said Gladys. Sladka stood by with his practiced cross-armed menace.

"Will everyone please calm down? Will someone tell us what this about?" I asked.

Of course, I posed the wrong question, which caused the volume to increase. I then asked for a few people to step forward and explain their concerns. The mob was not prepared for this reaction.

"You really don't care. You just want to stop us."

"I'm warning you, you bums," said Gladys.

"Wait. Are you Gladys Pierson? *The* Gladys Pierson?"

"Yes. In person. And you are?"

"Do you know my sister, Brenda Cullen?"

"Probably. Sounds familiar." The fellow never gave his name to Gladys.

"Hey, everybody. This is *the* Gladys Pierson. Don't mess with her."

The crowded quieted. A few took the opportunity to steal away, making Sladka's presence a mere ornament.

"We want our frequent flyer miles that are due to us."

"No ferretocracy."

"OK, what the hell is a ferretocracy?"

"It's a play on words on meritocracy."

"A bit lame, don't you think?" I asked.

"Maybe."

"OK, can you please pick a few people to speak on your behalf to discuss this?"

Heads swiveled, stares ensued, many looked like they regretted not wearing a balaclava or having attended at all. Clearly, they were not prepared for a negotiation. After some silence, one man yelled from the back, "Are you going to need our names?"

"If I come in, do I have sit near the window where Collins went flying? Maybe someone else will go out the window."

"The only way to know that is to come into the office."

Another asked, "Is this a trick?"

"Spaulding, the bastard, took away our frequent flyer miles for business trips and made us give them to the company."

Before this moment, I did not know that shortly before Spaulding died, he had demanded that Remora business travelers cede their frequent flyer miles to the company rather than retain them for themselves. As I did not see a divisional president, nor anyone else in a position of authority, I assumed they were exempt from this edict. When I worked in graphics, I had probably received the memo. But since I never traveled for the company, I ignored it.

Before me rose an adult middle-class rebellion. Usually, middle-class rebellions are led by their children. Not this one. Surprised at the turn of events, they started shouting again.

"Free Frequents now. Free Frequents now."

"No ferretocracy."

"OK, if you don't want to discuss this, I have other things I need to do."

"How many of us?" someone asked.

"As many as you want, but no more than four."

Five men volunteered to speak with me and eased into my office, eyes fixed on Gladys as if passing a viper. They looked around the Spaulding museum of testosterone with a keen interest on the windows.

"It's the pane whose color is slightly different," I said.

They responded with a sightly horrified and muted "oh" and turned their eyes back to me.

"Can we pretend this is the first day of school and introduce ourselves? I'm Rob Stone, the object of your insurrection." This seemed to calm things down a bit.

"I'm Doug Cullen, CEU, Chief Environmental Underwriter. I do a lot of traveling. So, I'm here to get my frequents back."

"I'm Mark Goodman, VP Surety, and I want my frequents back, too. This is not an insurrection. It's a loud request. I do a lot of traveling for the company."

"Do you work under Dom Oleoso?"

"Yes."

"It must be hard to work under someone who eats cheese in the corner of rooms," said Cullen.

"OK, yeah. But Dom knows his stuff," said Goodman.

"I'm Rich Schmidt. I work in accounting and I have to make sure this frequent flyer shit is allocated correctly. I mean, I'm responsible for making this program work properly."

"I'm Barry Martin, an associate attorney, Domestic Law Department. And this meritocracy business could harm my future."

"Ha, what future?" someone said.

"I'm Max Freed, associate compliance attorney and I'm wondering why we need this ferretocracy. Who are we going to trust to be fair and objective? How are you going to change people's behavior?"

Gladys walked in and asked the guys if they wanted something to drink or a snack. I knew Sladka continued to monitor the proceedings from a concealed perch or by telepathy.

Clearly, the entire group felt empowered by the perception that artists were not capable businesspeople. They probably did not know that Picasso paid his bills with checks. He knew his signature was usually worth more than the amount of the check and that many would remain uncashed.

Although I did not know their exact demands, I had many general considerations:

A. If I agreed immediately, that could reinforce their idea that

I was weak and would cave at the merest provocation. A dangerous precedent;

B. If I didn't give them back their frequents, it would amount to an arbitrary abuse of power with all sorts of consequences;

C. I could them tell them that I would consider their proposal and render a verdict at some unspecified time in the future, although that judgment would lose its immediacy and personal touch; or,

D. Return the frequents after some haggling and deflate their anger or create some theater and pretend not to be a pushover.

"What do you want to accomplish?" I asked.

"Before Spaulding died, he decreed that we had to surrender our frequent flyer miles to the company and we want them back," said Schmidt.

"Of course he did it before he died. Do you want Mr. Stone to think we're idiots?" said Goodman.

"So, you think your individual needs are greater than the company's?" I asked.

"You're not going to give us one of your airy-fairy art things, are you? Because we don't know nothing about art."

"Maybe I should make learning about art, a condition no matter what else we discuss."

When it comes to any ideas, airy-fairy or otherwise, ten percent of the people come up with the ideas. Eighty percent carry them out to varying degrees of their capability. And the last ten percent try to prevent the other ninety percent from succeeding, for reasons usually only known to them. The eighty percent sat in front of me with the potential of becoming the lowest ten percent.

"First, who paid for the plane tickets?" I asked.

"Of course, the company paid for the tickets, but don't forget, we're away from the office and our families. On 24-hour call for the company."

"And many of you enjoy that time away and eating at company expense."

"I thought you were an artist, a liberal."

"So, that's your best argument against the company retaining frequents—that I'm an artist and a liberal and should be more sympathetic? What people often forget is: 'What is important to you, is not necessarily important to others.' How are you going to make it important to others? To me?"

Rich Schmidt's shirt collar barely contained his neck. He probably played high school football and when he took off his tie at night, it must have been like a champagne cork popped. With a fading suntan and deeply veined hands, Mark Goodman looked like he spent considerable time outdoors. Doug Cullen seemed like a family type whose weekends centered around his kids playing sports and yelling at refs and umpires in person and on TV.

"We're the ones who are traveling, not the company. We're the ones who dedicate our days and hotel rooms to the company. We deserve some sort of perk for that," said Cullen.

"What he said. And it's tiring," echoed Goodman.

"And air travel is getting worse by the moment."

"What do you do with your frequents if air travel is so bad?"

"We use them to travel with our families."

"Travel is awful, but you use the frequents to take your families on vacations. Got it."

"Business travel is a stupid waste of my time. I could be doing more important stupid things back in the office," said Schmidt.

"Rich, how much time do you think you need to undo this thing and give everybody back what they deserve?" I asked.

"I dunno know. I'll devise something."

"Whatever it is, add a month. This way, if you finish earlier, you're a hero, and if you miscalculated, just a few people will know."

"What made you change your mind?"

"I really didn't know about this before today. Letting employees keep the frequents is more of a traditional perk than a logical use of allocations. But things are so one-sided in business, why the hell not? I just wanted to gauge how you guys would react to some situations and how you think."

"Is it true you used to give the higher-ups pieces of paper to eat when you first met them?"

"Yep."

"Why?"

"Usually, people have their prepared shtick when they start talking to me. Except you guys. But I always want to know how people think on their feet."

"I like that idea. For others," said Cullen. "Do you have management training?"

"None. I make up a lotta shit up as I go. I think being a worker gave me a pretty good idea what a manager should be and not be."

Schmidt stared at me and almost said, "You're not as stupid as you look." But didn't. A silent compliment.

Gladys brought the snacks and drinks. "Why are you guys here? I can't believe you would jeopardize your jobs for frequents."

"It's the old broken window theory but applied to business. If you let someone take advantage of you on the small stuff, where will it end?" said Goodman.

"Why didn't you protest when Spaulding was alive?" asked Gladys. When the crowd did not answer, she said, "Such little boys." And left.

Surely, I stood weaker compared to the sociopath Spaulding, but I hoped that was one of the reasons they chose me.

"And now, tell me what's wrong with a meritocracy?"

"No one knows how to act or what to do in a meritocracy. We would have to unlearn our current behavior and learn new behavior. Wouldn't that be a waste of the company's money? We learned under people who backstabbed and stole other people's work and took the credit. How do you change that? Are our bosses really going to rate us on our accomplishments? That means we'll never get ahead," said Martin.

"I studied to be a lawyer and we're trained to distinguish the facts and law from one legal matter to another and to smoke out bullshit," said Freed. "How am I supposed to smoke out bullshit if there is none? And we're also taught to be advocates. How can we do that if you take away some of our tools? Being fair is a waste of my education."

"I'm for a meritocracy," said Cullen. "The next level up is the Ole Boys Club, which is impossible to crack. This might help."

"I agree," said Goodman. "We've done what we can do and now we want to be part of the Ole Boys Club. There it's who you know, obedience to whatever they're doing that day, and the old 'what can you do for me' philosophy."

"Well, we are trying to institute a true meritocracy. But we shall see how that goes."

"Good luck with that."

"That sounds good."

"No, it doesn't," said Martin. "All those years of learning the tricks gone to waste."

"You guys who are for this meritocracy are like immigrants who arrive first and then are against the new immigrants. I got mine, tough shit. Why should I help you?" said Freed.

"Gentlemen, gentlemen," I said, not sure what to say next. I did not have a solution to many of these issues.

But neither did they.

"It's like any personal or institutional growth, you need different things at different times. In the end, we have to find an equitable solution," I said.

"How about a two-tiered system, so we both can get what we want?" asked Martin.

"How would that work?"

"You could give lawyers a waiver. No meritocracy for five years."

"You mean when lawyers start, they'll be allowed to backstab and steal other people's work? But other departments couldn't?"

"That's fair," said Freed.

"No, a meritocracy must apply to everyone," I said. "Don't you lawyers need to take Continuing Legal Education courses? So, isn't there one that teaches you how to act like other humans?"

"OK. And no more of that dumb-ass Kangaroo Court?"

"What Kangaroo Courts? I didn't know we started Kangaroo Courts," I blurted out, realizing I was undermining myself. "Wait. Did Barry Belette institute this?"

"Who else?"

"I mentioned something once in passing, months ago. He didn't tell me he started it. I guess things didn't go right. The whole idea was to settle minor disputes among the people instead of letting them fester or bother their immediate supervisor."

"You didn't hear about our own Salem Witch trial at Kangaroo Court?" asked Freed.

"No. Do I want to hear about this?"

"It seems a new employee is a Wiccan and she put candles and various spices in containers on her desk."

"It's better than photos of ugly grandchildren. Then you have to lie about how cute they are."

"And she intones daily rituals."

"So, someone objected ..."

"And the supervisor didn't want to get involved ..."

"And boom, a trial."

"In The Caf, right?"

"Right. It seems there are three judges who volunteered, and their names are randomly chosen."

"It became our Salem Witchcraft trial and a spectator sport. Instead of solving problems, everyone became aware of this problem, and they would heckle during and after the Kangaroo Court. One of the judges threatened to leave the company if the harassment didn't stop."

"That's the reason I like them," said Schmidt. "Free and good low-class entertainment, like those afternoon TV shows where people get into fist fights because they don't know who the father is."

"Don't tell Belette that. He'll want to televise them."

"People like it because we are taught to fear the witches, not the people who created the trial. But here's something else I'll have to reconsider."

"What was the outcome?"

"She could keep the crap on her desk but had to intone in silence."

"I told you they were stupid ideas," said Gladys as she entered the room again.

"Did you boys enjoy your drinks and snacks?" The muttering suggested agreement. "Good. Now, get the hell out and stop acting like spoiled little candy asses. Because here's the solution: get back to work and be glad you have jobs after this little demonstration. And I mean right now, before I tell Rob you can shove your frequent flyers and appoint Barry Belette czar of the new fairer and kinder rules. Three. Two. One."

Chapter 16

Lunch Meet

I OFTEN ATE LUNCH ALONE, which I enjoyed, but that was unusual for a CEO. People wanted a piece of your time or your presence to close a big deal. Instead, I remained a cypher to many and accordingly, not trustworthy. They were afraid I would speak of negative space, pentimento, or anything that would pop into my head that was not related to the subject at hand and either squelch the deal or make Remora seem inaccessible.

I had not had lunch with the old gang in months. And as that type of guilt stretches over time, it overwhelmed reasons to correct it and face the possible consequences. Despite that, I decided to visit The Caf unannounced. I rewrapped what remained of my sandwich and put it in the bottom drawer next to something that should have been thrown out a month ago. For some reason, people thought food stayed fresher longer in the bottom drawer or it was harder to find by others. I edged my way through the Caf and angled an unwieldy fifth chair between Lindsay and Gary and across from Karl and a newcomer.

"Does anyone see His Eminence, The CEO, sitting at our table?" asked Lindsay. The group looked over their shoulders and under the table and napkins, "Nope."

"Maybe I should find another table with better insults."

We then greeted one another with an undertone of both warmth and distance.

"This is your replacement, Peter Thaw. Peter went to the Rhode Island School of Design," said Lindsay before Karl interrupted.

"Riz-D to insiders."

"He was in the Peace Corp in Malawi where he taught agriculture and drawing."

"And then a year at École nationale supérieure des Beaux-Arts," added Lindsay.

"Nicole to insiders," said Gary.

"Not Nicole, École."

"Nice to meet you, Peter," I said. "Do you speak French?"

"No, they speak English in Rhode Island."

"Hello, Rob. Nice to meet you finally. These guys always talk about you."

"Not like you're dead or something ... just not here," said Karl.

"Peter's now filling pages of the Remora newsletters with photos that are perky as a teen's tits," said Gary.

"That next time you say that, Gary, you'll be fired," said Lindsay.

"He also changed the page-making software, which lets him create his own fonts. Boy, do these publications look different."

"I hope that didn't cost too much money?" I asked as if I cared.

"No, I have a buddy who's working on some beta software and will actually give Remora royalties if they can copyright a typeface we create," said Thaw.

"That brings up a different question. If there is a copyright, can it be copywrong?" asked Karl.

"How can you be copywrong? There is no such word."

"Yes, it's called copyright infringement," said Lindsay.

"No, that's different. Copywrong is something no one has considered," said Karl.

"Have you ever been infringed, Lindsay?" asked Gary.

"C'mon, Gary. You can get Rob fired by saying that in front of him."

"I get it. Last year it was a joke between us, and now I can bring down the entire company," said Gary.

"Yikes. I'm part of that and I don't even work here," said Karl.

"How come they still let you in?" asked Thaw.

"Habit. I got a job at another company, but the new people won't have lunch with me," said Karl.

As people continued to acknowledge my presence, I gave them the lower lip over the top lip greeting, which was more of a compromise than a smile.

"Hey, this is a good gig for an artist," I said to Peter. "The benefits are good. The hours are excellent. There's even a pension. What artist gets a pension? What type of artwork do you do when you're not here?"

"I like making gelatin silver prints. A friend lets me use his dark room. Been doing that for years. I also take different materials and then, with lights of various shapes and colors, I create shadows for a multi-dimensional sculpture."

"A great old-timey look and an homage to Yamashita. I'd like to see them some time."

"That would be great. What are you doing?"

"Dealing with matters I never imagined. My wife is the real artist. She makes incredible architectural models. She has an uncanny instinct and talent for it. Lately, I've been working with egg tempera." I'm not sure why I said that, since I had never worked in that medium, but I did know it was difficult.

"I would like to see them some day."

The lies that smooth relationships. As I looked around The Caf, I saw a number of younger people who would never have the benefits from the old and dead deceits of lunch. In the days before electronic contrivances ruled everyone's lives, if you did not want to speak to someone, you could call them during lunch hour knowing they were

Success Is Not An Option

out, let their phone ring, then you could honestly say you called. We did not even have voicemail. Another long gone lunch hour trick occurred before the universal use of credit cards. People would hide clothes in the wrong places in department stores so only they could find them on payday. Of course, I realized that younger people had their own more sophisticated deceits, but ours were grittier.

"Hey, Rob. Do you think an egg salad sandwich can be made into an intellectual property? And more important, how do you know how big a balloon will be before it's blown up?" asked Gary.

"Are those questions related?" said Karl.

"And, by the way, does the size of a balloon depend on whether it's a hot day or a cold day? If you're in the Alps, does the elevation change everything?" asked Gary.

"Actually," said Thaw, "A 9″ latex balloon will inflate to 9″ radius. An 11″ balloon will become 11″ radius," said Thaw.

"Did you learn that in Paris?"

"Nah, I used to do children's parties. It was a source of money and penitence."

"Hey Rob, did you know Peter works with greyhound rescue, cooks at a homeless shelter, is good friends with the Dalai Lama, and won an Iron Man competition?" said Gary.

Everyone wants the person who replaces them at work to be smarter, stupider, taller, smaller, more handsome, more hideous, overqualified, a complete moron, fifteen minutes out of college, ready for retirement, fit, fat, drunk, sober, a decision maker, a timid coward, a saint, a thief, guilty, innocent, sunny, and cloudy. If they did not make your office into a shrine, they lack the respect and credibility to do the job properly. Did they want someone different, the same, or just someone who is competent? I know I am the CEO, and I knew my reaction seemed petty, but they could have chosen someone who still needs his mittens attached to his sleeve by safety pins rather than someone who spends spring break with the friggin' Dalai Lama.

"What the hell are the cafeteria staff wearing? They look like they are being tortured," I said.

"They're leftover uniforms from the bar mitzvahs and weddings they've had here recently."

"Belette wants them to look more professional. So, he makes them wear those things like on *Downtown Abbie*."

"*Downton Abby*."

"Do you want to hear my Laura Linney impersonation?" said Lindsay.

"I can do the stuffy butler," said Karl.

"You sound like someone squeezing a bagpiper's balls. At least Lindsay's sounds like a person."

"They're wearing epaulets and hairnets."

"I hope wearing epaulets is not mandated by law," I said.

"Hello, Mr. Stone. Good to see you in The Caf again," said an employee I did not know.

I gave him the lower lip in response.

"Do you think he was being sincere or sarcastic?"

"Hard to say."

"How do sewers know in which direction to flow?" asked Karl.

"They're tilted toward the sea."

"How about in a city?"

"They have one-way signs."

"We heard you were reviewed. Who the hell reviews you, Rob?"

"Three consultants. They're the paid assassins of the Board."

"Did they know you're expert with an X-Acto knife?"

"Probably not. It's an instrument that's too precise for business."

"What did they say?"

"They said I need a better six-month and yearly plan."

"Anything else?"

"Not really. They want me to take a personality test."

"Why? Are they going to give you choices for a new one?" asked Lindsay.

"It's all bullshit. If I succeed, they'll say I followed their instructions and advice. And if I fail, I didn't follow their instructions and advice. Years of prejudice and subtle deception go into those reviews."

"Who reviews the consultants?"

"The Board? Whoever counts up their hours at MaKissMe?"

"See that man with a limp? He's missing a lung," said Gary.

"What the hell are you talking about?"

"He wants people to know he lost a lung. But because you can't see it, he limps."

"How do you know that?"

"It's obvious."

"I heard your office was attacked by a softball beer league who don't want to fly anymore for the company and others who hate your idea of a meritocracy," said Lindsay.

"Not everyone was pudgy," I said.

"They should be ashamed of themselves. There are scores of problems at Remora and they only care about themselves," said Gary. Then he looked a little sheepish when he realized I was responsible for fixing those problems.

"I have an idea," said Karl. "You're an old hippie. Why not get those guys to form a drum circle? Isn't that supposed to bring people together? They can smack the bottom of garbage cans or something."

"No one has wooden rulers anymore."

"How does it feel for an old hippie to be in charge of an insurance company of all things?"

"I'll let you know when I'm actually in charge."

"Maybe I should come and interview you for the newsletter?" said Lindsay.

"Only if I can use a pseudonym."

Scattered around The Caf, I saw Belette's changes. Under Spaulding, Belette served as a creature from a black and white

1930s horror movie, chanting his orders. Sycophants did not ordinarily act with independence. I feared I created a new type of monster but with a modern color scheme.

Above us hung Belette's disco ball, like a Damocles sword of poor taste and spasmodic dance moves. A folded bandstand leaned silent in a corner, ready to spring into a Hokey Pokey, YMCA, and other eternal wedding and bar mitzvah favorites at the slightest provocation.

Belette also started "The Caf Employee of the Month." Instead of a photo, and in recognition of the honor, he glued a snood personally worn by the winner to a plaque. Fortunately, at this point, there had been only two winners.

He also tinkered with the menu by adding what could only be described as his personal comfort foods: tapioca pudding and mass manufactured egg rolls. He could have made other changes, such as weeding out the grey peas and carrots or serving mac and cheese without pebbles of cheddar, but he chose not to. But he did introduce a dessert carousel like the one at Mt. Taygetus. An excellent example of a good intentions gone wrong.

I jumped up and asked, "Anyone want to share a slice of strawberry shortcake?" As the novelty of my appearance had worn thin, there were no immediate takers.

Lindsay finally agreed, "I'll go with you."

When I opened the door to the carousel, The Caf quieted. Everyone knew the dangers but me. Wanda The Lunch Lady and local Sheriff strutted over. "You know the rules." An incorrect assumption. "Only specified cafeteria staff members are permitted to take their own pies or cakes. Everyone else must use the special implements and wax paper provided." I admitted I had not read the countless handwritten and typed instructions, health warnings, payment restrictions, and mandatory punishments plastered to the glass of the carousel, obscuring most of the desserts.

"Do I need a haz-mat suit?" I said.

"You're not new here." All eyes, some with admiration, others with dread, shifted to Wanda. Two generations ago, her grandmothers ushered frightened children to their seats in darkened theaters with dimly-lit flashlights as they threatened expulsion from the movie house for the slightest transgression. Her mother drove a school bus with little tolerance for excess joy or seat changing.

"Com'on Wanda, you've known me for years. I simply want a slice of strawberry shortcake."

"You are a different person now. I don't know the person in front of me. The old Rob Stone would have done it the right way."

From somewhere far away in the crowd and behind Wanda's back, someone who had waited all their life to admonish any lunch lady, yelled out, "He's the fucking boss, you idiot."

Wanda looked at my face. She hesitated for a moment, vacillating between embarrassment and defiance; she realized that she had become the center of attention. And knew she would see these people every day until she retired.

"Alright. But just this one time. Let me show you the proper procedure for removing the cake." With the aplomb and delicacy of the bomb squad, she surgically removed a slice of lemon meringue and gently placed it on a plate, for which I thanked her.

"I know she gave me lemon meringue instead of strawberry, but she already made too many sacrifices for one day," I whispered to Lindsay.

"I'm deeply disappointed in you. You showed great equanimity. I hope this is not the new you. You know, I'm responsible for some of the changes in The Caf," said Lindsay.

"How's that?"

"Belette knew that you and I were friends, so he came to me for advice. He didn't want to do anything that would offend you."

"Well, that makes me feel better that he's still a sycophant. I was afraid for a moment that I had changed Belette for the better. I certainly wouldn't want that on my resume."

"I renamed The Caf, Tray Chic," said Lindsay.

"Barry actually admitted that to me but I knew it anyway. That name is beyond his wit. Maybe you can explain to him; it's not pronounced chick."

"I tried. Failure takes many forms."

"Is *Consommé de Marriage* your idea?"

"*Oui.*"

"Very clever. And the fewer people who get that joke, the better. I assume 'Three-Teared Cake' was also yours."

"But of course. I admit, however, that the 'Wall of Snoods' was his idea. Belette said that you liked the word 'snoods' and something about crossword puzzles. He made me swear that it wasn't a curse word," said Lindsay.

"The whole Tray Chic thing is my fault. Belette took a suggestion and is trying to make it into an empire. Although extra money would be helpful, it seems less people are using The Caf than in the past. Every day, more and more people seem to working from home," I said.

An employee passed by and asked, "Is everything OK, Mr. Stone? We never see you down here anymore."

"I'm just having lunch with friends I have neglected." I gave him the lower lip.

Karl stood up. "Well, good to see you, but we peasants have to get back to work. It was both weird and nice having you back."

Another employee stopped. "Hello Mr. Stone. How come you are down here? Everything OK?"

"Everything's fine. I'm just having lunch with old friends with whom I had lunch every day for years."

"Yes, but why are you here today?"

I knew even the lower lip would not work.

That was when I decided to officiate at Sir Reginald's and Quisling's wedding. I needed to be seen more.

Chapter 17

The Wedding

"I CANNOT THINK of two people more deserving of each other than Candy and Sir Reginald. They complement each other in ways we cannot even imagine. Fate is usually the culprit that brings couples together. But here, fate was just the footman, as a tragic accident coupled them with a deep and hypnotic appreciation of each other. In the words of John Muir, 'And into the woods I go, to lose my mind and find my soul.'"

A few audible "aahs" escaped from the gathered. I did not know what the Muir quote meant, so how could they? I was not even sure what the footman comment meant but it seemed poetic and appropriate enough. Lindsay, the apostle of paradox, helped draft the speech. As for myself, I thought, "Could I be a phony if my intention was ironic?" When I applied to be an officiant online, I found the qualifications less rigorous than buying a cheeseburger at McDonald's. This lack of diligence appealed to me and seemed more than appropriate to conduct this ceremony.

"Sir Reginald Pigot-Smythe, formerly Morris Plotnick of the Grand Concourse, The Bronx, do you promise to love, honor, cherish, and protect Candace Quisling, forsaking all others, and holding only unto her forevermore?"

"I do," said Sir Reginald. Then he whispered to me, "Hey

Guv, what's forsaking got to do with this? And can she still testify against me?"

"Can you just hold on for a minute until she says, 'I do?' And remember that I'm an on-line officiant, not an on-line lawyer."

"Candace Quisling of Yorkville, NY, and Yaphank, Long Island, do you promise to love, honor, cherish, and protect Sir Reginald Pigot-Smythe, forsaking all others, and holding only unto him forevermore?"

"I do."

"Mommy, why is that woman talking out of her bum?"

"I'm not sure, dear, but it's probably not the first time."

"By the power invested in me by the State of New York and some on-line ministry, I now pronounce you man and wife. You can kiss the bride or whatever you two do."

With Candy positioned in her usual reverse throne position with her ass toward the ceiling and her face toward the floor, Sir Reginald needed to go under her like a car mechanic changing the oil and other fluids to kiss her, to the delight of all.

"Thank you, Rob," said Candy.

As always, I was confused as to what direction I should thank her.

Sir Reginald confirmed my suspicion that affection and companionship were secondary to thwarting litigation. I assumed Candy consulted with her attorney to confirm whether Sir Reginald was not personally liable for her condition. Thus, she could respond to his proposal with a magnanimous gesture and gain a husband at the same time. One could only imagine the provisions of their pre-nup.

When Cassia and I met at Cooper Union, we pretended to understand the world. Although that was only partially true, it did not stop us from drawing, painting, and discussing it. The first time I saw Cassia, she was wearing a back-lit diaphanous gown, her hair flowed in waves, all behind a coy smile. Of course, she wore a flannel shirt, ripped jeans, and her boots' laces flopped about as she traipsed down the halls of Cooper Union. And still, that is the way I recollect her.

Cassia stood nearby me at the wedding as a protector, witness, and gatherer of intelligence. Although she knew she would attract undue attention, she did not hesitate to attend. This was not only out of loyalty, but she also wanted to see the sideshow I had been telling her about every night. After this, she could fill in her own coloring book with the faces and events. She smiled at strangers all night and did not reveal anything. She made small talk and even smaller talk. I rarely saw the politician in her, but she certainly enjoyed playing the role. She randomly greeted people with "Con mucho gusto," "Enchanté and Enchantée," and "Piacere di conoscerti" without knowing who they were. She also knew, "Where is the bathroom?" and "How much?" in those languages but that did not come up in today's conversations. She used these diversions to avoid answering any personal questions about either one of us.

During a quiet moment, I said, "You have taken to this First Lady thing with great aplomb."

"I'm channeling Michelle Obama and Edith Wilson."

"I get Michelle but why Edith Wilson?"

"She took over when Woodrow had a stroke. You said, 'by the powers invested in me by New York' during the ceremony."

"Did I? Not vested?"

"Invested."

"Do you think anyone else noticed?"

"I think this crowd liked it."

"Would you have married me if I'd said let's have our wedding in a cafeteria?"

"I'm not sure. They didn't have real mac and cheese back then or lox and cheese on a rice-cake coaster. We had our reception at your sister's house with a no-piece band and twelve people."

"I remember our cannoli wedding cake."

"That was good. And then we wasted all our money on a six-month hobo trip to Europe."

"We were young and stupid."

"We're still a bit stupid but older."

We could have held a Presidents Meeting at the wedding, every member attended with their designated Plus One. A most sterile term for someone with whom another had at least an emotional, if not a physical relationship. I guess it was better than being labeled a Minus One. The Presidents and their companions refused to have a good time. They apparently did not want to give the impression that they approved of the wedding or even liked Candy or Sir Reginald. They also threatened anyone who wanted to dance. Drinking, of course, was not only acceptable but encouraged. They pushed together the round cafeteria tables and sat in the approximate position where they sat at Presidents Meetings. It created a tilt-a-whirl of forbearance.

I spotted Gladys and her sister sitting with Sladka and the ever-grateful Tiffany. Sladka brought Find Dough, who many of the business types seemed to avoid. At least he was on a leash.

"Great job, Rob," said Gladys.

Her sister greeted me like an elderly aunt I never knew existed until now.

"I've seen your drawings," I told her. "They're quite good." Then realized I was not supposed to mention them.

Gladys's sister became flustered, as she did not have much contact with people other than those in her neighborhood. "You know," she said. "You're the son that Gladys never wanted. And she means that in the nicest way."

"Another mother would have confused me."

Gladys and her sister wore clothes from another era, sequined gowns and well-preserved mink stoles, to resemble each other in time and space. Their minks still had their heads on and had bought them when they also adorned the likes of Joan Crawford and Marilyn Monroe.

The bride and groom continued to ramble their way through Tray Chic. Someone murmured "nice job" from the Presidents' tables, probably a spouse. But I also heard, "Hey Reggie. Did your father fight in a British Thermal Unit?" And, "Hey, sexy lady. Is your bridal registry at Home Depot?"

I greeted Candy's mother, Mrs. Quisling, who remembered my visit to the hospital. I told her, "You know we have a Yiddish word for your relationship with Sir Reginald's parents: *machatunim*. The relationship of the four parents to one another."

"I didn't know that. Am I supposed to have a relationship with his family?" replied Mrs. Quisling. "I won't say anything bad today. My Candy couldn't find a husband even before her accident. What's that word again?"

"Machatunim. It's a little difficult to pronounce—mah-cha-TUHN-um. Try to say the 'cha' from the back of your throat." Candy's mother made a half-hearted attempt to repeat it, with the hope I would leave soon.

The mac and cheese glistened in their steam table wells, catching the light from the revolving disco ball. The cafeteria staff wore baseball caps that read Tray Chic and dished out the very best of what was renamed the "Retro-Caf Menu." It included burgers from the flattop, chicken fingers, and small containers of warm chocolate milk. While most guests waited in line behind the aluminum barrier and enjoyed the novelty and nostalgia of the food, a few others pushed their way to the front with plates in hand, worried their favorites would be gone.

Out-of-work actors and singers disguised as wait staff circulated with finger food made of the latest unknown ingredients. Some guests stabbed at the food with toothpicks as though this might be the last time that the canapes would ever come their way. The wedding had all the irony and outdated sophistication of a man lighting a woman's cigarette. "Here. Let me help you ... get cancer."

The DJ, secluded in his corner, played dance music at brain-splitting volume. Belette had unwittingly created a brilliant cacophony of sights and smells that could not be found elsewhere. While Belette scurried about to make sure people were fed and tables bussed, he occasionally lingered over some guests with a hope of a compliment. He mentioned to us how much the company would make, even though he gave an employee discount to Candy and Sir Reginald.

"Great idea to marry them. It makes you look like a *mensch*," Belette said to me.

"Thank you. I didn't realize you knew the word mensch."

"This is New York."

"Ah, Lindsay."

"You know, disco balls were invented in the early 1900s, but no one paid attention to them until the whole disco club thing blew up. I like to think of the disco ball as Remora's own little moon," said Belette.

"Why do you think the disco ball didn't catch on back then?" asked Cassia.

"I'm no dance expert, but I think people did less drugs then. And people danced with straighter backs."

"Was it hard to get a liquor license?" asked Cassia.

Belette cast a quick look at me and his face collapsed.

"Not too hard. Joe Black, the head of Maintenance, helped out. Said he knew someone."

"Do you have the license?" I asked.

"Joe said he had it."

"You don't have it?"

"I'm sure it's safe."

"Did you use company funds?"

"Of course."

"So, you do have the license in hand? Next time you schmear someone, make sure you schmear the right person."

"If I bribed the wrong person, is it still a crime?"

"And make sure you get over to Fraud on Monday and tell Greegan what you've done."

"He's already mad at me because he wasn't invited today."

From nowhere, Wanda The Lunch Lady grabbed my arm, put a

snood on my head, and led me to the dance floor. Fortunately, she could not move very fast. Unfortunately, when the crowd saw me, they formed a circle around Wanda and myself. Our dance moves emulated dishing out food and giving change at the register. The more I scowled and put my hands on my waist, the louder the laughs. When the music ended, I gave Wanda a big hug and kiss with the hope she would not hassle me the next time I bought a piece of cake. It was one of those moments, the stupider you acted, the better for everyone. Except the dance sweat stayed in your shirt collar all night.

"Should I be jealous?" asked Cassia.

"Are you usually jealous of stone-cold killers? It was a pre-emptive strike."

"The night seems to be going pretty well. Better than I thought from all your descriptions."

"Not bad, except for the bribe. But I was also afraid someone like Luca Brasi might ask me for a favor.

"The night is still young. What will happen with the bribe?" asked Cassia.

"Someone will take care of that. It is the price of doing business."

"Well, that's a different you."

Cassia and I went over to talk with the bride and groom. Cassia seemed comfortable talking to Candy's body parts. We were introduced to their families although only one of Sir Reginald's children attended. A short straw type of situation I guessed. Frozen smiles all around and they thanked me again for conducting the ceremony.

"I read about in-laws in preparation of my duties. Did you know that the term in-laws came from 14th-century Canon Law? That law dictated who you could and could not marry. But it wasn't until the 1890s that in-laws took on its full current meaning."

"That's fascinating, Rob," said Candy.

"Let me repeat that we're really chuffed that you married us.

I'd say that this means we're mates now, right?" asked Sir Reginald.

Whatever I would say would be the wrong answer for either one of us or both. "I would say we are eternally linked."

"I really am chuffed, but next time please keep that Morris Plotnick stuff just between us and then Bob's your uncle."

"No one was listening."

"Are you two lovebirds planning on having kids, starting tonight?" someone passing by asked in that traditional salacious wedding-night style.

"Her eggs aren't exactly Grade A," said Sir Reginald.

Dom Oleoso got separated from the pod of Presidents. Slightly drunk, he said, "Do you know why the others don't like you?"

"Is this multiple choice or an essay test?"

"There are good and bad reasons, mostly good. The most obvious reason is they all think they deserve your job. Whether they can do it or not doesn't matter. They think they deserve it. Just human nature, I guess. But they're afraid of you because you're not one of them."

"Who wants to be one of them?"

Oleoso continued, "When someone goes to a museum or reads a book, those guys think how the hell did they paint that or write a novel. But they also think, I bet I can do that if I put my mind to it. Of course, we all know it's bullshit. But please keep it up, whatever you're doing. You scare the shit out of a few of them. Not all of them. I never scare anybody. Whoever thought you could have a good time in a cafeteria?"

"Thank you."

"That was positive in a drunk sort of way. Especially for someone who's afraid of the world," I said to Cassia.

"Yeah. But I guess there is truth *in vino veritas*."

A little boy approached and said, "Are you Mr. Stone?"

"Yes, I am. What's your name?"

"Forest."

"That's a nice name. How old are you, Forest?"
"Six."
"Are you having a good time?"
"Yes. Are you, Mr. Stone?"
"Yes."
"My father says you're an artsy-fartsy Jew. What's that?" An elastic hand from nowhere reached in and pulled the child back into the crowd.

Chapter 18
The Mailroom

EVEN WITH THE popularity of working from home or a coffee shop, there are certain jobs that must be performed on the premises. This seemed like a perfect application for management-by-wandering, a technique where a supervisor does not have a specific destination and visits various employees in a random manner. This is supposed to accomplish many things, including gaining a familiarity with the humans of whom they are in charge as well as with their duties. It does, however, sound like a justification for lack of direction and an activity that is rarely conducted by upper management. Still, I thought it would be less intimidating than Find Dough on a leash.

As I walked down the corridors and, depending upon the orientation of the desks, I could only see one side of people's faces or their foreheads but rarely their backs. This confirmed the acceptance of the conventional wisdom: keep your head down and your nose clean.

I am convinced someone could walk around any office with a piece of paper in their hand with a practiced frown and a meaningful stride and no one would question what they were doing. I had no such paper in my hand.

I tried to engage those people who were rarely acknowledged

by others, such as the various accounting groups, regulatory units, and IT. These attempts on my part were abject failures; our stilted conversations declined rapidly into an office version of the platitudes exchanged at a funeral.

I came upon one area of legal where the workers were engaged in a job that no one would consider glamorous. After I introduced myself, the young woman in charge asked, "Is there a problem?"

"No, I'm just trying to learn what different people and different areas do."

Her eyes revealed skepticism, but her words were earnest. "Well, we file the rates and forms of the various policies for approval with the state insurance departments. Some states use the same application. Of course, now everything is done electronically, but we once mailed big fat packages of dead trees to each state separately. Then the states send their objections back to us, and we try to address them in consultation with the underwriters and the actuaries. It's like sending out junk mail, never knowing who will answer. You know, it's not easy outsmarting a bureaucrat. You have to get them to do something they don't want to do."

"It's a talent that has many applications. You could set up a booth at Motor Vehicles and advise people how to move the unmovable. You could make a fortune. Not that I'm telling you to leave the company."

I thanked her and wondered, what did a modern mailroom do these days? And what did it even look like? Even with all the electronic contrivances and fewer people at their desks, there must be a need for one. I asked a few people where the mailroom might be and they were unanimous in their uncertainty: the basement.

I headed to the basement, where I had never been. The walls were painted into white and grey halves with the precision of a drunk. The polished floor undulated with the same gray color. I followed the orange and blue pipes on the ceiling wondering what the colors meant. Why were the other pipes unpainted, and where do they all lead? From an open door down the hall, a cone of artificial light appeared, more like a breach of the building's exterior than a glimmer of hope. There, relegated to a dark corner and without a single sign indicating who lived there, I found the mailroom.

It was a survivor of different times and reigns. For decades, it had been a boot camp for upward mobility for those with ambition but without a college degree. But now the whispers of bigotry from an omnipresent caste system, founded in levels of education and preconceived abilities, ended all that.

Against one wall of the mailroom lay tiers of technology ranked by sophistication. At the bottom and forming the foundation were upside-down splintered oak cubbyholes, each with a faded name tag of long dead employees written in fountain pen. Above that rested a layer of fax and telex machines and crowned by the early generations of bulky computers.

Across from the debris, three Hispanic kids and their Hispanic supervisor worked with great attention, while nearby an elderly white man sat hunched over a newspaper.

"Hi, I'm Rob Stone," I said. "I just wanted to stop by and introduce myself."

Everyone's back stiffened and their pace increased except the old guy. Their eyes darted around looking for anything that might be incriminating, all focusing on a pile of packages. You could almost see one thinking, "Why?"

"Hello, Mr. Stone. I'm Hector, the mailroom supervisor." Hector shook my hand.

"Nice to meet you, Hector. Please call me Rob."

Hector introduced the younger men and skipped the old man, but kept staring at a heap of packages of what must have been contraband.

Without my asking, Hector said, "Let me explain. That stuff there? A lot of people have things delivered here. That way, no one can steal their deliveries because they're gone all day."

I walked over to the pile of parcels, all addressed to employees, most from well-known, on-line merchants. "A lot of dog treats and diapers," I said. "It makes us more employee-friendly." I honestly thought it was a good idea and did not want to create a rebellion of middle-class working mothers.

"Over there's the machine that x-rays the packages. You never know. That's what the last guy in charge said, 'You never know.' That machine slices off the tops of the envelopes and then we scan them over there and e-mail the images to the person by computer. If they want the letter, they can ask."

"Only one scanner?"

"Yeah, we don't get as much mail as we used to."

"Do you have any suggestions to improve things here?"

"A faster scanner and I think we can make some money. I think we can sell stamps, packing material, and pack people's stuff that has to be returned for a fee. I'm sure people would use it."

"Do they tip you for those services now?"

"Not the bosses. The regular people, sometimes."

"OK. Write up your suggestions and send them to me."

"Thank you. Those machines over there were once used for mass mailing. We keep them just in case they're ever needed again. Right now, all the mass mailings are done from some place in Pennsylvania. And this is the automatic mail opener. It slices open the tops of the envelopes," repeated Hector.

"Thank you all for doing a job that is truly needed. I'm happy to answer any questions."

When there were none, I walked over to the elderly man reading the *Wall Street Journal*. As I approached, I realized he wore a wig made of some sort of hair that was not exactly human and was thicker and darker than an eighteen-year-old's hair and a bit askew. He wore glasses that covered most of his face and sported a wispy Ho Chi Minh beard, a far different color than anything else on his body. I was not sure why he was disguised, but it was as bad as those used on that TV show where the head of a company posed as an outsider in order to mingle with the employees to find the scripted truth. Not much different than my mission.

A very nervous Hector interjected, "Mr. S. is just on break."

"Hi, I'm Rob Stone," I said to the elderly man and reached out my hand to shake his.

When the old man did not respond, Hector's eyes opened wider.

"I'm Rob Stone. I'm sorry, I didn't get your name."

Hector jumped in. "You should call Mr. Fine. He'll tell you. Here's his card."

Then the old man spoke, "Don't call Fine He'll just charge us for his time. You're Stone, right?"

"I'm Rob Stone. Who are you?"

"I'm not supposed to tell anyone who I am."

"Why not?"

"The stock will go down."

"What's your name?"

"Smith. Sam Smith. The kids call me, Mr. S."

His clothes looked as oddly familiar as the man himself.

"You're A.J. Spaulding, right? I know your face. I'm the one who pasted your head in an obituary," I said with great incredulity.

"Well, un-paste my head, man."

I questioned what I was seeing. The thought that A.J. Spaulding was sitting in front of me was absurd. All the kids and Hector stared intently at me.

"This makes no sense. You're supposed to be dead."

"How do you think it makes me feel?" said the old man.

"Call Mr. Fine," said Hector with great anxiety.

"Are you A.J. Spaulding?"

"You're Stone, right?"

"Yes. And you're A.J Spaulding. The head of Remora for 40 years."

"OK, you got me. I'm Anthony Joseph Spaulding, I'm the

Chairman of the Board and Head Dispatcher. Do you have a package?"

"What are you doing here, Mr. Spaulding?"

"Do you have a package? FedEx comes soon."

"How long have you been here?"

"Since about 8:17 this morning."

"Why are you here?"

"Someone has to take care of the packages."

"Are you OK down here?"

"Yes. Hector and the boys treat me like a king. They even bring me lunch every day. Tuna salad from around the corner. But what kind of name is Jesus?" said the old man.

"Jesus, Mr. S., Jesus," said Hector.

"And what kind of name is Angel?"

"Angel, Mr. S., Angel."

"Do you have a package for me? Besides FedEx, we use UPS."

"Why are you here?"

"I don't know, but I agreed to it."

"You wait here," I said as if that order mattered. Addled, I looked back one more time before I left the mailroom. I did not want the others to think I was completely mad. I did not even say good-bye.

Gladys greeted me at the elevator door on our floor. "Hector called. You should have told me you were going to the mailroom."

"I didn't know I was walking into a private cemetery."

"Don't overreact."

The three consultants appeared in my office as if Scotty had beamed them up. They wore casual clothes including polo shirts with little animals near the shoulder. "Sorry we're dressed like this. We were going to an off-site."

"See, I told you so," said Gladys to the consultants. "You should have told him."

"Is that really Spaulding?" I asked.

"Yes, that's really Spaulding," said Gladys, slumped over. "I knew this moment was inevitable. I'm sorry Rob. I wanted to tell you earlier."

"He has withering facilities," said Fine.

"So, you kill him and bury him in the basement?"

"We did neither. We consider him 'media dead,' not dead dead. He has withering facilities and we couldn't take the chance that Wall Street would find out."

"So, you kill him and bury him in the basement?"

"As you can see, we did not kill him."

"We didn't want the market, the media, policy holders, or stakeholders to think he made decisions while he had those withering facilities. It could have killed the company stock price," said Bill.

"He thinks he is the Chairman/Head Dispatcher."

"He is actually. We never elected a new chairman."

"And Hector isn't the Head Dispatcher?"

"He's the ex-officio Head Dispatcher."

"Why didn't you just let Spaulding retire?"

"Who knows what type of investigations there would have been of him and Remora if the world found out about his mental state?"

"We couldn't take a chance that someone might find out. And he's being well taken care of. Everyday a nondescript car drives him to the back door in the alley of the building …"

"A Honda," said Fiona. "Nobody looks for a dead man in a Honda."

"… And he is led to his desk, where he sits all day. Back home, he has all his amenities, comforts, and someone to take care of him."

"You could have spent a little more on that disguise. What about his family?"

"They hardly talked to him when he was alive. We bought a corpse, legally might I add, like the ones medical students use, and had it cremated."

"You burnt a fake Spaulding to a crisp?"

"It's not homicide if we don't kill him. It's the opposite."

"CEO-cide. And I'm the CEO now."

"What about his estate?"

"We are trying to delay the probate."

"Isn't that fraud?"

"To some, maybe."

"To some? You mean like the DA? Now I'm part of your fraud. What about Hector?"

"He doesn't know, exactly, but suspects something. We gave him a bonus which he appreciated."

"And the three guys who work with him? They all know now."

"Only because of you they know now. And now they're all going to need bonuses and NDAs."

"You mean nada. And don't blame me. And Gladys, you knew."

"Yes, I'm sorry I didn't tell you. I feel guilty."

"I relied on you."

"Sorry."

"Well, I can't keep this position. I don't want to be involved in a fraud," I said.

"But you are now."

"By accident, I am. By accident."

"Just sit tight and we will extricate you from this situation. Don't do anything stupid. A lot of innocent people will lose their jobs."

"And some guilty ones, like you, will go to jail."

"Just don't go to the authorities. That can't be unraveled."

"I haven't heard the word authorities since *Casablanca*. And what happens when he really dies?"

"The paperwork is already done."

"We didn't cash in his life insurance."

"Why? Is insurance fraud beneath you?"

"We knew you wouldn't go along with the scheme."

"Yet here I am."

"I told you."

"So, since I started, I've been accused of murder, SEC violations, mismanagement, fraud, had an employee revolt, was almost assassinated, and now I'm part of a cover-up of someone who's dead but alive. And I haven't been here a year yet."

"You were never going to be assassinated."

Sladka also appeared. "I'm involved, too."

"He talks."

"I know he talks but I asked him not to."

"The old man liked to talk on TV, too. That's another reason we did what we did."

"Dead from New York! It's A.J. Spaulding! Look, I need some time to think about all this."

"Don't do anything stupid."

"Me? I'm not the one who's done stupid things."

While trying to settle myself, I went out for some comfort food, a distraction. I knew one of them was following me, afraid I would go anywhere but where I went. The delis in the area only sold crap bagels. Today was not the day for those phony bagels. I settled for burger deluxe to go. Sometimes, they made a mistake and fried up some excellent fries.

I returned to the office, still perturbed, and silently brushed past everyone and closed the door. The office that I had ironically inherited from Spaulding. I fought with the lunacy of their tortured logic and wondered how the hell did I get out of this mess? Still distracted, I stared at the lettuce, tomato, and onion on my burger. What the hell does lettuce, tomato, and onion have to do with a burger? That takes no culinary skill, other than a sharp blade. If I weren't in a snit, I doubt that I would I have raised the question. But many business decisions are often like lettuce, tomatoes, and raw onions—there is no need for many of them. If all businesses made the correct decisions, we would not need bankruptcy courts. Let alone hiding dead/alive people. I needed to be alone. I didn't want anyone to see me thinking like this.

I got promoted to a job for which I was clearly unqualified

and apparently emotionally unprepared. Even if you were a worker bee and stayed in the same area as a supervisor, being a boss was a very different world. You made mistakes at the expense of others and those who were innocent. The consultants and the Board chose me because I fit their scheme and they thought I could easily be manipulated.

When I first met the consultants, I told them businesses were dictatorships and there should be term limits for CEOs. Now, Caesar sat in the basement directing packages, while the Senate waited for me outside my office.

What hubris of me to think that I, an artist, could sow change. And in insurance, of all worlds. Insurance is the couch art of the economy. How Faustian of me. Companies outwardly laud innovation but reward conformity. Try something new, but do not fail. I felt that I did not fail as much as I did not succeed.

I decided to call an old lawyer friend who I did not see very often. "Hello, Rich. It's Rob Stone. I know we haven't spoken in a while. How's Karen?"

We all know a Rich Weinberg, the type who could have been the class valedictorian if he opened a book, or could work for a white-shoe law firm if he wore socks in the winter. He was a solo practitioner, and like most solo practitioners, he needed to work alone. Not due to greed, but to their deep need to live in a province they had created and only touch the outside world as needed. Weinberg accepted most new business that came through the door, but had a desk plate that read in Hebrew, "No assholes." He excelled, however, at representing the truly aggrieved. I was not sure he even had an admin or paralegal.

"Ah, yes, Rob Stone. The artist turned oligarch."

"Can I ask you a question?"

"And if I say no, where will you go?"

"I would go to Legal Aid. Even at their salary they dress better than you."

"OK, what?"

I explained the situation with Spaulding.

"How fucked up is that? I don't do criminal work, but if you turn them in now, you should be OK, and if you don't, you have to hope for the best. You, my friend, are an accessory after the fact. And I don't mean a handbag."

"That's kinda what I thought. I also signed a loyalty oath when I first started."

"A private employer loyalty oath?"

"Yes."

"It's probably bullshit. Why did they ask you to sign one?"

"I'm an artist and they didn't trust artists. And, in particular, didn't trust me although they weren't specific."

"And you signed it."

"Sure. What did I care?"

"Well, you were right; it's bullshit. Even a better dressed Legal Aid attorney could rip that oath to shit."

"You know, we're similar in our attitudes. We're both sandpaper in a world where people are trying to smooth things over," I said.

"Yes, but at least I pay my own phone bill," said Weinberg.

Chapter 19

Wish Your Sister Well

THE FOLLOWING MORNING, my office had that distinct smell and energy of a funeral home. The first mourner was Lindsay, who interrupted the awkward silence. "You're such a schmuck, Rob. You should've pretended it wasn't Spaulding."

"Did you know he was alive? How the hell was I supposed to know the old bastard was stashed away in the bowels of the building? I never even met him before; I only recognized him through his pictures. He looked like a clump of hair on a chair."

"They want me to write a press release about you leaving."

"Who said I was leaving?"

"The consultants were here late last night with some of their undertaker friends. They're telling everyone that you're leaving the company immediately to take care of your sick sister. And they're spreading the rumor rather quickly, so you can't tell people your truth."

"Very noble of me. Now, all I need is a sister."

"Rob, they never trusted you with their secret and they certainly don't trust you now."

"I rose to their level of intolerance. But they will tell each other I rose to my own level of incompetence."

Lindsay and I huddled for about an hour. I told her some of the things Cassia and I were thinking of doing, although nothing was definite. She said that she would use as many weasel words in her release to make me seem like a nice guy. We also spoke about some of my old art projects in the closet and Lindsay said that she would dust them off.

> After twenty-eight years at Remora, Robert Stone has left the company to pursue other interests. He began as a graphic designer and rose to the position of CEO, where he profoundly changed the company.
>
> He will now pursue his artistic interests and engage in philanthropic activities. His next art show, "Expressions" will be at the Wilderbeest Galleries on The Bowery. The exhibit is a series of pithy sayings created by spraying canned cheddar cheese onto pitted brick plaques. The plaques are then lacquered to preserve the cheese. One reads, "Be Kind. But you need not start right away."
>
> The entire Remora family thanks him for his many contributions and wishes him well.

I said to Lindsay as she was ready to leave, "I just want you to know that you are the object of my first empty promise, 'Let's get together very soon.'"

"Oh let's. And please wish your sister well," said Lindsay.

"Do you think we can have lunch without the others?"

"Only if you're nice to me and meet in another neighborhood."

Gladys peeked her head in. "Are we still friends?"

"Of course. I couldn't have been fired without you. You know I appreciate everything you did, even if it was a new and untested way to protect your financial interest."

"I couldn't tell you the truth. I hope you understand that."

"Stop it. I understand."

"My sister thinks you're cute."

"Your sister hasn't seen a living, breathing man since 1957."

"You have a full schedule," Gladys said to me.

"Hello, Gladys," Lee said, entering the room. "I'm here for Rob's exit interview."

"Weren't you the exit interview for Collins, too?" said Gladys.

"Sorry, Rob. We have to do this. There's a lot of ground to cover and a lot of documents to sign. So, let's get going," said Lee.

"Very efficient. I haven't even officially decided I was leaving. This just happened yesterday."

"Please, Rob, be realistic; you know you have to leave. I'm going over all of this just in case you're deposed in the future or questioned by the press."

"Or if you need my opinion."

"Well, we might need your opinion on the first one. The one you invented. A pet protection organization called *Dogs for Canines* contacted us and they do not like your term "'Dog Rule.'" They claim it sounds harsh and discriminatory against dogs."

"Tell them to go hump somebody else's leg. C'mon Mimi, you just can't capitulate to everyone with a myopic complaint. Is *Dogs for Canines* run by dogs? Do they declare they bark for the barkless?"

"You've created a monster. People now yell 'Dog Rule' at meetings, even when they just don't like what someone said. Or it's getting late or they're hungry. You've created free-for-alls."

"All great philosophers are misinterpreted. A few for the better."

"Here, initial this."

"Why?"

"To prove we talked about it."

"I thought we were friends."

"We are friends. Initial here. Speaking of friends, do you remember the woman who said that she lost her virginity to you on TV?"

"Did you think I forgot about a public humiliation about sex?

Do you think my wife forgot about it? By the way, she did not lose her virginity on TV. It happened when we were younger."

"Just a reminder. Be careful in the future."

"Don't worry. I counted up all the women who lost their virginity to me and there are none left who can appear on TV."

"That's interesting. I thought as an artist type you would be more ... more ..."

"Promiscuous?"

"Experienced. Initial here."

"How many asses are you covering with these initials?"

"I liked the good job you did at the wedding, considering the participants."

"Thank you."

"To be perfectly indelicate, I'm sure everyone is wondering how Quisling and Reggie do it. If they do it at all."

"I'm sure those two have considered repurposing medieval devices of torture. Mimi Lee, does your mother know you have such improper thoughts?"

"For your information, I'm human. At least when I'm not here. Besides, you've also been free with your words and thoughts today, Rob. And I have all sorts of legal concerns about weddings in The Caf, including absolute liability, ethnic exclusion, and Remora being a joint tortfeasor, among others."

"You must be a lot of laughs at parties. By the way, Belette bribed someone to get our liquor license."

"OK, I might have to stop this whole thing."

"That'll make Belette's heart stop. Tell him that if he doesn't straighten things out, you'll cut off his disco balls."

"You'd better sign your full name here."

"Can't you give me all of them at once?"

"Quisling is going to need another operation and paying for the first one set a bad precedent."

"Why can't we brag about being benevolent?"

"No, this is an insurance company. People will get the wrong impression. And legally, once you don't enforce an exclusion, you open yourself up to all sorts of legal precedents and claims problems. It makes it harder for whoever takes over."

"Are you taking over?"

"Right, an Asian woman lawyer without sales cojones."

"I could put in a good word for you."

"With whom? Aren't you leaving permanently at 5 PM?"

"Why don't we put Quisling on a layaway plan, until her operation has been paid off? We can garnish Sir Reginald's accent if she doesn't pay. How come nice is rarely an option?"

"Initial here."

"By the way, you've been officially cleared of being involved in that crazy numbering underwriting scheme."

"Thanks. I'll be able to sleep tonight."

"But we have to put in new protocols, so it wouldn't happen again."

"Didn't someone say that could affect business?"

"Yes, but this way it looks like we did something. I'll make sure the new rules will not interfere with the way we conduct business."

"A typical business overreaction to something. Issue an edict for the whole company for a problem that only affects three people. How does an insurance company become a criminal enterprise? How does this place make money?"

"New York City Council passed the Collins Law, which requires that large panes of industrial glass must withstand the force of a 300-pound object. They want you to attend the signing ceremony."

"A going-away party for the going-away party."

"And probably the most important thing. Just remember, even though you're leaving, you still could be part of a criminal investigation or an internal investigation of things we didn't discuss today."

"Well, thank you for both informing me and scaring me."

"You're welcome. But that's my job."

"What Harvey Knoll said about claims people also applies to lawyers. He said that they are some of the people at the circus who clean up the shit of others, including the elephants. Speaking of that, what happened to the exploding suppositories?"

"They never found the culprit, so the police are concerned about the 4th of July."

Lee handed me a document. "This sets forth the provisions of your leaving. We're not calling it termination, retirement, or any other recognizable term. You are leaving of your own accord. Initial by the yellow stickies."

There is a warning on the package of Q-tips that you should not stick them in your ear canal. Thus, you should not use it for the purpose you bought it. This applies to many things, including business. People posture and position themselves in a way that has very little to do with their actual function.

She then handed me another form. "This is an NDA. You cannot speak about anything that happened at Remora, especially regarding Spaulding. If you do, we'll bring a legal action against you for breach. Again, sign by the yellow stickies. ... This form shows the amount Remora will pay you for severance."

"You mean silence."

"Severance."

"Severance pay, you say? If I don't sign the NDA, do I get my severance pay?"

"This form is for health insurance for you and your wife for life."

"That's good. How much is the co-pay?"

"You can read it later."

"If I have an objection, will you change it?"

"We might. Do you know there are people who are both glad and unhappy you're leaving? Many for the same reasons."

"I already know the reasons. A drunk told me. But here's the irony. Artists realize that making a lot of money is an unrealistic dream, while businesspeople think it's possible with the next deal. The irony is the artists are realistic and the hard-nosed business types are the dreamers when it comes to money."

"There's nothing wrong with making honest money. In fact, without the money of businesspeople, who would support all those museums and symphony halls? How about all those donors' names etched in gold?"

"Stairway to heaven."

"A bit of ironic gossip before I go. Someone nominated Spaulding for the

Insurance Hall of Fame."

"There's an Insurance Hall of Fame? Now playing third base and leading the league in fraud premium and debauchery, A.J. Spaulding." I did a poor imitation of a crowd roaring.

"The Insurance Hall of Fame is in Alabama."

"No shit. Alabama? Did they put it there to make doubly sure no one would ever visit?"

"There's a little one here in New York."

"Really? Do you have to pay to get in?"

"I doubt it. I think any interest would be welcome."

"I have a question for you. Can I pardon or absolve someone?"

"As long as it's not a real crime and needs the authority of the Board, or violates the by-laws of the company, I don't see why not."

"So long, Mimi, and stop being so afraid of everything."

"Too late to start now. Good luck, Rob."

If this had all occurred years ago, I would have considered myself an abject failure. But now that I was older, I thought I was a roaring success. Hardly anyone died under my watch. Well, at least none that were directly my fault. I tried to improve working conditions. If I was younger, my mistakes would follow me for decades ahead of any explanation I might offer. Have you ever heard of anyone offering an explanation or excuse on a resume?

The three consultants came next, as if they had the next number at the appetizer counter.

"We're here to wish you well," said Bill.

"Yes," said Fiona.

"Of course," said Quinn.

"The stock did well under your tenure and you weathered an assortment of unexpected events."

"We do wish you good luck."

"Thank you. Whatever you want to discuss with me will cost you $450 an hour plus expenses. I'm a free agent now."

"We disclosed what we thought was necessary. We were trying to protect you. This Spaulding business is tricky."

"The dead are annoying. Especially when they're still alive. They leave all sorts of legacies, true and false," I said.

"We warned you about being flippant and how that would get you into trouble."

"A random walk in the basement is the height of flippancy?"

All consultants openly act like they are not telling you everything and they have yet to tell you the most important thing. It is hard to know if it is an act or if tomorrow will cost a fortune.

"You almost proved that someone like yourself can lead a large company."

"AHH. But it was your little secret that led to my demise. Are you going to still use your new 'CEO as Liberal' model? Because if you do, I'm entitled to royalties."

"We serve at the pleasure of the Board. You know the official reason you're leaving."

"Yes, yes. To take care of my nonexistent sister, while you look after the live and almost kicking Spaulding."

"When we were kids in Brooklyn, we would go out early on the morning of July 5 to pick up the firecrackers that hadn't gone off. We then waited a year to see which ones might go off. While I have some clue what I'm leaving behind, I also have no clue which ones are duds and which are not."

After some more awkward moments and stilted chatter, we shook hands and exchanged a few more goodbyes.

During a lull, I checked my e-mails and there was a message from Harvey Knoll. I liked Harvey; he did not need face-to-face meetings.

I know you're leaving, so you can pass this bullshit onto the next guy, probably Jr. Jr.

Of course, you remember Louella Small the gun-toting claims adjuster from the Stretchpants, OK, office who seduced our young Philip Dent? Well, she's now the subject of a lawsuit. They claim she intimidated clients. Did she ever point that thing at anyone? Isn't that the whole point of an open carry state? We don't want to be associated with either side of a gun controversy, but goddammit, this is the first time we ever benefitted from a civilian carrying a gun and it works against us. We don't want to offend the pro-gun people; they have clout.

Young Dent has requested a transfer to the Stretchpants office and permission to carry a gun. I think he and Small want to get married. Does that come under the Mann Act? I hope he's of age and I'm assuming insurance is not an immoral enterprise. At least not in Oklahoma. So, I gave him permission.

Sorry to see you go and I hope your sister gets well soon. HA! HA!

In response, I wrote:

Thank you. Please do everything in your power to make sure that Louella and Young Dent don't have children.

Sladka appeared out of nowhere, as was his wont.

"You can speak," I told him.

"I just wanted to say it was a pleasure protecting you with my life," he said in that voice that sounded like a car problem.

"Thank you."

"Do you know who I'll have to protect next?"

"Sorry, I don't. But I'm sure you'll be willing to lay down your life for him. Or her. Probably a him. How's Tiffany and Find Dough?"

"Both are very happy and I owe them both to you. I heard you're leaving to take care of your sister."

The situation required lying. Whether he knew the truth or not mattered little. We chatted a bit more and I thanked him again for his loyalty and then I said, "One question."

"Anything."

"What's in your blue satchel?"

"Sorry, can't tell you that." And he vanished.

Then the unmistakable clank of Candy Quisling grew louder and louder until she and Sir Reginald appeared. "Guv, we came to wish you the best. We're gutted you're leaving."

"Thank you."

"Are you going to do other things?" asked Candy.

"Work on my art."

"That's great. I have a slogan for you, 'Art is good.'"

"Thank you. I'm not sure when I'll use it, but I'm sure some occasion will arise."

"Well, once again, we were both chuffed for the wedding. Maybe we can get together at my local for a bevvy some time."

"Sure."

The empty gesture just got emptier, although I was not sure Reggie understood that.

"Cheers and ta-ta."

"Yes, cheers and ta-ta to you two too."

Gladys came in. "You know there's no going-away party, so you don't have to hang around and act surprised."

"That's good. I think they're just about to cut off my computer access anyway."

"You were so honest, you couldn't be trusted."

"They wanted me to laugh at their jokes, like we were on a first date."

"You know, you were pathetic when you got here. You pushed my limits. But then, you turned it around and did pretty good. Well, at least you did until you found the old man."

"Thank you. You know what bothers me most, Gladys, far

more people are fired for being morons than for being incompetent. And the main reason why people change jobs is their immediate boss. I am leaving for none of those."

"I wouldn't worry about any of that. People will think of you as they want to think of you. I wrote a poem for the occasion."

I knew you would not last
You were not a member of the cast
You were far too nice of a guy
But some wanted to see you fry
But I tried to help best I could
My first attempt at motherhood
As a Mom I was not authorized
Because you were circumcised
They wanted more and more
And finally showed you the door
Good luck and all of that
Now I'll retire too so I can grow fat

"You're retiring?"

"Yes, I'm retiring. Whoever is next, 'good luck.' I don't need this tsouris anymore. I have more money than I ever thought I would have, including 20-something years of uncollected pension. So, Mary and me are going on a round-the-world cruise. First class. The whole works."

"Say hello to the gang in our St. Petersburg office."

"I heard they found a replacement for the guy they almost killed."

"Wonder if Remora gave him a sales quota too?"

"So long. Thanks and have a wonderful, wonderful trip and life."

We hugged and she asked Cassia and myself to her house for dinner before their adventure.

I did not have many items for my cardboard departure box, as I never felt comfortable in Spaulding's old office. A tchotchke here or there, even a painting of mine would not have made a difference. Nor did I steal anything on my way out that Spaulding had left behind.

I did wish I could have done more to change the company culture like having people appreciate evocative thinking, or hiring liberal arts majors and teaching them the industry, or gaining a sense of proportion as to what was important. Or even understanding how hard it was to create something but how easy to destroy it. I never even raised the issue of sabbaticals, which was now ironic.

One of the differences between artists and business people is, artists are suicidal and business people are homicidal. Artists look inward for the reason for their mistakes, while business people use a shotgun hoping to hit someone, anyone. Unless they have a particular target in mind. Then a Glock would do.

Just as I was about to leave, Belette arrived with flowers in his hand. He handed them to me, then stood at a distance as if not to be contaminated. And that's how life works. The person you least want to see, always appears at their convenience. And you must be nice as the onus remains on the sane.

"Very kind of you. I'll be sending out acknowledgement cards shortly." He thanked me for opportunities Spaulding never gave him. I was not sure whether to be proud of that or not. I was a hero to a weasel.

"Goodbye, Barry. I absolve you of all your mistakes." I wondered whether, if his father had done this decades ago, he would have been a different person and would never have been standing in front of me.

"Does that include the rumor I spread about Manny Friedman that got him fired?"

"I didn't know about that one."

"Before your time, I guess. Do you know who's taking over? And if you do know, can you put in a good word for me?"

"As soon as I see him or her, I'll give them all the good words I can muster."

"Since Candy's wedding, requests have shot through the roof. In fact, whoever takes over, I am going to ask if we can open a second and bigger Tray Chic."

I did not bother to correct his pronunciation.

"I heard you're leaving to take care of your uncle. Give him my best."

"My sister, Barry, my sister."

Epilogue

Snow Day

A SNOW DAY is a day off you did not earn. It is all about the convergence of different weather conditions, nothing a human did. No one feels guilty, as they take advantage of the company for not working. Some might be anxious because they had to do this or that, but they are the exception. Those who work from home, ironically, are unaffected, as are people who live in places like Florida and Arizona. I had the biggest snow day that one can imagine. And I took it without any compunctions.

In return for my leaving the company, I received $7.5 million. I did not know how they arrived at that figure. Believe it or not, then I got offers to be the CEO of other companies. Imitation is the laziest form of flattery.

We kept our rent-stabilized apartment in NYC because we were just not sure where we were going or what we would be doing or when we would be back. We were invited to Stretchpants, OK, for the wedding of Louella Sample and young Phil Dent. We just might go. Candy and Sir Reginald asked me to perform a *bris* on their newborn daughter. Clearly, they did not understand this Jewish rite but I was toying with the idea of saying yes. And a publisher wanted me to a write a memoir called

Negative Space. I would probably say no, but I would like to illustrate it.

Thank you MaKissMe and everyone at Remora for my snow day.

Final Note

Obviously you have purchased this book, but can you please recommend this book to others? I need the sales to offset the court costs for my breach of the NDA agreement precipitated by what you are reading.

Thanks again.

About the Author

Warren Alexander is a novelist, short story writer, and poet who was born and still lives in New York City. His satiric novel, *Cousins' Club,* was a semi-finalist for 2017 Book Life Award for General Fiction. *Wrong Train* was a finalist for the 2016 Rick DeMarinis Short Story Award. His poems have appeared in numerous journals. He received an M.A. in Creative Writing from NYU where he studied with Thomas Keneally, E.L. Doctorow, and Peter Carey.

He is currently working on a novel and a screenplay about relatively obscure people.

He was also a Vice President at as major insurance company.

~

To learn more about Warren Alexander and discover more Next Chapter authors, visit our website at www.nextchapter.pub.

Printed in Great Britain
by Amazon